INTERNATIONAL

BOOKS BY VLADIMIR NABOKOV

NOVELS

Mary

King, Queen, Knave

The Defense

The Eye

Glory

Laughter in the Dark

Despair

Invitation to a Beheading

The Gift

The Real Life of Sebastian Knight

Bend Sinister

Lolita

Pnin

Pale Fire

Ada or Ardor: A Family Chronicle

Transparent Things

Look at the Harlequins!

SHORT FICTION

Nabokov's Dozen

A Russian Beauty and Other Stories

Tyrants Destroyed and Other Stories

Details of a Sunset and Other Stories

The Enchanter

DRAMA

The Waltz Invention

Lolita: A Screenplay

The Man from the USSR and Other Plays

AUTOBIOGRAPHY AND INTERVIEWS

Speak, Memory: An Autobiography Revisited

Strong Opinions

BIOGRAPHY AND CRITICISM
Nikolai Gogol
Lectures on Literature
Lectures on Russian Literature
Lectures on Don Quixote

TRANSLATIONS
Three Russian Poets: Translations of Pushkin,
Lermontov, and Tiutchev
A Hero of Our Time (Mikhail Lermontov)
The Song of Igor's Campaign (Anon.)
Eugene Onegin (Alexander Pushkin)

LETTERS
Dear Bunny, Dear Volodya:
The Nabokov–Wilson Letters, 1940–1971
Vladimir Nabokov: Selected Letters, 1940–1977

MISCELLANEOUS
Poems and Problems
The Annotated Lolita

PALE FIRE

A NOVEL BY

VLADIMIR NABOKOV

VINTAGE INTERNATIONAL
VINTAGE BOOKS   A DIVISION OF RANDOM HOUSE, INC.
NEW YORK

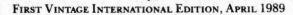

First Vintage International Edition, April 1989

Copyright © 1962 by Vera Nabokov and Dmitri Nabokov

All rights reserved under International and Pan-American Copyright Conventions. Published in the United States by Random House, Inc., New York. Originally published in hardcover by the Putnam Publishing Group in 1962. This edition published by arrangement with the Estate of Vladimir Nabokov.

Library of Congress Cataloging-in-Publication Data
Nabokov, Vladimir Vladimirovich, 1899–1977.
Pale fire: a novel / by Vladimir Nabokov.—1st Vintage international ed.
p.   cm.—(Vintage international)
ISBN 0-679-72342-0
I. Title.
PS3527.A15P3   1989   88-40532
813'.54—dc19   CIP

Manufactured in the United States of America
50th Printing

To Véra

This reminds me of the ludicrous account he gave Mr. Langton, of the despicable state of a young gentleman of good family. "Sir, when I heard of him last, he was running about town shooting cats." And then in a sort of kindly reverie, he bethought himself of his own favorite cat, and said, "But Hodge shan't be shot: no, no, Hodge shall not be shot."

JAMES BOSWELL, the Life of Samuel Johnson

Contents

Foreword

[11]

Pale Fire

A POEM IN FOUR CANTOS

[31]

Commentary

[71]

Index

[305]

Foreword

Pale Fire, a poem in heroic couplets, of nine hundred ninety-nine lines, divided into four cantos, was composed by John Francis Shade (born July 5, 1898, died July 21, 1959) during the last twenty days of his life, at his residence in New Wye, Appalachia, U.S.A. The manuscript, mostly a Fair Copy, from which the present text has been faithfully printed, consists of eighty medium-sized index cards, on each of which Shade reserved the pink upper line for headings (canto number, date) and used the fourteen light-blue lines for writing out with a fine nib in a minute, tidy, remarkably clear hand, the text of his poem, skipping a line to indicate double space, and always using a fresh card to begin a new canto.

The short (166 lines) Canto One, with all those amusing birds and parhelia, occupies thirteen cards. Canto Two, your favorite, and that shocking tour de force, Canto Three, are identical in length (334 lines) and cover twenty-seven cards each. Canto Four reverts to One in length and occupies again thirteen cards, of which the last four used on the day of his death give a Corrected Draft instead of a Fair Copy.

A methodical man, John Shade usually copied out his daily quota of completed lines at midnight but even if he recopied them again later, as I suspect he sometimes did, he marked his card or cards not with the date of his final adjustments, but with that of his Corrected Draft or first Fair Copy. I mean, he preserved the date of actual creation rather than that of second or third thoughts. There is a very loud amusement park right in front of my present lodgings.

We possess in result a complete calendar of his work. Canto One was begun in the small hours of July 2 and completed on July 4. He started the next canto on his birthday and finished it on July 11. Another week was devoted to

Canto Three. Canto Four was begun on July 19, and as already noted, the last third of its text (lines 949-999) is supplied by a Corrected Draft. This is extremely rough in appearance, teeming with devastating erasures and cataclysmic insertions, and does not follow the lines of the card as rigidly as the Fair Copy does. Actually, it turns out to be beautifully accurate when you once make the plunge and compel yourself to open your eyes in the limpid depths under its confused surface. It contains not one gappy line, not one doubtful reading. This fact would be sufficient to show that the imputations made (on July 24, 1959) in a newspaper interview with one of our professed Shadeans—who affirmed *without having seen the manuscript of the poem* that it "consists of disjointed drafts none of which yields a definite text" —is a malicious invention on the part of those who would wish not so much to deplore the state in which a great poet's work was interrupted by death as to asperse the competence, and perhaps honesty, of its present editor and commentator.

Another pronouncement publicly made by Prof. Hurley and his clique refers to a structural matter. I quote from the same interview: "None can say how long John Shade planned his poem to be, but it is not improbable that what he left represents only a small fraction of the composition he saw in a glass, darkly." Nonsense again! Aside from the veritable clarion of internal evidence ringing throughout Canto Four, there exists Sybil Shade's affirmation (in a document dated July 25, 1959) that her husband "never intended to go beyond four parts." For him the third canto was the penultimate one, and thus I myself have heard him speak of it, in the course of a sunset ramble, when, as if thinking aloud, he reviewed the day's work and gesticulated in pardonable self-approbation while his discreet companion kept trying in vain to adapt the swing of a long-limbed gait to the disheveled old poet's jerky shuffle. Nay, I shall even assert (as our shadows still walk without us) that there remained to be written only *one* line of the poem (namely verse 1000) which would have been identical to line 1 and would have completed the symmetry of the structure, with its two identical central parts, solid and ample, forming together with the shorter flanks twin wings of five hundred verses each, and damn that music. Knowing Shade's combinational turn of mind and subtle sense of harmonic balance, I cannot imagine that he intended to deform the faces of his crystal by meddling with its predictable growth. And if all this were not enough—and it is, it is enough—I have had the dramatic occasion of hearing my poor friend's own voice proclaim on the evening of July 21 the end, or almost the end, of his labors. (See my note to line 991.)

This batch of eighty cards was held by a rubber band which I now religiously put back after examining for the last time their precious contents. Another, much thinner, set of a dozen cards, clipped together and enclosed in the same manila envelope as the main batch, bears some additional couplets running their brief and sometimes smudgy course among a chaos of first drafts. As a rule, Shade destroyed drafts the moment he ceased to need them: well do I recall seeing him from my porch, on a brilliant morning, burning a whole stack of them in the pale fire of the incinerator before which he stood with bent head like an official mourner among the wind-borne black butterflies of that backyard auto-da-fé. But he saved those twelve cards because of the unused felicities shining among the dross of used draftings. Perhaps, he vaguely expected to replace certain passages in the Fair Copy with some of the lovely rejections in his files, or, more probably, a sneaking fondness for this or that vignette, suppressed out of architectonic considerations, or because it had annoyed Mrs. S., urged him to put off its disposal till the time when the marble finality of an immaculate typescript would have confirmed it or made the most delightful variant seem cumbersome and impure. And perhaps, let me add in all modesty, he intended to ask my advice after reading his poem to me as I know he planned to do.

In my notes to the poem the reader will find these canceled readings. Their places are indicated, or at least suggested, by the draftings of established lines in their immediate neighborhood. In a sense, many of them are more valuable artistically and historically than some of the best passages in the final text. I must now explain how *Pale Fire* came to be edited by me.

Immediately after my dear friend's death I prevailed on his distraught widow to forelay and defeat the commercial passions and academic intrigues that were bound to come swirling around her husband's manuscript (transferred by me to a safe spot even before his body had reached the grave) by signing an agreement to the effect that he had turned over the manuscript to me; that I would have it published without delay, with my commentary, by a firm of my choice; that all profits, except the publisher's percentage, would accrue to her; and that on publication day the manuscript would be handed over to the Library of Congress for permanent preservation. I defy any serious critic to find this contract unfair. Nevertheless, it has been called (by Shade's former lawyer) "a fantastic farrago of evil," while another person (his former literary agent) has wondered with a sneer if Mrs. Shade's tremulous signature might not have been penned "in some peculiar kind of red ink." Such hearts, such brains, would be unable to comprehend that one's attachment to a masterpiece may be utterly overwhelming, especially when it is the underside of the weave that entrances the beholder and only begetter, whose own past intercoils there with the fate of the innocent author.

As mentioned, I think, in my last note to the poem, the depth charge of Shade's death blasted such secrets and caused so many dead fish to float up, that I was forced to leave New Wye soon after my last interview with the jailed killer. The writing of the commentary had to be postponed until I could find a new incognito in quieter surroundings, but practical matters concerning the poem had to be settled at once. I took a plane to New York, had the manuscript photographed, came to terms with one of Shade's publishers, and was on the point of clinching the deal when, quite casually, in the midst of a vast sunset (we sat in a cell of walnut and glass fifty stories above the progression of scarabs), my interlocutor observed: "You'll be happy to know, Dr. Kinbote, that Professor So-and-so [one of the members of the Shade committee] has consented to act as our adviser in editing the stuff."

Now "happy" is something extremely subjective. One of our sillier Zemblan proverbs says: *the lost glove is happy*. Promptly I refastened the catch of my briefcase and betook myself to another publisher.

Imagine a soft, clumsy giant; imagine a historical personage whose knowledge of money is limited to the abstract billions of a national debt; imagine an exiled prince who is unaware of the Golconda in his cuff links! This is to say— oh, hyperbolically—that I am the most impractical fellow in the world. Between such a person and an old fox in the book publishing business, relations are at first touchingly carefree and chummy, with expansive banterings and all sorts of amiable tokens. I have no reason to suppose that anything will ever happen to prevent this initial relationship with good old Frank, my present publisher, from remaining a permanent fixture.

Frank has acknowledged the safe return of the galleys I had been sent here and has asked me to mention in my Preface—and this I willingly do—that I alone am responsible for any mistakes in my commentary. Insert before a professional. A professional proofreader has carefully rechecked the printed text of the poem against the phototype of the manuscript, and has found a few trivial misprints I had missed; that has been all in the way of outside assistance. Needless to say how much I had been looking forward to Sybil Shade's providing me with abundant biographical data; unfortunately she left New Wye even before I did, and is dwelling now with relatives in Quebec. We might have had, of course, a most fruitful correspondence, but the Shadeans were not to be shaken off. They headed for Canada in droves to pounce on the poor lady as soon as I had lost contact with her and her changeful moods. Instead of answering a month-old letter from my cave in Cedarn, listing some of my most desperate queries, such as the real name of "Jim Coates" etc., she suddenly shot me a wire, requesting me to accept Prof. H. (!) and Prof. C. (!!) as co-editors of her husband's poem. How deeply this surprised and pained me! Naturally, it precluded collaboration with my friend's misguided widow.

And he was a very dear friend indeed! The calendar says I had known him only for a few months but there exist friendships which develop their own inner duration, their own eons of transparent time, independent of rotating, malicious music. Never shall I forget how elated I was upon learning, as mentioned in a note my reader shall find, that the suburban house (rented for my use from Judge Goldsworth who had gone on his Sabbatical to England) into which I moved on February 5, 1959, stood next to that of the celebrated American poet whose verses I had tried to put into Zemblan two decades earlier! Apart from this glamorous neighborhood, the Goldsworthian château, as I was soon to discover, had little to recommend it. The heating system was a farce, depending as it did on registers in the floor wherefrom the tepid exhalations of a throbbing and groaning basement furnace were transmitted to the rooms with the faintness of a moribund's last breath. By occluding the apertures upstairs I attempted to give more energy to the register in the living room but its climate proved to be incurably vitiated by there being nothing between it and the arctic regions save a sleezy front door without a vestige of vestibule—either because the house had been built in midsummer by a naïve settler who could not imagine the kind of winter New Wye had in store for him, or because old-time gentility required that a chance caller at the open door could satisfy himself from the threshold that nothing unseemly was going on in the parlor.

February and March in Zembla (the two last of the four "white-nosed months," as we call them) used to be pretty rough too, but even a peasant's room there presented a solid of uniform warmth—not a reticulation of deadly drafts. It is true that, as usually happens to newcomers, I was told I had chosen the worst winter in years—and this at the latitude of Palermo. On one of my first mornings there, as I was preparing to leave for college in the powerful red car I had just acquired, I noticed that Mr. and Mrs. Shade, neither of whom I had yet met socially (I was to learn later that they assumed I wished to be left alone), were having trouble with their old Packard in the slippery driveway where it emitted whines of agony but could not extricate one tortured rear wheel out of a concave inferno of ice. John Shade busied himself clumsily with a bucket from which, with the gestures of a sower, he distributed handfuls of brown sand over the blue glaze. He wore snowboots, his vicuña collar was up, his abundant gray hair looked berimed in the sun. I knew he had been ill a few months before, and thinking to offer my neighbors a ride to the campus in my powerful machine, I hurried out toward them. A lane curving around the slight eminence on which my rented castle stood separated it from my neighbors' driveway, and I was about to cross that lane when I lost my footing and sat down on the surprisingly hard snow. My fall acted as a chemical reagent on the Shades' sedan, which forthwith budged and almost ran over me as it swung into the lane with John at the wheel strenuously grimacing and Sybil fiercely talking to him. I am not sure either saw me.

A few days later, however, namely on Monday, February 16, I was introduced to the old poet at lunch time in the faculty club. "At last presented credentials," as noted, a little ironically, in my agenda. I was invited to join him and four or five other eminent professors at his usual table, under an enlarged photograph of Wordsmith College as it was, stunned and shabby, on a remarkably gloomy summer day in 1903. His laconic suggestion that I "try the pork" amused me. I am a strict vegetarian, and I like to cook my own meals. Consuming something that had been handled by a fellow creature was, I explained to the rubicund convives, as repulsive to me as eating any creature, and that would include—lowering my voice—the pulpous pony-tailed girl student who served us and licked her pencil. Moreover, I had already finished the fruit brought with me in my briefcase, so I would content myself, I said, with a bottle of good college ale. My free and simple demeanor set everybody at ease. The usual questions were fired at me about eggnogs and milkshakes being or not being acceptable to one of my persuasion. Shade said that with him it was the other way around: he must make a definite effort to partake of a vegetable. Beginning a salad, was to him like stepping into sea water on a chilly day, and he had always to brace himself in order to attack the fortress of an apple. I was not yet used to the rather fatiguing jesting and teasing that goes on among American intellectuals of the inbreeding academic type and so abstained from telling John Shade in front of all those grinning old males how much I admired his work lest a serious discussion of literature degenerate into mere facetiation. Instead I asked him about one of my newly acquired students who also attended his course, a moody, delicate, rather wonderful boy; but with a resolute shake of his hoary forelock the old poet answered that he had ceased long ago to memorize faces and names of students and that the only person in his poetry class whom he could visualize was an extramural lady on crutches. "Come, come," said Professor Hurley, "do you mean, John, you really don't have a mental or visceral picture of that stunning blonde in the black leotard who haunts Lit. 202?" Shade, all his wrinkles beaming, benignly tapped Hurley on the wrist to make him stop. Another tormentor inquired if it was true that I had installed two ping-pong tables in my basement. I asked, was it a crime? No, he said, but why two? "Is *that* a crime?" I countered, and they all laughed.

Despite a wobbly heart (see line 735), a slight limp, and a certain curious contortion in his method of progress, Shade had an inordinate liking for long walks, but the snow bothered him, and he preferred, in winter, to have his wife call for him after classes with the car. A few days later, as I was about to leave Parthenocissus Hall—or Main Hall (or now Shade Hall, alas), I saw him waiting outside for Mrs. Shade to fetch him. I stood beside him for a minute, on the steps of the pillared porch, while pulling my gloves on, finger by finger, and looking away, as if waiting to review a regiment: "That was a thorough job," commented the poet. He consulted his wrist watch. A snowflake settled upon it. "Crystal to crystal," said Shade. I offered to take him home in my powerful Kramler. "Wives, Mr. Shade, are forgetful." He cocked his shaggy head to look at the library clock. Across the bleak expanse of snow-covered turf two radiant lads in colorful winter clothes passed, laughing and sliding. Shade glanced at his watch again and, with a shrug, accepted my offer.

I wanted to know if he did not mind being taken the longer way, with a stop at Community Center where I wanted to buy some chocolate-coated cookies and a little caviar. He said it was fine with him. From the inside of the supermarket, through a plate-glass window, I saw the old chap pop into a liquor store. When I returned with my purchases, he was back in the car, reading a tabloid newspaper which I had thought no poet would deign to touch. A comfortable burp told me he had a flask of brandy concealed about his warmly coated person. As we turned into the driveway of his house, we saw Sybil pulling up in front of it. I got out with courteous vivacity. She said: "Since my husband does not believe in introducing people, let us do it ourselves: You are Dr. Kinbote, aren't you? And I am Sybil Shade." Then she addressed her husband saying he might have waited in his office another minute: she had honked and called, and walked all the way up, et cetera. I turned to go, not wishing to listen to a marital scene, but she called me back: "Have a drink with us," she said, "or rather with me, because John is forbidden to touch alcohol." I explained I could not stay long as I was about to have a kind of little seminar at home followed by some table tennis, with two charming identical twins and another boy, another boy.

Henceforth I began seeing more and more of my celebrated neighbor. The view from one of my windows kept providing me with first-rate entertainment, especially when I was on the wait for some tardy guest. From the second story of my house the Shades' living-room window remained clearly visible so long as the branches of the deciduous trees between us were still bare, and almost every evening I could see the poet's slippered foot gently rocking. One inferred from it that he was sitting with a book in a low chair but one never managed to glimpse more than that foot and its shadow moving up and down to the secret rhythm of mental absorption, in the concentrated lamplight. Always at the same time the brown morocco slipper would drop from the wool-socked foot which continued to oscillate, with, however, a slight slackening of pace. One knew that bedtime was closing in with all its terrors; that in a few minutes the toe would prod and worry the slipper, and then disappear with it from my golden field of vision traversed by the black bendlet of a branch. And sometimes Sybil Shade would trip by with the velocity and swinging arms of one flouncing out in a fit of temper, and would return a little later, at a much slower gait, having, as it were, pardoned her husband for his friendship with an eccentric neighbor; but the riddle of her behavior was entirely solved one night when by dialing their number and watching their window at the same time I magically induced her to go through the hasty and quite innocent motions that had puzzled me.

Alas, my peace of mind was soon to be shattered. The thick venom of envy began squirting at me as soon as academic suburbia realized that John Shade valued my society above that of all other people. Your snicker, my dear Mrs. C., did not escape our notice as I was helping the tired old poet to find his galoshes after that dreary get-together party at your house. One day I happened to enter the English Literature office in quest of a magazine with the picture of the Royal Palace in Onhava, which I wanted my friend to see, when I overheard a young instuctor in a green velvet jacket, whom I shall mercifully call Gerald Emerald, carelessly saying in answer to something the secretary had asked: "I guess Mr. Shade has already left with the Great Beaver." Of course, I am quite tall, and my brown beard is of a rather rich tint and texture; the silly cognomen evidently applied to me, but was not worth noticing, and after calmly taking the magazine from a pamphlet-cluttered table, I contented myself on my way out with pulling Gerald Emerald's bow-tie loose with a deft jerk of my fingers as I passed by him. There was also the morning when Dr. Nattochdag, head of the department to which I was attached, begged me in a formal voice to be seated, then closed the door, and having regained, with a downcast frown, his swivel chair, urged me "to be more careful." In what sense, careful? A boy had complained to his adviser. Complained of what, good Lord? That I had criticized a literature course he attended ("a ridiculous survey of ridiculous works, conducted by a ridiculous mediocrity"). Laughing in sheer relief, I embraced my good Netochka, telling him I would never be naughty again. I take this opportunity to salute him. He always behaved with such exquisite courtesy toward me that I sometimes wondered if he did not suspect what Shade suspected, and what only three people (two trustees and the president of the college) definitely knew.

Oh, there were many such incidents. In a skit performed by a group of drama students I was pictured as a pompous woman hater with a German accent, constantly quoting Housman and nibbling raw carrots; and a week before Shade's death, a certain ferocious lady at whose club I had refused to speak on the subject of "The Hally Vally" (as she put it, confusing Odin's Hall with the title of a Finnish epic), said to me in the middle of a grocery store, "You are a remarkably disagreeable person. I fail to see how John and Sybil can stand you," and, exasperated by my polite smile, she added: "What's more, you are insane."

But let me not pursue the tabulation of nonsense. Whatever was thought, whatever was said, I had my full reward in John's friendship. This friendship was the more precious for its tenderness being intentionally concealed, especially when we were not alone, by that gruffness which stems from what can be termed the dignity of the heart. His whole being constituted a mask. John Shade's physical appearance was so little in keeping with the harmonies hiving in the man, that one felt inclined to dismiss it as a coarse disguise or passing fashion; for if the fashions of the Romantic Age subtilized a poet's manliness by baring his attractive neck, pruning his profile and reflecting a mountain lake in his oval gaze, present-day bards, owing perhaps to better opportunities of aging, look like gorillas or vultures. My sublime neighbor's face had something about it that might have appealed to the eye, had it been only leonine or only Iroquoian; but unfortunately, by combining the two it merely reminded one of a fleshy Hogarthian tippler of indeterminate sex. His misshapen body, that gray mop of abundant hair, the yellow nails of his pudgy fingers, the bags under his lusterless eyes, were only intelligible if regarded as the waste products eliminated from his intrinsic self by the same forces of perfection which purified and chiseled his verse. He was his own cancellation.

I have one favorite photograph of him. In this color snapshot taken by a onetime friend of mine, on a brilliant spring day, Shade is seen leaning on a sturdy cane that had belonged to his aunt Maud (see line 86). I am wearing a white windbreaker acquired in a local sports shop and a pair of lilac slacks hailing from Cannes. My left hand is half raised—not to pat Shade on the shoulder as seems to be the intention, but to remove my sunglasses which, however, it never reached in *that* life, the life of the picture; and the library book under my right arm is a treatise on certain Zemblan calisthenics in which I proposed to interest that young roomer of mine who snapped the picture. A week later he was to betray my trust by taking sordid advantage of my absence on a trip to Washington whence I returned to find he had been entertaining a fiery-haired whore from Exton who had left her combings and reek in all three bathrooms. Naturally, we separated at once, and through a chink in the window curtains I saw bad Bob standing rather pathetically, with his crewcut, and shabby valise, and the skis I had given him, all forlorn on the roadside, waiting for a fellow student to drive him away forever. I can forgive everything save treason.

We never discussed, John Shade and I, any of my personal misfortunes. Our close friendship was on that higher, exclusively intellectual level where one can rest from emotional troubles, not share them. My admiration for him was for me a sort of alpine cure. I experienced a grand sense of wonder whenever I looked at him, especially in the presence of other people, inferior people. This wonder was enhanced by my awareness of their not feeling what I felt, of their not seeing what I saw, of their taking Shade for granted, instead of drenching every nerve, so to speak, in the romance of his presence. Here he is, I would say to myself, that is his head, containing a brain of a different brand than that of the synthetic jellies preserved in the skulls around him. He is looking from the terrace (of Prof. C.'s house on that March evening) at the distant lake. I am looking at him. I am witnessing a unique physiological phenomenon: John Shade perceiving and transforming the world, taking it in and taking it apart, re-combining its elements in the very process of storing them up so as to produce at some unspecified date an organic miracle, a fusion of image and music, a line of verse. And I experienced the same thrill as when in my early boyhood I once watched across the tea table in my uncle's castle a conjurer who had just given a fantastic performance and was now quietly consuming a vanilla ice. I stared at his powdered cheeks, at the magical flower in his buttonhole where it had passed through a succession of different colors and had now become fixed as a white carnation, and especially at his marvelous fluid-looking fingers which could if he chose make his spoon dissolve into a sunbeam by twiddling it, or turn his plate into a dove by tossing it up in the air.

Shade's poem is, indeed, that sudden flourish of magic: my gray-haired friend, my beloved old conjurer, put a pack of index cards into his hat—and shook out a poem.

To this poem we now must turn. My Foreword has been, I trust, not too skimpy. Other notes, arranged in a running commentary, will certainly satisfy the most voracious reader. Although those notes, in conformity with custom, come after the poem, the reader is advised to consult them first and then study the poem with their help, rereading them of course as he goes through its text, and perhaps, after having done with the poem, consulting them a third time so as to complete the picture. I find it wise in such cases as this to eliminate the bother of back-and-forth leafings by either cutting out and clipping together the pages with the text of the thing, or, even more simply, purchasing two copies of the same work which can then be placed in adjacent positions on a comfortable table—not like the shaky little affair on which my typewriter is precariously enthroned now, in this wretched motor lodge, with that carrousel inside and outside my head, miles away from New Wye. Let me state that without my notes Shade's text simply has no human reality at all since the human reality of such a poem as his (being too skittish and reticent for an autobiographical work), with the omission of many pithy lines carelessly rejected by him, has to depend entirely on the reality of its author and his surroundings, attachments and so forth, a reality that only my notes can provide. To this statement my dear poet would probably not have subscribed, but, for better or worse, it is the commentator who has the last word.

CHARLES KINBOTE

Oct. 19, 1959, Cedarn, Utana

Pale Fire

A POEM IN FOUR CANTOS

CANTO ONE

1   I was the shadow of the waxwing slain
By the false azure in the windowpane;
I was the smudge of ashen fluff—and I
Lived on, flew on, in the reflected sky.
And from the inside, too, I'd duplicate
Myself, my lamp, an apple on a plate:
Uncurtaining the night, I'd let dark glass
Hang all the furniture above the grass,
And how delightful when a fall of snow
10   Covered my glimpse of lawn and reached up so
As to make chair and bed exactly stand
Upon that snow, out in that crystal land!

Retake the falling snow: each drifting flake
Shapeless and slow, unsteady and opaque,
A dull dark white against the day's pale white
And abstract larches in the neutral light.
And then the gradual and dual blue
As night unites the viewer and the view,
And in the morning, diamonds of frost
20   Express amazement: Whose spurred feet have crossed
From left to right the blank page of the road?
Reading from left to right in winter's code:
A dot, an arrow pointing back; repeat:
Dot, arrow pointing back . . . A pheasant's feet!
Torquated beauty, sublimated grouse,

Finding your China right behind my house.
Was he in *Sherlock Holmes*, the fellow whose
Tracks pointed back when he reversed his shoes?

All colors made me happy: even gray.
30 My eyes were such that literally they
Took photographs. Whenever I'd permit,
Or, with a silent shiver, order it,
Whatever in my field of vision dwelt—
An indoor scene, hickory leaves, the svelte
Stilettos of a frozen stillicide—
Was printed on my eyelids' nether side
Where it would tarry for an hour or two,
And while this lasted all I had to do
Was close my eyes to reproduce the leaves,
40 Or indoor scene, or trophies of the eaves.

I cannot understand why from the lake
I could make out our front porch when I'd take
Lake Road to school, whilst now, although no tree
Has intervened, I look but fail to see
Even the roof. Maybe some quirk in space
Has caused a fold or furrow to displace
The fragile vista, the frame house between
Goldsworth and Wordsmith on its square of green.

I had a favorite young shagbark there
50 With ample dark jade leaves and a black, spare,
Vermiculated trunk. The setting sun
Bronzed the black bark, around which, like undone
Garlands, the shadows of the foliage fell.

It is now stout and rough; it has done well.
White butterflies turn lavender as they
Pass through its shade where gently seems to sway
The phantom of my little daughter's swing.

The house itself is much the same. One wing
We've had revamped. There's a solarium. There's
60   A picture window flanked with fancy chairs.
TV's huge paperclip now shines instead
Of the stiff vane so often visited
By the naïve, the gauzy mockingbird
Retelling all the programs she had heard;
Switching from *chippo-chippo* to a clear
To-wee, to-wee; then rasping out: *come here,
Come here, come herrr*'; flirting her tail aloft,
Or gracefully indulging in a soft
Upward hop-flop, and instantly (*to-wee!*)
70   Returning to her perch—the new TV.

I was an infant when my parents died.
They both were ornithologists. I've tried
So often to evoke them that today
I have a thousand parents. Sadly they
Dissolve in their own virtues and recede,
But certain words, chance words I hear or read,
Such as "bad heart" always to him refer,
And "cancer of the pancreas" to her.

A preterist: one who collects cold nests.
80   Here was my bedroom, now reserved for guests.
Here, tucked away by the Canadian maid,

I listened to the buzz downstairs and prayed
For everybody to be always well,
Uncles and aunts, the maid, her niece Adèle
Who'd seen the Pope, people in books, and God.

I was brought up by dear bizarre Aunt Maud,
A poet and a painter with a taste
For realistic objects interlaced
With grotesque growths and images of doom.
90   She lived to hear the next babe cry. Her room
We've kept intact. Its trivia create
A still life in her style: the paperweight
Of convex glass enclosing a lagoon,
The verse book open at the Index (Moon,
Moonrise, Moor, Moral), the forlorn guitar,
The human skull; and from the local *Star*
A curio: *Red Sox Beat Yanks 5-4*
On *Chapman's Homer*, thumbtacked to the door.

My God died young. Theolatry I found
100 Degrading, and its premises, unsound.
No free man needs a God; but was I free?
How fully I felt nature glued to me
And how my childish palate loved the taste
Half-fish, half-honey, of that golden paste!

My picture book was at an early age
The painted parchment papering our cage:
Mauve rings around the moon; blood-orange sun;
Twinned Iris; and that rare phenomenon
The iridule—when, beautiful and strange,
110 In a bright sky above a mountain range

One opal cloudlet in an oval form
Reflects the rainbow of a thunderstorm
Which in a distant valley has been staged—
For we are most artistically caged.

And there's the wall of sound: the nightly wall
Raised by a trillion crickets in the fall.
Impenetrable! Halfway up the hill
I'd pause in thrall of their delirious trill.
That's Dr. Sutton's light. That's the Great Bear.
120 A thousand years ago five minutes were
Equal to forty ounces of fine sand.
Outstare the stars. Infinite foretime and
Infinite aftertime: above your head
They close like giant wings, and you are dead.

The regular vulgarian, I daresay,
Is happier: he sees the Milky Way
Only when making water. Then as now
I walked at my own risk: whipped by the bough,
Tripped by the stump. Asthmatic, lame and fat,
130 I never bounced a ball or swung a bat.

I was the shadow of the waxwing slain
By feigned remoteness in the windowpane.
I had a brain, five senses (one unique),
But otherwise I was a cloutish freak.
In sleeping dreams I played with other chaps
But really envied nothing—save perhaps
The miracle of a lemniscate left
Upon wet sand by nonchalantly deft
Bicycle tires.

A thread of subtle pain,
140 Tugged at by playful death, released again,
But always present, ran through me. One day,
When I'd just turned eleven, as I lay
Prone on the floor and watched a clockwork toy—
A tin wheelbarrow pushed by a tin boy—
Bypass chair legs and stray beneath the bed,
There was a sudden sunburst in my head.

And then black night. That blackness was sublime.
I felt distributed through space and time:
One foot upon a mountaintop, one hand
150 Under the pebbles of a panting strand,
One ear in Italy, one eye in Spain,
In caves, my blood, and in the stars, my brain.
There were dull throbs in my Triassic; green
Optical spots in Upper Pleistocene,
An icy shiver down my Age of Stone,
And all tomorrows in my funnybone.

During one winter every afternoon
I'd sink into that momentary swoon.
And then it ceased. Its memory grew dim.
160 My health improved. I even learned to swim.
But like some little lad forced by a wench
With his pure tongue her abject thirst to quench,
I was corrupted, terrified, allured,
And though old doctor Colt pronounced me cured
Of what, he said, were mainly growing pains,
The wonder lingers and the shame remains.

CANTO TWO

There was a time in my demented youth
When somehow I suspected that the truth
About survival after death was known
To every human being: I alone
Knew nothing, and a great conspiracy
Of books and people hid the truth from me.

There was the day when I began to doubt
Man's sanity: How could he live without
Knowing for sure what dawn, what death, what doom
Awaited consciousness beyond the tomb?

And finally there was the sleepless night
When I decided to explore and fight
The foul, the inadmissible abyss,
Devoting all my twisted life to this
One task. Today I'm sixty-one. Waxwings
Are berry-pecking. A cicada sings.

The little scissors I am holding are
A dazzling synthesis of sun and star.
I stand before the window and I pare
My fingernails and vaguely am aware
Of certain flinching likenesses: the thumb,
Our grocer's son; the index, lean and glum
College astronomer Starover Blue;

190 The middle fellow, a tall priest I knew;
The feminine fourth finger, an old flirt;
And little pinky clinging to her skirt.
And I make mouths as I snip off the thin
Strips of what Aunt Maud used to call "scarf-skin."

Maud Shade was eighty when a sudden hush
Fell on her life. We saw the angry flush
And torsion of paralysis assail
Her noble cheek. We moved her to Pinedale,
Famed for its sanitarium. There she'd sit
200 In the glassed sun and watch the fly that lit
Upon her dress and then upon her wrist.
Her mind kept fading in the growing mist.
She still could speak. She paused, and groped, and found
What seemed at first a serviceable sound,
But from adjacent cells impostors took
The place of words she needed, and her look
Spelt imploration as she sought in vain
To reason with the monsters in her brain.

What moment in the gradual decay
210 Does resurrection choose? What year? What day?
Who has the stopwatch? Who rewinds the tape?
Are some less lucky, or do all escape?
A syllogism: *other men die; but I
Am not another; therefore I'll not die.*
Space is a swarming in the eyes; and time,
A singing in the ears. In this hive I'm
Locked up. Yet, *if* prior to life we had
Been able to imagine life, what mad,

Impossible, unutterably weird,
220 Wonderful nonsense it might have appeared!

So why join in the vulgar laughter? Why
Scorn a hereafter none can verify:
The Turk's delight, the future lyres, the talks
With Socrates and Proust in cypress walks,
The seraph with his six flamingo wings,
And Flemish hells with porcupines and things?
It isn't that we dream too wild a dream:
The trouble is we do not make it seem
Sufficiently unlikely; for the most
230 We can think up is a domestic ghost.

How ludicrous these efforts to translate
Into one's private tongue a public fate!
Instead of poetry divinely terse,
Disjointed notes, Insomnia's mean verse!

Life is a message scribbled in the dark.
Anonymous.
                    Espied on a pine's bark,
As we were walking home the day she died,
An empty emerald case, squat and frog-eyed,
Hugging the trunk; and its companion piece,
240 A gum-logged ant.
                    That Englishman in Nice,
A proud and happy linguist: *je nourris*
Les pauvres cigales—meaning that he
Fed the poor sea gulls!

41

                    Lafontaine was wrong:
Dead is the mandible, alive the song.

And so I pare my nails, and muse, and hear
Your steps upstairs, and all is right, my dear.

Sybil, throughout our high-school days I knew
Your loveliness, but fell in love with you
During an outing of the senior class
250   To New Wye Falls. We luncheoned on damp grass.
Our teacher of geology discussed
The cataract. Its roar and rainbow dust
Made the tame park romantic. I reclined
In April's haze immediately behind
Your slender back and watched your neat small head
Bend to one side. One palm with fingers spread,
Between a star of trillium and a stone,
Pressed on the turf. A little phalange bone
Kept twitching. Then you turned and offered me
260   A thimbleful of bright metallic tea.

Your profile has not changed. The glistening teeth
Biting the careful lip; the shade beneath
The eye from the long lashes; the peach down
Rimming the cheekbone; the dark silky brown
Of hair brushed up from temple and from nape;
The very naked neck; the Persian shape
Of nose and eyebrow, you have kept it all—
And on still nights we hear the waterfall.

Come and be worshiped, come and be caressed,
270   My dark Vanessa, crimson-barred, my blest

My Admirable butterfly! Explain
How could you, in the gloom of Lilac Lane,
Have let uncouth, hysterical John Shade
Blubber your face, and ear, and shoulder blade?

We have been married forty years. At least
Four thousand times your pillow has been creased
By our two heads. Four hundred thousand times
The tall clock with the hoarse Westminster chimes
Has marked our common hour. How many more
280 Free calendars shall grace the kitchen door?

I love you when you're standing on the lawn
Peering at something in a tree: "It's gone.
It was so small. It might come back" (all this
Voiced in a whisper softer than a kiss).
I love you when you call me to admire
A jet's pink trail above the sunset fire.
I love you when you're humming as you pack
A suitcase or the farcical car sack
With round-trip zipper. And I love you most
290 When with a pensive nod you greet her ghost
And hold her first toy on your palm, or look
At a postcard from her, found in a book.

She might have been you, me, or some quaint blend:
Nature chose me so as to wrench and rend
Your heart and mine. At first we'd smile and say:
"All little girls are plump" or "Jim McVey
(The family oculist) will cure that slight
Squint in no time." And later: "She'll be quite
Pretty, you know"; and, trying to assuage

³⁰⁰ The swelling torment: "That's the awkward age."
"She should take riding lessons," you would say
(Your eyes and mine not meeting). "She should play
Tennis, or badminton. Less starch, more fruit!
She may not be a beauty, but she's cute."

It was no use, no use. The prizes won
In French and history, no doubt, were fun;
At Christmas parties games were rough, no doubt,
And one shy little guest might be left out;
But let's be fair: while children of her age
³¹⁰ Were cast as elves and fairies on the stage
That *she*'d helped paint for the school pantomime,
My gentle girl appeared as Mother Time,
A bent charwoman with slop pail and broom,
And like a fool I sobbed in the men's room.

Another winter was scrape-scooped away.
The Toothwort White haunted our woods in May.
Summer was power-mowed, and autumn, burned.
Alas, the dingy cygnet never turned
Into a wood duck. And again your voice:
³²⁰ "But this is prejudice! You should rejoice
That she is innocent. Why overstress
The physical? She *wants* to look a mess.
Virgins have written some *resplendent* books.
Lovemaking is not everything. Good looks
Are not *that* indispensable!" And still
Old Pan would call from every painted hill,
And still the demons of our pity spoke:
No lips would share the lipstick of her smoke;
The telephone that rang before a ball

330 Every two minutes in Sorosa Hall
For her would never ring; and, with a great
Screeching of tires on gravel, to the gate
Out of the lacquered night, a white-scarfed beau
Would never come for her; she'd never go,
A dream of gauze and jasmine, to that dance.
We sent her, though, to a château in France.

And she returned in tears, with new defeats,
New miseries. On days when all the streets
Of College Town led to the game, she'd sit
840 On the library steps, and read or knit;
Mostly alone she'd be, or with that nice
Frail roommate, now a nun; and, once or twice,
With a Korean boy who took my course.
She had strange fears, strange fantasies, strange force
Of character—as when she spent three nights
Investigating certain sounds and lights
In an old barn. She twisted words: pot, top,
Spider, redips. And "powder" was "red wop."
She called you a didactic katydid.
850 She hardly ever smiled, and when she did,
It was a sign of pain. She'd criticize
Ferociously our projects, and with eyes
Expressionless sit on her tumbled bed
Spreading her swollen feet, scratching her head
With psoriatic fingernails, and moan,
Murmuring dreadful words in monotone.

She was my darling: difficult, morose—
But still my darling. You remember those
Almost unruffled evenings when we played

45

360 Mah-jongg, or she tried on your furs, which made
Her almost fetching; and the mirrors smiled,
The lights were merciful, the shadows mild.
Sometimes I'd help her with a Latin text,
Or she'd be reading in her bedroom, next
To my fluorescent lair, and you would be
In your own study, twice removed from me,
And I would hear both voices now and then:
"Mother, what's *grimpen?*" "What is what?"
                                         "Grim Pen."
Pause, and your guarded scholium. Then again:
370 "Mother, what's *chtonic?*" That, too, you'd explain,
Appending: "Would you like a tangerine?"
"No. Yes. And what does *sempiternal* mean?"
You'd hesitate. And lustily I'd roar
The answer from my desk through the closed door.

It does not matter what it was she read
(some phony modern poem that was said
In English Lit to be a document
"Engazhay and compelling"—what this meant
Nobody cared); the point is that the three
380 Chambers, *then* bound by you and her and me,
Now form a tryptich or a three-act play
In which portrayed events forever stay.

I think she always nursed a small mad hope.

I'd finished recently my book on Pope.
Jane Dean, my typist, offered her one day
To meet Pete Dean, a cousin. Jane's fiancé

Would then take all of them in his new car
A score of miles to a Hawaiian bar.
The boy was picked up at a quarter past
390   Eight in New Wye. Sleet glazed the roads. At last
They found the place—when suddenly Pete Dean
Clutching his brow exclaimed that he had clean
Forgotten an appointment with a chum
Who'd land in jail if he, Pete, did not come,
Et cetera. She said she understood.
After he'd gone the three young people stood
Before the azure entrance for awhile.
Puddles were neon-barred; and with a smile
She said she'd be *de trop*, she'd much prefer
400   Just going home. Her friends escorted her
To the bus stop and left; but she, instead
Of riding home, got off at Lochanhead.

You scrutinized your wrist: "It's eight fifteen.
[And here time forked.] I'll turn it on." The screen
In its blank broth evolved a lifelike blur,
And music welled.

                He took one look at her,
And shot a death ray at well-meaning Jane.

A male hand traced from Florida to Maine
The curving arrows of Aeolian wars.
410   You said that later a quartet of bores,
Two writers and two critics, would debate
The Cause of Poetry on Channel 8.
A nymph came pirouetting, under white

Rotating petals, in a vernal rite
To kneel before an altar in a wood
Where various articles of toilet stood.
I went upstairs and read a galley proof,
And heard the wind roll marbles on the roof.
"See the blind beggar dance, the cripple sing"
420 Has unmistakably the vulgar ring
Of its preposterous age. Then came your call,
My tender mockingbird, up from the hall.
I was in time to overhear brief fame
And have a cup of tea with you: my name
Was mentioned twice, as usual just behind
(one oozy footstep) Frost.

                              "Sure you don't mind?
I'll catch the Exton plane, because you know
If I don't come by midnight with the dough—"

And then there was a kind of travelog:
430 A host narrator took us through the fog
Of a March night, where headlights from afar
Approached and grew like a dilating star,
To the green, indigo and tawny sea
Which we had visited in thirty-three,
Nine months before her birth. Now it was all
Pepper-and-salt, and hardly could recall
That first long ramble, the relentless light,
The flock of sails (one blue among the white
Clashed queerly with the sea, and two were red),
440 The man in the old blazer, crumbing bread,
The crowding gulls insufferably loud,
And one dark pigeon waddling in the crowd.

"Was that the phone?" You listened at the door.
Nothing. Picked up the program from the floor.
More headlights in the fog. There was no sense
In window-rubbing: only some white fence
And the reflector poles passed by unmasked.

"Are we quite sure she's acting right?" you asked.
"It's technically a blind date, of course.
450 Well, shall we try the preview of *Remorse?*"
And we allowed, in all tranquillity,
The famous film to spread its charmed marquee;
The famous face flowed in, fair and inane:
The parted lips, the swimming eyes, the grain
Of beauty on the cheek, odd gallicism,
And the soft form dissolving in the prism
Of corporate desire.
             "*I think,*" *she said,*
"*I'll get off here.*" "*It's only Lochanhead.*"
"*Yes, that's okay.*" *Gripping the stang, she peered*
460 *At ghostly trees. Bus stopped. Bus disappeared.*

Thunder above the Jungle. "No, not that!"
Pat Pink, our guest (antiatomic chat).
Eleven struck. You sighed. "Well, I'm afraid
There's nothing else of interest." You played
Network roulette: the dial turned and trk'ed.
Commercials were beheaded. Faces flicked.
An open mouth in midsong was struck out.
An imbecile with sideburns was about
To use his gun, but you were much too quick.
470 A jovial Negro raised his trumpet. Trk.

Your ruby ring made life and laid the law.
Oh, switch it off! And as life snapped we saw
A pinhead light dwindle and die in black
Infinity.

      Out of his lakeside shack
A watchman, Father Time, all gray and bent,
Emerged with his uneasy dog and went
Along the reedy bank. He came too late.

You gently yawned and stacked away your plate.
We heard the wind. We heard it rush and throw
480 Twigs at the windowpane. Phone ringing? No.
I helped you with the dishes. The tall clock
Kept on demolishing young root, old rock.

"Midnight," you said. What's midnight to the young?
And suddenly a festive blaze was flung
Across five cedar trunks, snowpatches showed,
And a patrol car on our bumpy road
Came to a crunching stop. Retake, retake!

People have thought she tried to cross the lake
At Lochan Neck where zesty skaters crossed
490 From Exe to Wye on days of special frost.
Others supposed she might have lost her way
By turning left from Bridgeroad; and some say
She took her poor young life. I know. You know.

It was a night of thaw, a night of blow,
With great excitement in the air. Black spring

Stood just around the corner, shivering
In the wet starlight and on the wet ground.
The lake lay in the mist, its ice half drowned.
A blurry shape stepped off the reedy bank
500 Into a crackling, gulping swamp, and sank.

L'*if*, lifeless tree! Your great Maybe, Rabelais:
The grand potato.
                              I.P.H., a lay
Institute (I) of Preparation (P)
For the Hereafter (H), or If, as we
Called it—big if!—engaged me for one term
To speak on death ("to lecture on the Worm,"
Wrote President McAber).
                              You and I,
And she, then a mere tot, moved from New Wye
To Yewshade, in another, higher state.
⁵¹⁰ I love great mountains. From the iron gate
Of the ramshackle house we rented there
One saw a snowy form, so far, so fair,
That one could only fetch a sigh, as if
It might assist assimilation.
                              Iph
Was a larvorium and a violet:
A grave in Reason's early spring. And yet
It missed the gist of the whole thing; it missed
What mostly interests the preterist;
For we die every day; oblivion thrives
⁵²⁰ Not on dry thighbones but on blood-ripe lives,
And our best yesterdays are now foul piles
Of crumpled names, phone numbers and foxed files.
I'm ready to become a floweret

Or a fat fly, but never, to forget.
And I'll turn down eternity unless
The melancholy and the tenderness
Of mortal life; the passion and the pain;
The claret taillight of that dwindling plane
Off Hesperus; your gesture of dismay
On running out of cigarettes; the way
You smile at dogs; the trail of silver slime
Snails leave or flagstones; this good ink, this rhyme,
This index card, this slender rubber band
Which always forms, when dropped, an ampersand,
Are found in Heaven by the newlydead
Stored in its strongholds through the years.

                                        Instead

The Institute assumed it might be wise
Not to expect too much of paradise:
What if there's nobody to say hullo
To the newcomer, no reception, no
Indoctrination? What if you are tossed
Into a boundless void, your bearings lost,
Your spirit stripped and utterly alone,
Your task unfinished, your despair unknown,
Your body just beginning to putresce,
A non-undressable in morning dress,
Your widow lying prone on a dim bed,
Herself a blur in your dissolving head!

While snubbing gods, including the big G,
Iph borrowed some peripheral debris
From mystic visions; and it offered tips
(The amber spectacles for life's eclipse)—
How not to panic when you're made a ghost:

Sidle and slide, choose a smooth surd, and coast,
Meet solid bodies and glissade right through,
Or let a person circulate through you.
How to locate in blackness, with a gasp,
Terra the Fair, an orbicle of jasp.
How to keep sane in spiral types of space.
560 Precautions to be taken in the case
Of freak reincarnation: what to do
On suddenly discovering that you
Are now a young and vulnerable toad
Plump in the middle of a busy road,
Or a bear cub beneath a burning pine,
Or a book mite in a revived divine.

Time means succession, and succession, change:
Hence timelessness is bound to disarrange
Schedules of sentiment. We give advice
570 To widower. He has been married twice:
He meets his wives; both loved, both loving, both
Jealous of one another. Time means growth,
And growth means nothing in Elysian life.
Fondling a changeless child, the flax-haired wife
Grieves on the brink of a remembered pond
Full of a dreamy sky. And, also blond,
But with a touch of tawny in the shade,
Feet up, knees clasped, on a stone balustrade
The other sits and raises a moist gaze
580 Toward the blue impenetrable haze.
How to begin? Which first to kiss? What toy
To give the babe? Does that small solemn boy
Know of the head-on crash which on a wild

March night killed both the mother and the child?
And she, the second love, with instep bare
In ballerina black, why does she wear
The earrings from the other's jewel case?
And why does she avert her fierce young face?

For as we know from dreams it is so hard
590   To speak to our dear dead! They disregard
Our apprehension, queaziness and shame—
The awful sense that they're not quite the same.
And our school chum killed in a distant war
Is not surprised to see us at his door,
And in a blend of jauntiness and gloom
Points at the puddles in his basement room.

But who can teach the thoughts we should roll-call
When morning finds us marching to the wall
Under the stage direction of some goon
600   Political, some uniformed baboon?
We'll think of matters only known to us—
Empires of rhyme, Indies of calculus;
Listen to distant cocks crow, and discern
Upon the rough gray wall a rare wall fern;
And while our royal hands are being tied,
Taunt our inferiors, cheerfully deride
The dedicated imbeciles, and spit
Into their eyes just for the fun of it.

Nor can one help the exile, the old man
610   Dying in a motel, with the loud fan
Revolving in the torrid prairie night

And, from the outside, bits of colored light
Reaching his bed like dark hands from the past
Offering gems; and death is coming fast.
He suffocates and conjures in two tongues
The nebulae dilating in his lungs.

A wrench, a rift—that's all one can foresee.
Maybe one finds *le grand néant*; maybe
Again one spirals from the tuber's eye.

620   As you remarked the last time we went by
The Institute: "I really could not tell
The difference between this place and Hell."

We heard cremationists guffaw and snort
At Grabermann's denouncing the Retort
As detrimental to the birth of wraiths.
We all avoided criticizing faiths.
The great Starover Blue reviewed the role
Planets had played as landfalls of the soul.
The fate of beasts was pondered. A Chinese
630   Discanted on the etiquette at teas
With ancestors, and how far up to go.
I tore apart the fantasies of Poe,
And dealt with childhood memories of strange
Nacreous gleams beyond the adults' range.
Among our auditors were a young priest
And an old Communist. Iph could at least
Compete with churches and the party line.

In later years it started to decline:
Buddhism took root. A medium smuggled in

640 Pale jellies and a floating mandolin.
Fra Karamazov, mumbling his inept
All is allowed, into some classes crept;
And to fulfill the fish wish of the womb,
A school of Freudians headed for the tomb.

That tasteless venture helped me in a way.
I learnt what to ignore in my survey
Of death's abyss. And when we lost our child
I knew there would be nothing: no self-styled
Spirit would touch a keyboard of dry wood
650 To rap out her pet name; no phantom would
Rise gracefully to welcome you and me
In the dark garden, near the shagbark tree.

"What is that funny creaking—do you hear?"
"It is the shutter on the stairs, my dear."

"If you're not sleeping, let's turn on the light.
I hate that wind! Let's play some chess." "All right."

"I'm sure it's not the shutter. There—again."
"It is a tendril fingering the pane."

"What glided down the roof and made that thud?"
660 "It is old winter tumbling in the mud."

"And now what shall I do? My knight is pinned."

Who rides so late in the night and the wind?
It is the writer's grief. It is the wild
March wind. It is the father with his child.

Later came minutes, hours, whole days at last,
When she'd be absent from our thoughts, so fast
Did life, the woolly caterpillar run.
We went to Italy. Sprawled in the sun
On a white beach with other pink or brown
670   Americans. Flew back to our small town.
Found that my bunch of essays *The Untamed*
Seahorse was "universally acclaimed"
(It sold three hundred copies in one year).
Again school started, and on hillsides, where
Wound distant roads, one saw the steady stream
Of carlights all returning to the dream
Of college education. You went on
Translating into French Marvell and Donne.
It was a year of Tempests: Hurricane
680   Lolita swept from Florida to Maine.
Mars glowed. Shahs married. Gloomy Russians spied.
Lang made your portrait. And one night I died.

The Crashaw Club had paid me to discuss
Why Poetry Is Meaningful to Us.
I gave my sermon, a dull thing but short.
As I was leaving in some haste, to thwart
The so-called "question period" at the end,
One of those peevish people who attend
Such talks only to say they disagree
690   Stood up and pointed with his pipe at me.

And then it happened—the attack, the trance,
Or one of my old fits. There sat by chance
A doctor in the front row. At his feet

Patly I fell. My heart had stopped to beat,
It seems, and several moments passed before
It heaved and went on trudging to a more
Conclusive destination. Give me now
Your full attention.

               I can't tell you how
I knew—but I did know that I had crossed
700   The border. Everything I loved was lost
But no aorta could report regret.
A sun of rubber was convulsed and set;
And blood-black nothingness began to spin
A system of cells interlinked within
Cells interlinked within cells interlinked
Within one stem. And dreadfully distinct
Against the dark, a tall white fountain played.

I realized, of course, that it was made
Not of our atoms; that the sense behind
710   The scene was not our sense. In life, the mind
Of any man is quick to recognize
Natural shams, and then before his eyes
The reed becomes a bird, the knobby twig
An inchworm, and the cobra head, a big
Wickedly folded moth. But in the case
Of my white fountain what it did replace
Perceptually was something that, I felt,
Could be grasped only by whoever dwelt
In the strange world where I was a mere stray.

720   And presently I saw it melt away:
Though still unconscious, I was back on earth.

The tale I told provoked my doctor's mirth.
He doubted very much that in the state
He found me in "one could hallucinate
Or dream in any sense. Later, perhaps,
But not during the actual collapse.
No, Mr. Shade."

But, Doctor, I was dead!
He smiled. "Not quite: just half a shade," he said.

However, I demurred. In mind I kept
730   Replaying the whole thing. Again I stepped
Down from the platform, and felt strange and hot,
And saw that chap stand up, and toppled, not
Because a heckler pointed with his pipe,
But probably because the time was ripe
For just that bump and wobble on the part
Of a limp blimp, an old unstable heart.

My vision reeked with truth. It had the tone,
The quiddity and quaintness of its own
Reality. It *was*. As time went on,
740   Its constant vertical in triumph shone.
Often when troubled by the outer glare
Of street and strife, inward I'd turn, and there,
There in the background of my soul it stood,
Old Faithful! And its presence always would
Console me wonderfully. Then, one day,
I came across what seemed a twin display.

It was a story in a magazine
About a Mrs. Z. whose heart had been
Rubbed back to life by a prompt surgeon's hand.

750 She told her interviewer of "The Land
Beyond the Veil" and the account contained
A hint of angels, and a glint of stained
Windows, and some soft music, and a choice
Of hymnal items, and her mother's voice;
But at the end she mentioned a remote
Landscape, a hazy orchard—and I quote:
"Beyond that orchard through a kind of smoke
I glimpsed a tall white fountain—and awoke."

If on some nameless island Captain Schmidt
760 Sees a new animal and captures it,
And if, a little later, Captain Smith
Brings back a skin, that island is no myth.
Our fountain was a signpost and a mark
Objectively enduring in the dark,
Strong as a bone, substantial as a tooth,
And almost vulgar in its robust truth!

The article was by Jim Coates. To Jim
Forthwith I wrote. Got her address from him.
Drove west three hundred miles to talk to her.
770 Arrived. Was met by an impassioned purr.
Saw that blue hair, those freckled hands, that rapt
Orchideous air—and knew that I was trapped.

"Who'd miss the opportunity to meet
A poet so distinguished?" It was sweet
Of me to come! I desperately tried
To ask my questions. They were brushed aside:
"Perhaps some other time." The journalist
Still had her scribblings. I should not insist.

She plied me with fruit cake, turning it all
780   Into an idiotic social call.
"I can't believe," she said, "that it is *you*!
I loved your poem in th*:* *Blue Review*.
That one about *Mon Blon*. I have a niece
Who's climbed the Matterhorn. The other piece
I could not understand. I mean the sense.
Because, of course, the sound—But I'm so dense!"

She was. I might have persevered. I might
Have made her tell me more about the white
Fountain we both had seen "beyond the veil"
790   But if (I thought) I mentioned that detail
She'd pounce upon it as upon a fond
Affinity, a sacramental bond,
Uniting mystically her and me,
And in a jiffy our two souls would be
Brother and sister trembling on the brink
Of tender incest. "Well," I said, "I think
It's getting late. . . ."
                I also called on Coates.
He was afraid he had mislaid her notes.
He took his article from a steel file:
800   "It's accurate. I have not changed her style.
There's one misprint—not that it matters much:
Mountain, not *fountain*. The majestic touch."

Life Everlasting—based on a misprint!
I mused as I drove homeward: take the hint,
And stop investigating my abyss?
But all at once it dawned on me that *this*
Was the real point, the contrapuntal theme;

Just this: not text, but texture; not the dream
But topsy-turvical coincidence,
810 Not flimsy nonsense, but a web of sense.
Yes! It sufficed that I in life could find
Some kind of link-and-bobolink, some kind
Of correlated pattern in the game,
Plexed artistry, and something of the same
Pleasure in it as they who played it found.

It did not matter who they were. No sound,
No furtive light came from their involute
Abode, but there they were, aloof and mute,
Playing a game of worlds, promoting pawns
820 To ivory unicorns and ebon fauns;
Kindling a long life here, extinguishing
A short one there; killing a Balkan king;
Causing a chunk of ice formed on a high-
Flying airplane to plummet from the sky
And strike a farmer dead; hiding my keys,
Glasses or pipe. Coordinating these
Events and objects with remote events
And vanished objects. Making ornaments
Of accidents and possibilities.

830 Stormcoated, I strode in: Sybil, it is
My firm conviction—"Darling, shut the door.
Had a nice trip?" Splendid—but what is more
I have returned convinced that I can grope
My way to some—to some—"Yes, dear?" Faint hope.

Now I shall spy on beauty as none has
Spied on it yet. Now I shall cry out as
None has cried out. Now I shall try what none
Has tried. Now I shall do what none has done.
And speaking of this wonderful machine:
840   I'm puzzled by the difference between
Two methods of composing: A, the kind
Which goes on solely in the poet's mind,
A testing of performing words, while he
Is soaping a third time one leg, and B,
The other kind, much more decorous, when
He's in his study writing with a pen.

In method B the hand supports the thought,
The abstract battle is concretely fought.
The pen stops in mid-air, then swoops to bar
850   A canceled sunset or restore a star,
And thus it physically guides the phrase
Toward faint daylight through the inky maze.

But method A is agony! The brain
Is soon enclosed in a steel cap of pain.
A muse in overalls directs the drill
Which grinds and which no effort of the will
Can interrupt, while the automaton

Is taking off what he has just put on
Or walking briskly to the corner store
860   To buy the paper he has read before.

Why is it so? Is it, perhaps, because
In penless work there is no pen-poised pause
And one must use three hands at the same time,
Having to choose the necessary rhyme,
Hold the completed line before one's eyes,
And keep in mind all the preceding tries?
Or is the process deeper with no desk
To prop the false and hoist the poetesque?
For there are those mysterious moments when
870   Too weary to delete, I drop my pen;
I ambulate—and by some mute command
The right word flutes and perches on my hand.

My best time is the morning; my preferred
Season, midsummer. I once overheard
Myself awakening while half of me
Still slept in bed. I tore my spirit free,
And caught up with myself—upon the lawn
Where clover leaves cupped the topaz of dawn,
And where Shade stood in nightshirt and one shoe.
880   And then I realized that *this* half too
Was fast asleep; both laughed and I awoke
Safe in my bed as day its eggshell broke,
And robins walked and stopped, and on the damp
Gemmed turf a brown shoe lay! My secret stamp,
The Shade impress, the mystery inborn.
Mirages, miracles, midsummer morn.

Since my biographer may be too staid
Or know too little to affirm that Shade
Shaved in his bath, here goes:

> "He'd fixed a sort

890 Of hinge-and-screw affair, a steel support
Running across the tub to hold in place
The shaving mirror right before his face
And with his toe renewing tap-warmth, he'd
Sit like a king there, and like Marat bleed."

The more I weigh, the less secure my skin;
In places it's ridiculously thin;
Thus near the mouth: the space between its wick
And my grimace, invites the wicked nick.
Or this dewlap: some day I must set free
900 The Newport Frill inveterate in me.
My Adam's apple is a prickly pear:
Now I shall speak of evil and despair
As none has spoken. Five, six, seven, eight,
Nine strokes are not enough. Ten. I palpate
Through strawberry-and-cream the gory mess
And find unchanged that patch of prickliness.

I have my doubts about the one-armed bloke
Who in commercials with one gliding stroke
Clears a smooth path of flesh from ear to chin,
910 Then wipes his face and fondly tries his skin.
I'm in the class of fussy bimanists.
As a discreet ephebe in tights assists
A female in an acrobatic dance,
My left hand helps, and holds, and shifts its stance.

Now I shall speak . . . Better than any soap
Is the sensation for which poets hope
When inspiration and its icy blaze,
The sudden image, the immediate phrase
Over the skin a triple ripple send
920   Making the little hairs all stand on end
As in the enlarged animated scheme
Of whiskers mowed when held up by Our Cream.

Now I shall speak of evil as none has
Spoken before. I loathe such things as jazz;
The white-hosed moron torturing a black
Bull, rayed with red; abstractist bric-a-brac;
Primitivist folk-masks; progressive schools;
Music in supermarkets; swimming pools;
Brutes, bores, class-conscious Philistines, Freud, Marx,
930   Fake thinkers, puffed-up poets, frauds and sharks.

And while the safety blade with scrape and screak
Travels across the country of my cheek,
Cars on the highway pass, and up the steep
Incline big trucks around my jawbone creep,
And now a silent liner docks, and now
Sunglassers tour Beirut, and now I plough
Old Zembla's fields where my gray stubble grows,
And slaves make hay between my mouth and nose.

Man's life as commentary to abstruse
940   *Unfinished poem. Note for further use.*

Dressing in all the rooms, I rhyme and roam
Throughout the house with, in my fist, a comb

Or a shoehorn, which turns into the spoon
I eat my egg with. In the afternoon
You drive me to the library. We dine
At half past six. And that odd muse of mine,
My versipel, is with me everywhere,
In carrel and in car, and in my chair.

And all the time, and all the time, my love,
950   You too are there, beneath the word, above
The syllable, to underscore and stress
The vital rhythm. One heard a woman's dress
Rustle in days of yore. I've often caught
The sound and sense of your approaching thought.
And all in you is youth, and you make new,
By quoting them, old things I made for you.

Dim Gulf was my first book (free verse); *Night Rote*
Came next; then *Hebe's Cup*, my final float
In that damp carnival, for now I term
960   Everything "Poems," and no longer squirm.
(But *this* transparent thingum does require
Some moondrop title. Help me, Will! *Pale Fire*.)

Gently the day has passed in a sustained
Low hum of harmony. The brain is drained
And a brown ament, and the noun I meant
To use but did not, dry on the cement.
Maybe my sensual love for the *consonne
D'appui*, Echo's fey child, is based upon
A feeling of fantastically planned,
970   Richly rhymed life.
                    I feel I understand

Existence, or at least a minute part
Of my existence, only through my art,
In terms of combinational delight;
And if my private universe scans right,
So does the verse of galaxies divine
Which I suspect is an iambic line.
I'm reasonably sure that we survive
And that my darling somewhere is alive,
As I am reasonably sure that I
980   Shall wake at six tomorrow, on July
The twenty-second, nineteen fifty-nine,
And that the day will probably be fine;
So this alarm clock let me set myself,
Yawn, and put back Shade's "Poems" on their shelf.

But it's not bedtime yet. The sun attains
Old Dr. Sutton's last two windowpanes.
The man must be—what? Eighty? Eighty-two?
Was twice my age the year I married you.
Where are you? In the garden. I can see
990   Part of your shadow near the shagbark tree.
Somewhere horseshoes are being tossed. Click. Clunk.
(Leaning against its lamppost like a drunk.)
A dark Vanessa with a crimson band
Wheels in the low sun, settles on the sand
And shows its ink-blue wingtips flecked with white.
And through the flowing shade and ebbing light
A man, unheedful of the butterfly—
Some neighbor's gardener, I guess—goes by
Trundling an empty barrow up the lane.

Commentary

Lines 1-4:   I was the shadow of the waxwing slain, etc.

The image in these opening lines evidently refers to a bird knocking itself out, in full flight, against the outer surface of a glass pane in which a mirrored sky, with its slightly darker tint and slightly slower cloud, presents the illusion of continued space. We can visualize John Shade in his early boyhood, a physically unattractive but otherwise beautifully developed lad, experiencing his first eschatological shock, as with incredulous fingers he picks up from the turf that compact ovoid body and gazes at the wax-red streaks ornamenting those gray-brown wings and at the graceful tail feathers tipped with yellow as bright as fresh paint. When in the last year of Shade's life I had the fortune of being his neighbor in the idyllic hills of New Wye (see Foreword), I often saw those particular birds most convivially feeding on the chalk-blue berries of junipers growing at the corner of his house. (See also lines 181-182.)

My knowledge of garden Aves had been limited to those of northern Europe but a young New Wye gardener, in whom I was interested (see note to line 998), helped me to identify the profiles of quite a number of tropical-looking little strangers and their comical calls; and, naturally, every tree top plotted its dotted line toward the ornithological work on my desk to which I would gallop from the lawn in nomenclatorial agitation. How hard I found to fit the name "robin" to the suburban impostor, the gross fowl, with its untidy dull-red livery and the revolting gusto it showed when consuming long, sad, passive worms!

Incidentally, it is curious to note that a crested bird called in Zemblan *sampel* ("silktail"), closely resembling a waxwing in shape and shade, is the model of one of the three heraldic creatures (the other two being respectively a reindeer proper and a merman azure, crined or) in the armorial bearings of the Zemblan King, Charles the Beloved (born 1915), whose glorious misfortunes I discussed so often with my friend.

The poem was begun at the dead center of the year, a few minutes after midnight July 1, while I played chess with a young Iranian enrolled in our summer school; and I do not doubt that our poet would have understood his annotator's temptation to synchronize a certain fateful fact, the departure from Zembla of the would-be regicide Gradus, with that date. Actually, Gradus left Onhava on the Copenhagen plane on July 5.

Line 12: that crystal land

Perhaps an allusion to Zembla, my dear country. After this, in the disjointed, half-obliterated draft which I am not at all sure I have deciphered properly:

> Ah, I must not forget to say something
> That my friend told me of a certain king.

Alas, he would have said a great deal more if a domestic anti-Karlist had not controlled every line he communicated to her! Many a time have I rebuked him in bantering fashion: "You really should promise to use all that wonderful stuff, you bad gray poet, you!" And we would both giggle like boys. But then, after the inspiring evening stroll, we had to part, and grim night lifted the drawbridge between his impregnable fortress and my humble home.

That King's reign (1936-1958) will be remembered by at least a few discerning historians as a peaceful and elegant one. Owing to a fluid system of judicious alliances, Mars in his time never marred the record. Internally, until corruption, betrayal, and Extremism penetrated it, the People's Place (parliament) worked in perfect harmony with the Royal Council. Harmony, indeed, was the reign's password. The polite arts and pure sciences flourished. Technicology, applied physics, industrial chemistry and so forth were suffered to thrive. A small skyscraper of ultramarine glass was steadily rising in Onhava. The climate seemed to be improving. Taxation had become a thing of beauty. The poor were getting a little richer, and the rich a little poorer (in accordance with what may be known some day as Kinbote's Law). Medical care was spreading to the confines of the state: less and less often, on his tour of the country, every autumn, when the rowans hung coral-heavy, and the puddles tinkled with Muscovy glass, the friendly and eloquent monarch would be interrupted by a pertussal "backdraucht" in a crowd of schoolchildren. Parachuting had become a popular sport. Everybody, in a word, was content—even the political mischiefmakers who were contentedly making mischief paid by a contented *Sosed* (Zembla's gigantic neighbor). But let us not pursue this tiresome subject.

To return to the King: take for instance the question of personal culture. How often is it that kings engage in some special research? Conchologists among them can be counted on the fingers of one maimed hand. The last king of Zembla —partly under the influence of his uncle Conmal, the great translator of Shakespeare (see notes to lines 39-40 and 962), had become, despite frequent migraines, passionately addicted to the study of literature. At forty, not long before the collapse of his throne, he had attained such a degree of scholarship that he dared accede to his venerable uncle's raucous dying request: "Teach, Karlik!" Of course, it would have been unseemly for a monarch to appear in the robes of learning at a university lectern and present to rosy youths *Finnigan's Wake* as a monstrous extension of Angus Mac-Diarmid's "incoherent transactions" and of Southey's Lingo-Grande ("Dear Stumparumper," etc.) or discuss the Zemblan variants, collected in 1798 by Hodinski, of the *Kongs-skugg-sio* (*The Royal Mirror*), an anonymous masterpiece of the twelfth century. Therefore he lectured under an assumed name and in a heavy make-up, with wig and false whiskers. All brown-bearded, apple-cheeked, blue-eyed Zem-blans look alike, and I who have not shaved now for a year, resemble my disguised king (see also note to line 894).

During these periods of teaching, Charles Xavier made it a rule to sleep at a *pied-à-terre* he had rented, as any scholarly citizen would, in Coriolanus Lane: a charming, central-heated studio with adjacent bathroom and kitchenette. One recalls with nostalgic pleasure its light gray carpeting and pearl-gray walls (one of them graced with a solitary copy of Picasso's *Chandelier, pot et casserole émaillée*), a shelfful of calf-bound poets, and a virginal-looking daybed under its rug of imitation panda fur. How far from this limpid simplicity seemed the palace and the odious Council Chamber with its unsolvable problems and frightened councilors!

Line 17:   And then the gradual;   *Line* 29:   gray

By an extraordinary coincidence (inherent perhaps in the
contrapuntal nature of Shade's art) our poet seems to name
here (gradual, gray) a man, whom he was to see for one
fatal moment three weeks later, but of whose existence at
the time (July 2) he could not have known. Jakob Gradus
called himself variously Jack Degree or Jacques de Grey, or
James de Gray, and also appears in police records as Ravus,
Ravenstone, and d'Argus. Having a morbid affection for the
ruddy Russia of the Soviet era, he contended that the real
origin of his name should be sought in the Russian word for
grape, *vinograd,* to which a Latin suffix had adhered, making
it Vinogradus. His father, Martin Gradus, had been a Protes-
tant minister in Riga, but except for him and a maternal
uncle (Roman Tselovalnikov, police officer and part-time
member of the Social-Revolutionary party), the whole clan
seems to have been in the liquor business. Martin Gradus
died in 1920, and his widow moved to Strasbourg where she
soon died, too. Another Gradus, an Alsatian merchant, who
oddly enough was totally unrelated to our killer but had
been a close business friend of his kinsmen for years, adopted
the boy and raised him with his own children. It would seem
that at one time young Gradus studied pharmacology in
Zurich, and at another, traveled to misty vineyards as an itin-
erant wine taster. We find him next engaging in petty subversive activities—printing peevish pamphlets, acting as messenger for obscure syndicalist groups, organizing strikes at
glass factories, and that sort of thing. Sometime in the forties
he came to Zembla as a brandy salesman. There he married
a publican's daughter. His connection with the Extremist
party dates from its first ugly writhings, and when the revolu-

tion broke out, his modest organizational gifts found some appreciation in various offices. His departure for Western Europe, with a sordid purpose in his heart and a loaded gun in his pocket, took place on the very day that an innocent poet in an innocent land was beginning Canto Two of *Pale Fire*. We shall accompany Gradus in constant thought, as he makes his way from distant dim Zembla to green Appalachia, through the entire length of the poem, following the road of its rhythm, riding past in a rhyme, skidding around the corner of a run-on, breathing with the caesura, swinging down to the foot of the page from line to line as from branch to branch, hiding between two words (see note to line 596), reappearing on the horizon of a new canto, steadily marching nearer in iambic motion, crossing streets, moving up with his valise on the escalator of the pentameter, stepping off, boarding a new train of thought, entering the hall of a hotel, putting out the bedlight, while Shade blots out a word, and falling asleep as the poet lays down his pen for the night.

Line 27: Sherlock Holmes

A hawk-nosed, lanky, rather likable private detective, the main character in various stories by Conan Doyle. I have no means to ascertain at the present time which of these is referred to here but suspect that our poet simply made up this Case of the Reversed Footprints.

Lines 34-35: Stilettos of a frozen stillicide

How persistently our poet evokes images of winter in the beginning of a poem which he started composing on a balmy summer night! The mechanism of the associations is easy to make out (glass leading to crystal and crystal to ice) but the prompter behind it retains his incognito. One is too modest to suppose that the fact that the poet and his future commentator first met on a winter day somehow impinges here on the actual season. In the lovely line heading this comment the reader should note the last word. My dictionary defines it as "a succession of drops falling from the eaves, eavesdrop, cavesdrop." I remember having encountered it for the first time in a poem by Thomas Hardy. The bright frost has eternalized the bright eavesdrop. We should also note the cloak-and-dagger hint-glint in the "svelte stilettos" and the shadow of regicide in the rhyme.

Lines 39-40: Was close my eyes, etc.

These lines are represented in the drafts by a variant reading:

39 . . . . and home would haste my thieves,
40 The sun with stolen ice, the moon with leaves

One cannot help recalling a passage in *Timon of Athens* (Act IV, Scene 3) where the misanthrope talks to the three marauders. Having no library in the desolate log cabin where I live like Timon in his cave, I am compelled for the purpose of quick citation to retranslate this passage into English prose from a Zemblan poetical version of *Timon* which, I hope, sufficiently approximates the text, or is at least faithful to its spirit:

> The sun is a thief: she lures the sea
> and robs it. The moon is a thief:
> he steals his silvery light from the sun.
> The sea is a thief: it dissolves the moon.

For a prudent appraisal of Conmal's translations of Shakespeare's works, see note to line 962.

Line 42: I could make out

By the end of May I could make out the outlines of some of my images in the shape his genius might give them; by mid-June I felt sure at last that he would recreate in a poem the dazzling Zembla burning in my brain. I mesmerized him with it, I saturated him with my vision, I pressed upon him, with a drunkard's wild generosity, all that I was helpless myself to put into verse. Surely, it would not be easy to discover in the history of poetry a similar case—that of two men, different in origin, upbringing, thought associations, spiritual intonation and mental mode, one a cosmopolitan scholar, the other a fireside poet, entering into a secret compact of this kind. At length I knew he was ripe with my Zembla, bursting with suitable rhymes, ready to spurt at the brush of an eyelash. I kept urging him at every opportunity to surmount his habitual sloth and start writing. My little pocket diary contains such jottings as: "Suggested to him the heroic measure"; "retold the escape"; "offered the use of a quiet room in my house"; "discussed making recordings of my voice for his use"; and finally, under date of July 3: "poem begun!"

Although I realize only too clearly, alas, that the result, in its pale and diaphanous final phase, cannot be regarded as a direct echo of my narrative (of which, incidentally, only a few fragments are given in my notes—mainly to Canto One), one can hardly doubt that the sunset glow of the story acted as a catalytic agent upon the very process of the sustained creative effervescence that enabled Shade to produce a 1000-line poem in three weeks. There is, moreover, a symptomatic family resemblance in the coloration of both poem and story. I have reread, not without pleasure, my comments to his lines, and in many cases have caught myself borrowing a kind of opalescent light from my poet's fiery orb, and unconsciously aping the prose style of his own critical essays. But his widow, and his colleagues, may stop worrying and enjoy in full the fruit of whatever advice they gave my good-natured poet. Oh yes, the final text of the poem is entirely his.

If we discount, as I think we should, three casual allusions to royalty (605, 822, and 894) and the Popian "Zembla" in line 937, we may conclude that the final text of *Pale Fire* has been deliberately and drastically drained of every trace of the material I contributed; but we also find that despite the control exercised upon my poet by a domestic censor and God knows whom else, he has given the royal fugitive a refuge in the vaults of the variants he has preserved; for in his draft as many as thirteen verses, superb singing verses (given by me in note to lines 70, 79, and 130, all in Canto

One, which he obviously worked at with a greater degree of creative freedom than he enjoyed afterwards) bear the specific imprint of my theme, a minute but genuine star ghost of my discourse on Zembla and her unfortunate king.

Lines 47-48: the frame house between Goldsworth and Wordsmith

The first name refers to the house in Dulwich Road that I rented from Hugh Warren Goldsworth, authority on Roman Law and distinguished judge. I never had the pleasure of meeting my landlord but I came to know his handwriting almost as well as I do Shade's. The second name denotes, of course, Wordsmith University. In seeming to suggest a midway situation between the two places, our poet is less concerned with spatial exactitude than with a witty exchange of syllables invoking the two masters of the heroic couplet, between whom he embowers his own muse. Actually, the "frame house on its square of green" was five miles west of the Wordsmith campus but only fifty yards or so distant from my east windows.

In the Foreword to this work I have had occasion to say something about the amenities of my habitation. The charming, charmingly vague lady (see note to line 691), who secured it for me, sight unseen, meant well, no doubt, especially since it was widely admired in the neighborhood for its "old-world spaciousness and graciousness." Actually, it was an old, dismal, white-and-black, half-timbered house, of the type termed *wodnaggen* in my country, with carved gables, drafty bow windows and a so-called "semi-noble" porch, surmounted by a hideous veranda. Judge Goldsworth had a wife and four daughters. Family photographs met me in the hallway and pursued me from room to room, and although I am sure that Alphina (9), Betty (10), Candida (12), and Dee (14) will soon change from horribly cute little school-girls to smart young ladies and superior mothers, I must confess that their pert pictures irritated me to such an extent that finally I gathered them one by one and dumped them all in a closet under the gallows row of their cellophane-shrouded winter clothes. In the study I found a large picture of their parents, with sexes reversed, Mrs. G. resembling Malenkov, and Mr. G. a Medusa-locked hag, and this I replaced by the reproduction of a beloved early Picasso: earth boy leading raincloud horse. I did not bother, though, to do much about the family books which were also all over the house—four sets of different Children's Encyclopedias, and a stolid grown-up one that ascended all the way from shelf to shelf along a flight of stairs to burst an appendix in the attic. Judging by the novels in Mrs. Goldsworth's boudoir, her intellectual interests were fully developed, going as they did from Amber to Zen. The head of this alphabetic family had a library too, but this consisted mainly of legal works and a lot of conspicuously lettered ledgers. All the layman could glean for instruction and entertainment was a morocco-bound album in which the judge had lovingly pasted the life histories and pictures of people he had sent to prison or condemned to death: unforgettable faces of imbecile hood-lums, last smokes and last grins, a strangler's quite ordinary-looking hands, a self-made widow, the close-set merciless eyes of a homicidal maniac (somewhat resembling, I admit, the late Jacques d'Argus), a bright little parricide aged seven ("Now, sonny, we want you to tell us—"), and a sad pudgy old pederast who had blown up his blackmailer. What rather surprised me was that he, my learned landlord, and not his "missus," directed the household. Not only had he left me a detailed inventory of all such articles as cluster around a new tenant like a mob of menacing natives, but he had taken stupendous pains to write out on slips of paper recommendations, explanations, injunctions and supplementary lists. Whatever I touched on the first day of my stay yielded a specimen of Goldsworthiana. I unlocked the medicine chest in the second bathroom, and out fluttered a message advising me that the slit for discarded safety blades was too full for use. I opened the icebox, and it warned me with a bark that "no national specialties with odors hard to get rid of" should be placed therein. I pulled out the middle drawer of the desk in the study—and discovered a *catalogue raisonné* of its meager contents which included an assortment of ashtrays, a damask paperknife (described as "one ancient dagger brought by Mrs. Goldsworth's father from the Orient"), and an old but unused pocket diary optimistically maturing there until its calendric correspondencies came around again. Among various detailed notices affixed to a special board in the pantry, such as plumbing instructions, dissertations on electricity, discourses on cactuses and so forth, I found the diet of the black cat that came with the house:

> Mon, Wed, Fri: Liver
> Tue, Thu, Sat: Fish
> Sun: Ground meat

(All it got from me was milk and sardines; it was a likable little creature but after a while its movements began to grate on my nerves and I farmed it out to Mrs. Finley, the cleaning woman.) But perhaps the funniest note concerned the manipulations of the window curtains which had to be drawn in different ways at different hours to prevent the sun from getting at the upholstery. A description of the position of the sun, daily and seasonal, was given for the several windows, and if I had heeded all this I would have been kept as busy as a participant in a regatta. A footnote, however, generously suggested that instead of manning the curtains, I might prefer to shift and reshift out of sun range the more precious pieces of furniture (two embroidered armchairs and a heavy "royal console") but should do it carefully lest I scratch the wall moldings. I cannot, alas, reproduce the meticulous schedule of these transposals but seem to recall that I was supposed to castle the long way before going to bed and the short way first thing in the morning. My dear Shade roared with laughter when I led him on a tour of inspection and had him find some of those bunny eggs for himself. Thank God, his robust hilarity dissipated the atmosphere of *damnum infectum* in which I was supposed to dwell. On his part, he regaled me with a number of anecdotes concerning the judge's dry wit and courtroom mannerisms; most of these anecdotes were doubtless folklore exaggerations, a few were evident inventions, and all were harmless. He did not bring up, my sweet old friend never did, ridiculous stories about the terrifying shadows that Judge Goldsworth's gown threw across the underworld, or about this or that beast lying in prison and positively dying of *raghdirst* (thirst for revenge)—crass banalities circulated by the scurrilous and the heartless—by all those for whom romance, remoteness, sealskin-lined scarlet skies, the darkening dunes of a fabulous kingdom, simply do not exist. But

enough of this. Let us turn to our poet's windows. I have
no desire to twist and batter an unambiguous *apparatus
criticus* into the monstrous semblance of a novel.

Today it would be impossible for me to describe Shade's
house in terms of architecture or indeed in any term other
than those of peeps and glimpses, and window-framed opportunities. As previously mentioned (see Foreword), the
coming of summer presented a problem in optics: the encroaching foliage did not always see eye to eye with me: it
confused a green monocle with an opaque occludent, and the
idea of protection with that of obstruction. Meanwhile (on
July 3 according to my agenda) I had learned—not from
John but from Sybil—that my friend had started to work on
a long poem. After not having seen him for a couple of days,
I happened to be bringing him some third-class mail from
his box on the road, adjacent to Goldsworth's (which I used
to ignore, crammed as it was with leaflets, local advertisements, commercial catalogues, and that kind of trash) and
ran into Sybil whom a shrub had screened from my falcon
eye. Straw-hatted and garden-gloved, she was squatting on
her hams in front of a flower bed and pruning or tying up
something, and her close-fitting brown trousers reminded
me of the mandolin tights (as I jokingly called them) that
my own wife used to wear. She said not to bother him with
those ads and added the information about his having "begun a really big poem." I felt the blood rush to my face and
mumbled something about his not having shown any of it to
me yet, and she straightened herself, and swept the black
and gray hair off her forehead, and stared at me, and said:
"What do you mean—shown any of it? He never shows anything unfinished. Never, never. He will not even discuss it
with you until it is quite, quite finished." I could not believe

it, but soon discovered on talking to my strangely reticent
friend that he had been well coached by his lady. When I
endeavored to draw him out by means of good-natured sallies
such as: "People who live in glass houses should not write
poems," he would only yawn and shake his head, and retort
that "foreigners ought to keep away from old saws." Nevertheless the urge to find out what he was doing with all the
live, glamorous, palpitating, shimmering material I had lav-
ished upon him, the itching desire to see him at work (even
if the fruit of his work was denied me), proved to be utterly
agonizing and uncontrollable and led me to indulge in an
orgy of spying which no considerations of pride could stop.

Windows, as well known, have been the solace of first-
person literature throughout the ages. But this observer
never could emulate in sheer luck the eavesdropping *Hero
of Our Time* or the omnipresent one of *Time Lost.* Yet I
was granted now and then scraps of happy hunting. When
my casement window ceased to function because of an elm's
gross growth, I found, at the end of the veranda, an ivied
corner from which I could view rather amply the front of the
poet's house. If I wanted to see its south side I could go
down to the back of my garage and look from behind a tulip
tree across the curving downhill road at several precious
bright windows, for he never pulled down the shades (*she*
did). If I yearned for the opposite side, all I had to do was
walk uphill to the top of my garden where my bodyguard of
black junipers watched the stars, and the omens, and the
patch of pale light under the lone streetlamp on the road
below. By the onset of the season here conjured up, I had
surmounted the very special and very private fears that are
discussed elsewhere (see note to line 62) and rather enjoyed
following in the dark a weedy and rocky easterly projection

of my grounds ending in a locust grove on a slightly higher level than the north side of the poet's house.

Once, three decades ago, in my tender and terrible boyhood, I had the occasion of seeing a man in the act of making contact with God. I had wandered into the so-called Rose Court at the back of the Ducal Chapel in my native Onhava, during an interval in hymnal practice. As I mooned there, lifting and cooling my bare calves by turns against a smooth column, I could hear the distant sweet voices interblending in subdued boyish merriment which some chance grudge, some jealous annoyance with one particular lad, prevented me from joining. The sound of rapid steps made me raise my morose gaze from the sectile mosaic of the court—realistic rose petals cut out of rodstein and large, almost palpable thorns cut out of green marble. Into these roses and thorns there walked a black shadow: a tall, pale, long-nosed, dark-haired young minister whom I had seen around once or twice strode out of the vestry and without seeing me stopped in the middle of the court. Guilty disgust contorted his thin lips. He wore spectacles. His clenched hands seemed to be gripping invisible prison bars. But there is no bound to the measure of grace which man may be able to receive. All at once his look changed to one of rapture and reverence. I had never seen such a blaze of bliss before but was to perceive something of that splendor, of that spiritual energy and divine vision, now, in another land, reflected upon the rugged and homely face of old John Shade. How glad I was that the vigils I had kept all through the spring had prepared me to observe him at his miraculous midsummer task! I had learned exactly when and where to find the best points from which to follow the contours of his inspiration. My binoculars would seek him out and focus upon him from afar in his various places of labor: at night, in the violet glow of his upstairs study where a kindly mirror reflected for me his hunched-up shoulders and the pencil with which he kept picking his ear (inspecting now and then the lead, and even tasting it); in the forenoon, lurking in the ruptured shadows of his first-floor study where a bright goblet of liquor quietly traveled from filing cabinet to lectern, and from lectern to bookshelf, there to hide if need be behind Dante's bust; on a hot day, among the vines of a small arborlike portico, through the garlands of which I could glimpse a stretch of oilcloth, his elbow upon it, and the plump cherubic fist propping and crimpling his temple. Incidents of perspective and lighting, interference by framework or leaves, usually deprived me of a clear view of his face; and perhaps nature arranged it that way so as to conceal from a possible predator the mysteries of generation; but sometimes when the poet paced back and forth across his lawn, or sat down for a moment on the bench at the end of it, or paused under his favorite hickory tree, I could distinguish the expression of passionate interest, rapture and reverence, with which he followed the images wording themselves in his mind, and I knew that whatever my agnostic friend might say in denial, at *that* moment Our Lord was with him.

On certain nights, when long before its inhabitants' usual bedtime the house would be dark on the three sides I could survey from my three vantage points, that very darkness kept telling me they were at home. Their car stood near its garage—but I could not believe they had gone out on foot, since in that case they would have left the porch light turned on. Later considerations and deductions have persuaded me that the night of great need on which I decided to check the matter was July 11, the date of Shade's completing his Sec-

ond Canto. It was a hot, black, blustery night. I stole through
the shrubbery to the rear of their house. At first I thought
that this fourth side was also dark, thus clinching the matter,
and had time to experience a queer sense of relief before
noticing a faint square of light under the window of a little
back parlor where I had never been. It was wide open. A tall
lamp with a parchment-like shade illuminated the bottom of
the room where I could see Sybil and John, her on the edge of
a divan, sidesaddle, with her back to me, and him on a
hassock near the divan upon which he seemed to be slowly
collecting and stacking scattered playing cards left after a
game of patience. Sybil was alternatively huddle-shaking
and blowing her nose; John's face was all blotchy and wet.
Not being aware at the time of the exact type of writing
paper my friend used, I could not help wondering what on
earth could be so tear-provoking about the outcome of a
game of cards. As I strained to see better, standing up to my
knees in a horribly elastic box hedge, I dislodged the sono-
rous lid of a garbage can. This of course might have been
mistaken for the work of the wind, and Sybil hated the
wind. She at once left her perch, closed the window with a
great bang, and pulled down its strident blind.

I crept back to my cheerless domicile with a heavy heart
and a puzzled mind. The heart remained heavy but the puz-
zle was solved a few days later, very probably on St. Swithin's
Day, for I find in my little diary under that date the anticipa-
tory *"promnad vespert mid J.S.,"* crossed out with a petu-
lance that broke the lead in midstroke. Having waited and
waited for my friend to join me in the lane, until the red of
the sunset had turned to the ashes of dusk, I walked over to
his front door, hesitated, assessed the gloom and the silence,
and started to walk around the house. This time not a glint

came from the back parlor, but by the bright prosaic light in the kitchen I distinguished one end of a whitewashed table and Sybil sitting at it with so rapt a look on her face that one might have supposed she had just thought up a new recipe. The back door was ajar, and as I tapped it open and launched upon some gay airy phrase, I realized that Shade, sitting at the other end of the table, was in the act of reading to her something that I guessed to be a part of his poem. They both started. An unprintable oath escaped from him and he slapped down on the table the stack of index cards he had in his hand. Later he was to attribute this temperamental outburst to his having mistaken, with his reading glasses on, a welcome friend for an intruding salesman; but I must say it shocked me, it shocked me greatly, and disposed me at the time to read a hideous meaning into everything that followed. "Well, sit down," said Sybil, "and have some coffee" (victors are generous). I accepted, as I wanted to see if the recitation would be continued in my presence. It was not. "I thought," I said to my friend, "you were coming out with me for a stroll." He excused himself saying he felt out of sorts, and continued to clean the bowl of his pipe as fiercely as if it were my heart he was hollowing out.

Not only did I understand *then* that Shade regularly read to Sybil cumulative parts of his poem but it also dawns upon me *now* that, just as regularly, she made him tone down or remove from his Fair Copy everything connected with the magnificent Zemblan theme with which I kept furnishing him and which, without knowing much about the growing work, I fondly believed would become the main rich thread in its weave!

Higher up on the same wooded hill stood, and still stands I trust, Dr. Sutton's old clapboard house and, at the very top, eternity shall not dislodge Professor C.'s ultramodern villa from whose terrace one can glimpse to the south the larger and sadder of the three conjoined lakes called Omega, Ozero, and Zero (Indian names garbled by early settlers in such a way as to accommodate specious derivations and commonplace allusions). On the northern side of the hill Dulwich Road joins the highway leading to Wordsmith University to which I shall devote here only a few words partly because all kinds of descriptive booklets should be available to the reader by writing to the University's Publicity Office, but mainly because I wish to convey, in making this reference to Wordsmith briefer than the notes on the Goldsworth and Shade houses, the fact that the college was considerably farther from them than they were from one another. It is probably the first time that the dull pain of distance is rendered through an effect of style and that a topographical idea finds its verbal expression in a series of foreshortened sentences.

After winding for about four miles in a general eastern direction through a beautifully sprayed and irrigated residential section with variously graded lawns sloping down on both sides, the highway bifurcates: one branch goes left to New Wye and its expectant airfield; the other continues to the campus. Here are the great mansions of madness, the impeccably planned dormitories—bedlams of jungle music—the magnificent palace of the Administration, the brick walls, the archways, the quadrangles blocked out in velvet green and chrysoprase, Spencer House and its lily pond, the Chapel, New Lecture Hall, the Library, the prisonlike edifice containing our classrooms and offices (to be called from now on Shade Hall), the famous avenue of all the trees mentioned by Shakespeare, a distant droning sound, the hint of a haze, the turquoise dome of the Observatory, wisps and pale plumes of cirrus, and the poplar-curtained Roman-tiered football field, deserted on summer days except for a dreamy-eyed youngster flying—on a long control line in a droning circle—a motor-powered model plane.

Dear Jesus, do something.

Line 49: shagbark

A hickory. Our poet shared with the English masters the noble knack of transplanting trees into verse with their sap and shade. Many years ago Disa, our King's Queen, whose favorite trees were the jacaranda and the maidenhair, copied out in her album a quatrain from John Shade's collection of short poems *Hebe's Cup*, which I cannot refrain from quoting here (from a letter I received on April 6, 1959, from southern France):

> THE SACRED TREE
> The ginkgo leaf, in golden hue, when shed,
>   A muscat grape,
>   Is an old-fashioned butterfly, ill-spread,
>   In shape.

When the new Episcopal church in New Wye (see note to line 549) was built, the bulldozers spared an arc of those sacred trees planted by a landscaper of genius (Repburg) at the end of the so-called Shakespeare Avenue, on the campus. I do not know if it is relevant or not but there is a cat-and-mouse game in the second line, and "tree" in Zemblan is *grados*.

Line 57: The phantom of my little daughter's swing

After this Shade crossed out lightly the following lines in the draft:

The light is good; the reading lamps, long-necked;
All doors have keys. Your modern architect
Is in collusion with psychanalysts:
When planning parents' bedrooms, he insists
On lockless doors so that, when looking back,
The future patient of the future quack
May find, all set for him, the Primal Scene.

Line 61: TV's huge paperclip

In the otherwise empty, and pretty fatuous, obituary mentioned in my notes to lines 71-72, there happens to be quoted a manuscript poem (received from Sybil Shade) which is said to have been "composed by our poet apparently at the end of June, thus less than a month before our poet's death, thus being the last short piece that our poet wrote."

Here it is:

THE SWING
The setting sun that lights the tips
Of TV's giant paperclips
  Upon the roof;

The shadow of the doorknob that
At sundown is a baseball bat
  Upon the door;

> The cardinal that likes to sit
> And make chip-wit, chip-wit, chip-wit
>   Upon the tree;
>
> The empty little swing that swings
> Under the tree: these are the things
>   That break my heart.

I leave *my* poet's reader to decide whether it is likely he would have written this only a few days before he repeated its miniature themes in this part of the poem. I suspect it to be a much earlier effort (it has not year subscript but should be dated soon after his daughter's death) which Shade dug out from among his old papers to see what he could use for *Pale Fire* (the poem our necrologist does not know).

Line 62: often

Often, almost nightly, throughout the spring of 1959, I had feared for my life. Solitude is the playfield of Satan. I cannot describe the depths of my loneliness and distress. There was naturally my famous neighbor just across the lane, and at one time I took in a dissipated young roomer (who generally came home long after midnight). Yet I wish to stress that cold hard core of loneliness which is not good for a displaced soul. Everybody knows how given to regicide Zemblans are: two Queens, three Kings, and fourteen Pretenders died violent deaths, strangled, stabbed, poisoned, and drowned, in the course of only one century (1700–1800).

The Goldsworth castle became particularly solitary after that turning point at dusk which resembles so much the nightfall of the mind. Stealthy rustles, the footsteps of yester-year leaves, an idle breeze, a dog touring the garbage cans—everything sounded to me like a bloodthirsty prowler. I kept moving from window to window, my silk nightcap drenched with sweat, my bared breast a thawing pond, and sometimes, armed with the judge's shotgun, I dared beard the terrors of the terrace. I suppose it was then, on those masquerading spring nights with the sounds of new life in the trees cru-elly mimicking the cracklings of old death in my brain, I suppose it was then, on those dreadful nights, that I got used to consulting the windows of my neighbor's house in the hope for a gleam of comfort (see notes to lines 47-48). What would I not have given for the poet's suffering another heart attack (see line 691 and note) leading to my being called over to their house, all windows ablaze, in the middle of the night, in a great warm burst of sympathy, coffee, telephone calls, Zemblan herbal receipts (they work wonders!), and a resurrected Shade weeping in my arms ("There, there, John"). But on those March nights their house was as black as a coffin. And when physical exhaustion and the sepulchral cold drove me at last upstairs to my solitary double bed, I would lie awake and breathless—as if only now living con-sciously through those perilous nights in my country, where at any moment, a company of jittery revolutionists might enter and hustle me off to a moonlit wall. The sound of a rapid car or a groaning truck would come as a strange mix-ture of friendly life's relief and death's fearful shadow: would that shadow pull up at my door? Were those phantom thugs coming for me? Would they shoot me at once—or would they smuggle the chloroformed scholar back to Zembla, Rodnaya Zembla, to face there a dazzling decanter and a row of judges exulting in their inquisitorial chairs?

At times I thought that only by self-destruction could I hope to cheat the relentlessly advancing assassins who were in me, in my eardrums, in my pulse, in my skull, rather than on that constant highway looping up over me and around my heart as I dozed off only to have my sleep shattered by that drunken, impossible, unforgettable Bob's return to Candida's or Dee's former bed. As briefly mentioned in the foreword, I finally threw him out; after which for several nights neither wine, nor music, nor prayer could allay my fears. On the other hand, those mellowing spring days were quite sufferable, my lectures pleased everybody, and I made it a point of attending all the social functions available to me. But after the gay evening there came again the insidious approach, the oblique shuffle, that creeping up, and that pause, and the resumed crepitation.

The Goldsworth château had many outside doors, and no matter how thoroughly I inspected them and the window shutters downstairs at bedtime, I never failed to discover next morning something unlocked, unlatched, a little loose, a little ajar, something sly and suspicious-looking. One night the black cat, which a few minutes before I had seen rippling down into the basement where I had arranged toilet facilities for it in an attractive setting, suddenly reappeared on the threshold of the music room, in the middle of my insomnia and a Wagner record, arching its back and sporting a neck bow of white silk which it could certainly never have put on all by itself. I telephoned 11111 and a few minutes later was discussing possible culprits with a policeman who relished greatly my cherry cordial, but whoever had broken in had left no trace. It is so easy for a cruel person to make the victim of his ingenuity believe that he has persecution mania, or is really being stalked by a killer, or is suffering from hallucinations. Hallucinations! Well did I know that among certain youthful instructors whose advances I had rejected there was at least one evil practical joker; I knew it ever since the time I came home from a very enjoyable and successful meeting of students and teachers (at which I had exuberantly thrown off my coat and shown several willing pupils a few of the amusing holds employed by Zemblan wrestlers) and found in my coat pocket a brutal anonymous note saying: "You have hal.....s real bad, chum," meaning evidently "hallucinations," although a malevolent critic might infer from the insufficient number of dashes that little Mr. Anon, despite teaching Freshman English, could hardly spell.

I am happy to report that soon after Easter my fears disappeared never to return. Into Alphina's or Betty's room another lodger moved, Balthasar, Prince of Loam, as I dubbed him, who with elemental regularity fell asleep at nine and by six in the morning was planting heliotropes (*Heliotropium turgenevi*). This is the flower whose odor evokes with timeless intensity the dusk, and the garden bench, and a house of painted wood in a distant northern land.

Line 70: The new TV

After this, in the draft (dated July 3), come a few unnumbered lines that may have been intended for some later parts of the poem. They are not actually deleted but are accompanied by a question mark in the margin and encircled with a wavy line encroaching upon some of the letters:

> There are events, strange happenings, that strike
> The mind as emblematic. They are like
> Lost similes adrift without a string,
> Attached to nothing. Thus that northern king,
> Whose desperate escape from prison was
> Brought off successfully only because
> Some forty of his followers that night
> Impersonated him and aped his flight—

He never would have reached the western coast had not a fad spread among his secret supporters, romantic, heroic daredevils, of impersonating the fleeing king. They rigged themselves out to look like him in red sweaters and red caps, and popped up here and there, completely bewildering the revolutionary police. Some of the pranksters were much younger than the King, but this did not matter since his pictures in the huts of mountain folks and in the myopic shops of hamlets, where you could buy worms, ginger bread and *zhiletka* blades, had not aged since his coronation. A charming cartoon touch was added on the famous occasion when from the terrace of the Kronblik Hotel, whose chairlift takes tourists to the Kron glacier, one merry mime was seen floating up, like a red moth, with a hapless, and capless, policeman riding two seats behind him in dream-slow pursuit. It gives one pleasure to add that before reaching the staging point, the false king managed to escape by climbing down one of the pylons that supported the traction cable (see also notes to lines 149 and 171).

Line 71:   parents

With commendable alacrity, Professor Hurley produced
an Appreciation of John Shade's published works within a
month after the poet's death. It came out in a skimpy literary review, whose name momentarily escapes me, and was
shown to me in Chicago where I interrupted for a couple of
days my automobile journey from New Wye to Cedarn, in
these grim autumnal mountains.

A Commentary where placid scholarship should reign is
not the place for blasting the preposterous defects of that
little obituary. I have only mentioned it because that is
where I gleaned a few meager details concerning the poet's
parents. His father, Samuel Shade, who died at fifty, in 1902,
had studied medicine in his youth and was vice-president of
a firm of surgical instruments in Exton. His chief passion,
however, was what our eloquent necrologist calls "the study
of the feathered tribe," adding that "a bird had been named
for him: *Bombycilla Shadei*" (this should be *"shadei,"* of
course). The poet's mother, nee Caroline Lukin, assisted
him in his work and drew the admirable figures of his *Birds
of Mexico*, which I remember having seen in my friend's
house. What the obituarist does not know is that Lukin
comes from Luke, as also do Locock and Luxon and Lukash-
evich. It represents one of the many instances when the
amorphous-looking but live and personal hereditary patro-
nymic grows, sometimes in fantastic shapes, around the common pebble of a Christian name. The Lukins are an old
Essex family. Other names derive from professions such as
Rymer, Scrivener, Limner (one who illuminates parch-
ments), Botkin (one who makes bottekins, fancy footwear)
and thousands of others. My tutor, a Scotsman, used to call

any old tumble-down building "a hurley-house." But enough of this.

A few other items concerning John Shade's university studies and the middle years of his singularly uneventful life can be looked up by his reader in the professor's article. It would have been on the whole a dull piece had it not been enlivened, if that is the term, by certain special features. Thus, there is only one allusion to my friend's masterpiece (the neatly stacked batches of which, as I write this, lie in the sun on my table as so many ingots of fabulous metal) and this I transcribe with morbid delight: "Just before our poet's untimely death he seems to have been working on an autobiographical poem." The circumstances of this death are completely distorted by the professor, a faithful follower of the gentlemen of the daily press who—perhaps for political reasons—had falsified the culprit's motives and intentions without awaiting his trial—which unfortunately was not to take place in this world (see eventually my ultimate note). But, of course, the most striking characteristic of the little obituary is that it contains *not one reference* to the glorious friendship that brightened the last months of John's life.

My friend could not evoke the image of his father. Similarly the King, who also was not quite three when his father, King Alfin, died, was unable to recall his face, although oddly he did remember perfectly well the little monoplane of chocolate that he, a chubby babe, happened to be holding in that very last photograph (Christmas 1918) of the melancholy, riding-breeched aviator in whose lap he reluctantly and uncomfortably sprawled.

Alfin the Vague (1873-1918; regnal dates 1900-1918, but 1900-1919 in most biographical dictionaries, a fumble due to the coincident calendar change from Old Style to New) was given his cognomen by Amphitheatricus, a not unkindly writer of fugitive poetry in the liberal gazettes (who was also responsible for dubbing my capital Uranograd!). King Alfin's absent-mindedness knew no bounds. He was a wretched linguist having at his disposal only a few phrases of French and Danish, but every time he had to make a speech to his subjects—to a group of gaping Zemblan yokels in some remote valley where he had crash-landed—some uncontrollable switch went into action in his mind, and he reverted to those phrases, flavoring them for topical sense with a little Latin. Most of the anecdotes relating to his naïve fits of abstraction are too silly and indecent to sully these pages; but one of them that I do not think especially funny induced such guffaws from Shade (and returned to me, via the Common Room, with such obscene accretions) that I feel inclined to give it here as a sample (and as a corrective). One summer before the first world war, when the emperor of a great foreign realm (I realize how few there are to choose from) was paying an extremely unusual and flattering visit to our little hard country, my father took him and a young Zemblan interpreter (whose sex I leave open) in a newly purchased custom-built car on a jaunt in the countryside. As usual, King Alfin traveled without a vestige of escort, and this, and his brisk driving, seemed to trouble his guest. On their way back, some twenty miles from Onhava, King Alfin decided to stop for repairs. While he tinkered with the motor, the emperor and the interpreter sought the shade of some pines by the highway, and only when King Alfin was back in Onhava, did he gradually realize from a reiteration of rather frantic questions that he had left somebody behind ("What emperor?" has remained his only memorable *mot*). Generally speaking, in respect of any of my contributions (or what I thought to be contributions) I repeatedly enjoined my poet to record them in writing, by all means, but not to spread them in idle speech; even poets, however, are human.

King Alfin's absent-mindedness was strangely combined with a passion for mechanical things, especially for flying apparatuses. In 1912, he managed to rise in an umbrella-like Fabre "hydroplane" and almost got drowned in the sea between Nitra and Indra. He smashed two Farmans, three Zemblan machines, and a beloved Santos Dumont *Demoiselle*. A very special monoplane, Blenda IV, was built for him in 1916 by his constant "aerial adjutant," Colonel Peter Gusev (later a pioneer parachutist and, at seventy, one of the greatest jumpers of all time), and this was his bird of doom. On the serene, and not too cold, December morning that the angels chose to net his mild pure soul, King Alfin was in the act of trying solo a tricky vertical loop that Prince Andrey Kachurin, the famous Russian stunter and War One hero, had shown him in Gatchina. Something went wrong, and the little Blenda was seen to go into an uncontrolled dive. Behind and above him, in a Caudron biplane, Colonel Gusev (by then Duke of Rahl) and the Queen snapped several pictures of what seemed at first a noble and graceful evolution but then turned into something else. At the last moment, King Alfin managed to straighten out his machine and was again master of gravity when, immediately afterwards, he flew smack into the scaffolding of a huge hotel which was being constructed in the middle of a coastal heath as if for the special purpose of standing in a king's way. This uncompleted and badly gutted building was ordered razed by Queen Blenda who had it replaced by a tasteless monument of granite surmounted by an improbable type of aircraft made of bronze. The glossy prints of the enlarged photographs depicting the entire catastrophe were discovered one day by eight-year-old Charles Xavier in the drawer of a secretary bookcase. In some of these ghastly pictures one could make out the shoulders and leathern casque of the strangely unconcerned aviator, and in the penultimate one of the series, just before the white-blurred shattering crash, one distinctly saw him raise one arm in triumph and reassurance. The boy had hideous dreams after that but his mother never found out that he had seen those infernal records.

Her he remembered—more or less: a horsewoman, tall, broad, stout, ruddy-faced. She had been assured by a royal cousin that her son would be safe and happy under the tutelage of admirable Mr. Campbell who had taught several dutiful little princesses to spread butterflies and enjoy *Lord Ronald's Coronach*. He had immolated his life, so to speak, at the portable altars of a vast number of hobbies, from the study of book mites to bear hunting, and could reel off *Macbeth* from beginning to end during hikes; but he did not give a damn for his charges' morals, preferred ladies to laddies, and did not meddle in the complexities of Zemblan ingledom. He left, for some exotic court, after a ten-year stay, in 1932 when our Prince, aged seventeen, had begun dividing his time between the University and his regiment. It was the nicest period in his life. He never could decide what he enjoyed more: the study of poetry—especially English poetry—or attending parades, or dancing in masquerades with boy-girls and girl-boys. His mother died suddenly on July 21, 1936, from an obscure blood ailment that had also afflicted her mother and grandmother. She had been much better on the day before—and Charles Xavier had gone to an all-night ball in the so-called Ducal Dome in

Grindelwod: for the nonce, a formal heterosexual affair, rather refreshing after some previous sport. At about four in the morning, with the sun enflaming the tree crests and Mt. Falk, a pink cone, the King stopped his powerful car at one of the gates of the palace. The air was so delicate, the light so lyrical, that he and the three friends he had with him decided to walk through the linden bosquet the rest of the distance to the Pavonian Pavilion where guests were lodged. He and Otar, a platonic pal, wore tails but they had lost their top hats to the highway winds. A strange something struck all four of them as they stood under the young limes in the prim landscape of scarp and counterscarp fortified by shadow and countershadow. Otar, a pleasant and cultured adeling with a tremendous nose and sparse hair, had his two mistresses with him, eighteen-year-old Fifalda (whom he later married) and seventeen-year-old Fleur (whom we shall meet in two other notes), daughters of Countess de Fyler, the Queen's favorite lady in waiting. One involuntarily lingers over that picture, as one does when standing at a vantage point of time and knowing in retrospect that in a moment one's life would undergo a complete change. So here was Otar, looking with a puzzled expression at the distant windows of the Queen's quarters, and there were the two girls, side by side, thin-legged, in shimmering wraps, their kitten noses pink, their eyes green and sleepy, their earrings catching and loosing the fire of the sun. There were a few people around, as there always were, no matter the hour, at this gate, along which a road, connecting with the Eastern highway, ran. A peasant woman with a small cake she had baked, doubtlessly the mother of the sentinel who had not yet come to relieve the unshaven dark young *nattdett* (child of night) in his dreary sentry box, sat on a spur stone watching in feminine fascination the luciola-like tapers that moved from window to window; two workmen, holding their bicycles, stood staring too at those strange lights; and a drunk with a walrus mustache kept staggering around and patting the trunks of the lindens. One picks up minor items at such slowdowns of life. The King noticed that some reddish mud flecked the frames of the two bicycles and that their front wheels were both turned in the same direction, parallel to one another. Suddenly, down a steep path among the lilac bushes—a short cut from the Queen's quarters—the Countess came running and tripping over the hem of her quilted robe, and at the same moment, from another side of the palace, all seven councilors, dressed in their formal splendor and carrying like plum cakes replicas of various regalia, came striding down the stairs of stone, in dignified haste, but she beat them by one alin and spat out the news. The drunk started to sing a ribald ballad about "Karlie-Garlie" and fell into the demilune ditch. It is not easy to describe lucidly in short notes to a poem the various approaches to a fortified castle, and so, in my awareness of this problem, I prepared for John Shade, some time in June, when narrating to him the events briefly noticed in some of my comments (see note to line 130, for example), a rather handsomely drawn plan of the chambers, terraces, bastions and pleasure grounds of the Onhava Palace. Unless it has been destroyed or stolen, this careful picture in colored inks on a large (thirty by twenty inches) piece of cardboard might still be where I last saw it in mid-July, on the top of the big black trunk, opposite the old mangle, in a niche of the little corridor leading to the so-called fruit room. If it is not there, it might be looked for in his upper-floor study. I have written about this to Mrs. Shade but she does not reply to my letters. In case it still exists, I wish to beg her, without raising my voice, and very humbly, as humbly as the lowliest of the King's subjects might plead for an immediate restitution of his rights (the plan is mine and is clearly signed with a black chess-king crown after "Kinbote"), to send it, well packed, marked *not to be bent* on the wrapper, and by registered mail, to my publisher for reproduction in later editions of this work. Whatever energy I possessed has quite ebbed away lately, and these excruciating headaches now make impossible the mnemonic effort and eye strain that the drawing of another such plan would demand. The black trunk stands on another brown or brownish even larger one, and there is I think a stuffed fox or coyote next to them in their dark corner.

Line 79:   a preterist

Written against this in the margin of the draft are two lines of which only the first can be deciphered. It reads:

The evening is the time to praise the day

I feel pretty sure that my friend was trying to incorporate here something he and Mrs. Shade had heard me quote in my lighter-hearted moments, namely a charming quatrain from our Zemblan counterpart of the Elder Edda, in an anonymous English translation (Kirby's?):

The wise at nightfall praise the day,
The wife when she has passed away,
The ice when it is crossed, the bride
When tumbled, and the horse when tried.

Line 80: my bedroom

Our Prince was fond of Fleur as of a sister but with no soft shadow of incest or secondary homosexual complications. She had a small pale face with prominent cheekbones, luminous eyes, and curly dark hair. It was rumored that after going about with a porcelain cup and Cinderella's slipper for months, the society sculptor and poet Arnor had found in her what he sought and had used her breasts and feet for his *Lilith Calling Back Adam;* but I am certainly no expert in these tender matters. Otar, her lover, said that when you walked behind her, and she knew you were walking behind her, the swing and play of those slim haunches was something intensely artistic, something Arab girls were taught in special schools by special Parisian panders who were afterwards strangled. Her fragile ankles, he said, which she placed very close together in her dainty and wavy walk, were the "careful jewels" in Arnor's poem about a *miragarl* ("mirage girl"), for which "a dream king in the sandy wastes of time would give three hundred camels and three fountains."

On sagáren werém tremkín tri stána
Verbálala wod gév ut tri phantána

(I have marked the stress accents).

The Prince did not heed this rather kitschy prattle (all, probably, directed by her mother) and, let it be repeated, regarded her merely as a sibling, fragrant and fashionable, with a painted pout and a *maussade,* blurry, Gallic way of expressing the little she wished to express. Her unruffled rudeness toward the nervous and garrulous Countess amused him. He liked dancing with her—and only with her. He hardly squirmed at all when she stroked his hand or applied herself soundlessly with open lips to his cheek which the haggard after-the-ball dawn had already sooted. She did not seem to mind when he abandoned her for manlier pleasures; and she met him again in the dark of a car or in the half-glow of a cabaret with the subdued and ambiguous smile of a kissing cousin.

The forty days between Queen Blenda's death and his coronation was perhaps the most trying stretch of time in his life. He had had no love for his mother, and the hopeless and helpless remorse he now felt degenerated into a sickly physical fear of her phantom. The Countess, who seemed to be near him, to be rustling at his side, all the time, had him attend table-turning séances with an experienced American medium, séances at which the Queen's spirit, operating the same kind of planchette she had used in her lifetime to chat with Thormodus Torfaeus and A. R. Wallace, now briskly wrote in English: "Charles take take cherish love flower flower flower." An old psychiatrist so thoroughly bribed by the Countess as to look, even on the outside, like a putrid pear, assured him that his vices had subconsciously killed his mother and would continue "to kill her in him" if he did not renounce sodomy. A palace intrigue is a spectral spider that entangles you more nastily at every desperate jerk you try. Our Prince was young, inexperienced, and half-frenzied with insomnia. He hardly struggled at all. The Countess spent a fortune on buying his *kamergrum* (groom of the chamber), his bodyguard, and even the greater part of the Court Chamberlain. She took to sleeping in a small antechamber next to his bachelor bedroom, a splendid spacious circular apartment at the top of the high and massive South

West Tower. This had been his father's retreat and was still connected by a jolly chute in the wall with a round swimming pool in the hall below, so that the young Prince could start the day as his father used to start it by slipping open a panel beside his army cot and rolling into the shaft whence he whizzed down straight into bright water. For other needs than sleep Charles Xavier had installed in the middle of the Persian rug-covered floor a so-called patifolia, that is, a huge, oval, luxuriously flounced, swansdown pillow the size of a triple bed. It was in this ample nest that Fleur now slept, curled up in its central hollow, under a coverlet of genuine giant panda fur that had just been rushed from Tibet by a group of Asiatic well-wishers on the occasion of his ascension to the throne. The antechamber, where the Countess was ensconced, had its own inner staircase and bathroom, but also communicated by means of a sliding door with the West Gallery. I do not know what advice or command her mother had given Fleur; but the little thing proved a poor seducer. She kept trying, as one quietly insane, to mend a broken viola d'amore or sat in dolorous attitudes comparing two ancient flutes, both sad-tuned and feeble. Meantime, in Turkish garb, he lolled in his father's ample chair, his legs over its arm, flipping through a volume of *Historia Zemblica,* copying out passages and occasionally fishing out of the nether recesses of his seat a pair of old-fashioned motoring goggles, a black opal ring, a ball of silver chocolate wrapping, or the star of a foreign order.

It was warm in the evening sun. She wore on the second day of their ridiculous cohabitation nothing except a kind of buttonless and sleeveless pajama top. The sight of her four bare limbs and three mousepits (Zemblan anatomy) irritated him, and while pacing about and pondering his

coronation speech, he would toss towards her, without looking, her shorts or a terrycloth robe. Sometimes, upon returning to the comfortable old chair he would find her in it
contemplating sorrowfully the picture of a *bogtur* (ancient
warrior) in the history book. He would sweep her out of his
chair, his eyes still on his writing pad, and stretching herself
she would move over to the window seat and its dusty sunbeam; but after a while she tried to cuddle up to him, and
he had to push away her burrowing dark curly head with
one hand while writing with the other or detach one by one
her little pink claws from his sleeve or sash.

Her presence at night did not kill insomnia, but at least
kept at bay the strong ghost of Queen Blenda. Between exhaustion and drowsiness, he trifled with paltry fancies, such
as getting up and pouring out a little cold water from a decanter onto Fleur's naked shoulder so as to extinguish upon
it the weak gleam of a moonbeam. Stentoriously the Countess snored in her lair. And beyond the vestibule of his vigil
(here he began falling asleep), in the dark cold gallery, lying all over the painted marble and piled three or four deep
against the locked door, some dozing, some whimpering,
were his new boy pages, a whole mountain of gift boys from
Troth, and Tuscany, and Albanoland.

He awoke to find her standing with a comb in her hand
before his—or rather, his grandfather's—cheval glass, a trip-
tych of bottomless light, a really fantastic mirror, signed
with a diamond by its maker, Sudarg of Bokay. She turned
about before it: a secret device of reflection gathered an infinite number of nudes in its depths, garlands of girls in
graceful and sorrowful groups, diminishing in the limpid
distance, or breaking into individual nymphs, some of whom,
she murmured, must resemble her ancestors when they

were young—little peasant *garlien* combing their hair in shallow water as far as the eye could reach, and then the wistful mermaid from an old tale, and then nothing.

On the third night a great stomping and ringing of arms came from the inner stairs, and there burst in the Prime Councilor, three Representatives of the People, and the chief of a new bodyguard. Amusingly, it was the Representatives of the People whom the idea of having for queen the granddaughter of a fiddler infuriated the most. That was the end of Charles Xavier's chaste romance with Fleur, who was pretty yet not repellent (as some cats are less repugnant than others to the good-natured dog told to endure the bitter effluvium of an alien genus). With their white suitcases and obsolete musical instruments the two ladies wandered back to the annex of the Palace. There followed a sweet twang of relief—and then the door of the anteroom slid open with a merry crash and the whole heap of *putti* tumbled in.

He was to go through a far more dramatic ordeal thirteen years later with Disa, Duchess of Payn, whom he married in 1949, as described in notes to lines 275 and 433–434, which the student of Shade's poem will reach in due time; there is no hurry. A series of cool summers ensued. Poor Fleur was still around, though indistinctly so. Disa befriended her after the old Countess perished in the crowded vestibule of the 1950 Exposition of Glass Animals, when part of it was almost destroyed by fire, Gradus helping the fire brigade to clear a space in the square for the lynching of the non-union incendiaries, or at least of the persons (two baffled tourists from Denmark) who had been mistaken for them. Our young Queen may have felt some subtle sympathy for her pale lady in waiting whom from time to time the King glimpsed illuminating a concert program by the diagonal light of an ogival window, or heard making tinny music in Bower B. The beautiful bedroom of his bachelor days is alluded to again in a note to line 130, as the place of his "luxurious captivity" in the beginning of the tedious and unnecessary Zemblan Revolution.

Line 85:   Who'd seen the Pope

Pius X, Giuseppe Melchiorre Sarto, 1835-1914; Pope 1903-1914.

Lines 86-90:   Aunt Maud

Maud Shade, 1869-1950, Samuel Shade's sister. At her death, Hazel (born 1934) was not exactly a "babe" as implied in line 90. I found her paintings unpleasant but interesting. Aunt Maud was far from spinsterish, and the extravagant and sardonic turn of her mind must have shocked sometimes the genteel dames of New Wye.

Lines 90-93:   Her room, etc.

In the draft, instead of the final text:

.... her room
We've kept intact. Her trivia for us
Retrace her style: the leaf sarcophagus
(A Luna's dead and shriveled-up cocoon)

The reference is to what my dictionary defines as "a large, tailed, pale green moth, the caterpillar of which feeds on the hickory." I suspect Shade altered this passage because his moth's name clashed with "Moon" in the next line.

Line 91:   trivia

Among these was a scrapbook in which over a period of years (1937-1949) Aunt Maud had been pasting clippings of an involuntarily ludicrous or grotesque nature. John Shade allowed me one day to memorandum the first and the last of the series; they happened to intercommunicate most pleasingly, I thought. Both stemmed from the same family magazine *Life,* so justly famed for its pudibundity in regard to the mysteries of the male sex; hence one can well imagine how startled or titillated those families were. The first comes from the issue of May 10, 1937, p. 67, and advertises the Talon Trouser Fastener (a rather grasping and painful name, by the way). It shows a young gent radiating virility among several ecstatic lady-friends, and the inscription reads: *You'll be amazed that the fly of your trousers could be so dramatically improved.* The second comes from the issue of March 28, 1949, p. 126, and advertises Hanes Fig Leaf Brief. It shows a modern Eve worshipfully peeping from behind a potted tree of knowledge at a leering young Adam in rather ordinary but clean underwear, with the front of his advertised brief conspicuously and compactly shaded, and the inscription reads: *Nothing beats a fig leaf.*

I think there must exist a special subversive group of pseudo-cupids—plump hairless little devils whom Satan commissions to make disgusting mischief in sacrosanct places.

Line 92:   the paperweight

The image of those old-fashioned horrors strangely haunted our poet. I have clipped from a newspaper that recently reprinted it an old poem of his where the souvenir shop also preserves a landscape admired by the tourist:

> MOUNTAIN VIEW
> Between the mountain and the eye
> The spirit of the distance draws
> A veil of blue amorous gauze,
> The very texture of the sky.
> A breeze reaches the pines, and I
> Join in the general applause.
>
> But we all know it cannot last,
> The mountain is too weak to wait—
> Even if reproduced and glassed
> In me as in a paperweight.

Line 98:   On Chapman's Homer

A reference to the title of Keats' famous sonnet (often quoted in America) which, owing to a printer's absent-mindedness, has been drolly transposed, from some other article, into the account of a sports event. For other vivid misprints see note to line 802.

Line 101:   No free man needs a God

When one considers the numberless thinkers and poets in the history of human creativity whose freedom of mind was enhanced rather than stunted by Faith, one is bound to question the wisdom of this easy aphorism (see also note to line 549).

Line 109:   iridule

An iridescent cloudlet, Zemblan *muderperlwelk*. The term "iridule" is, I believe, Shade's own invention. Above it, in the Fair Copy (card 9, July 4) he has written in pencil "peacock-herl." The peacock-herl is the body of a certain sort of artificial fly also called "alder." So the owner of this motor court, an ardent fisherman, tells me. (See also the "strange nacreous gleams" in line 634.)

Line 119:   Dr. Sutton

This is a recombination of letters taken from two names, one beginning in "Sut," the other ending in "ton." Two distinguished medical men, long retired from practice, dwelt on our hill. Both were very old friends of the Shades; one had a daughter, president of Sybil's club—and this is the Dr. Sutton I visualize in my notes to lines 181 and 1000. He is also mentioned in Line 986.

Lines 120-121:   five minutes were equal to forty ounces, etc.

In the left margin, and parallel to it: "In the Middle Ages an hour was equal to 480 ounces of fine sand or 22,560 atoms."

I am unable to check either this statement or the poet's calculations in regard to five minutes, i.e., three hundred seconds, since I do not see how 480 can be divided by 300 or vice versa, but perhaps I am only tired. On the day (July 4) John Shade wrote this, Gradus the Gunman was getting ready to leave Zembla for his steady blunderings through two hemispheres (see note to line 181).

Line 130:   I never bounced a ball or swung a bat

Frankly I too never excelled in soccer and cricket; I am a passable horseman, a vigorous though unorthodox skier, a good skater, a tricky wrestler, and an enthusiastic rock-climber.

Line 130 is followed in the draft by four verses which Shade discarded in favor of the Fair Copy continuation (line 131 etc.). This false start goes:

> As children playing in a castle find
> In some old closet full of toys, behind
> The animals and masks, a sliding door
> [four words heavily crossed out] a secret corridor—

The comparison has remained suspended. Presumably our poet intended to attach it to the account of his stumbling upon some mysterious truth in the fainting fits of his boyhood. I cannot say how sorry I am that he rejected these lines. I regret it not only because of their intrinsic beauty, which is great, but also because the image they contain was suggested by something Shade had from me. I have already alluded in the course of these notes to the adventures of Charles Xavier, last King of Zembla, and to the keen interest my friend took in the many stories I told him about that king. The index card on which the variant has been preserved is dated July 4 and is a direct echo of our sunset rambles in the fragrant lanes of New Wye and Dulwich. "Tell me more," he would say as he knocked his pipe empty against a beech trunk, and while the colored cloud lingered, and while far away in the lighted house on the hill Mrs. Shade sat quietly enjoying a video drama, I gladly acceded to my friend's request.

In simple words I described the curious situation in which the King found himself during the first months of the rebellion. He had the amusing feeling of his being the only black piece in what a composer of chess problems might term a king-in-the-corner waiter of the *solus rex* type. The Royalists, or at least the Modems (Moderate Democrats), might have still prevented the state from turning into a commonplace modern tyranny, had they been able to cope with the tainted gold and the robot troops that a powerful police state from its vantage ground a few sea miles away was pouring into the Zemblan Revolution. Despite the hopelessness of the situation, the King refused to abdicate. A haughty and morose captive, he was caged in his rose-stone palace from a corner turret of which one could make out with the help of field glasses lithe youths diving into the swimming pool of a fairy tale sport club, and the English ambassador in old-fashioned flannels playing tennis with the Basque coach on a clay court as remote as paradise. How serene were the mountains, how tenderly painted on the western vault of the sky!

Somewhere in the mist of the city there occurred every day disgusting outbursts of violence, arrests and executions, but the great city rolled on as smoothly as ever, the cafés were full, splendid plays were being performed at the Royal Theater, and it was really the palace which contained the strongest concentrate of gloom. Stone-faced, square-shouldered *komizars* enforced strict discipline among the troops on duty within and without. Puritan prudence had sealed up the wine cellars and removed all the maid servants from the southern wing. The ladies in waiting had, of course, left long before, at the time the King exiled his Queen to her villa on the French Riviera. Thank heavens, she was spared those dreadful days in the polluted palace!

The door of every room was guarded. The banqueting hall had three custodians and as many as four loafed in the library whose dark recesses seemed to harbor all the shadows of treason. The bedrooms of the few remaining palace attendants had each its armed parasite, drinking forbidden rum with an old footman or taking liberties with a young page. And in the great Heralds' Hall one could always be sure of finding ribald jokers trying to squeeze into the steel panoply of its hollow knights. And what a smell of leather and goat in the spacious chambers once redolent of carnations and lilacs!

This tremendous company consisted of two main groups: ignorant, ferocious-looking but really quite harmless conscripts from Thule, and taciturn, very polite Extremists from the famous Glass Factory where the revolution had flickered first. One can now reveal (since he is safe in Paris) that this contingent included at least one heroic royalist so virtuosically disguised that he made his unsuspecting fellow guards look like mediocre imitators. Actually Odon happened to be one of the most prominent actors in Zembla and was winning applause in the Royal Theater on his off-duty nights. Through him the King kept in touch with numerous adherents, young nobles, artists, college athletes, gamblers, Black Rose Paladins, members of fencing clubs, and other men of fashion and adventure. Rumors rumbled. It was said that the captive would soon be tried by a special court; but it was also said that he would be shot while ostensibly being transported to another place of confinement. Although flight was discussed daily, the schemes of the conspirators had more aesthetic than practical value. A powerful motorboat had been prepared in a coastal cave near Blawick (Blue Cove) in western Zembla, beyond the chain of tall mountains which separated the city from the sea; the imagined reflections of the trembling transparent water on rock wall and boat were tantalizing, but none of

the schemers could suggest how the King could escape
from his castle and pass safely through its fortifications.

One August day, at the beginning of his third month of
luxurious captivity in the South West Tower, he was accused of using a fop's hand mirror and the sun's cooperative
rays to flash signals from his lofty casement. The vastness of
the view it commanded was denounced not only as conducive to treachery but as producing in the surveyor an airy
sense of superiority over his low-lodged jailers. Accordingly,
one evening the King's cot-and-pot were transferred to a
dismal lumber room on the same side of the palace but on
its first floor. Many years before, it had been the dressing
room of his grandfather, Thurgus the Third. After Thurgus
died (in 1900) his ornate bedroom was transformed into a
kind of chapel and the adjacent chamber, shorn of its full-
length multiple mirror and green silk sofa, soon degenerated
into what it had now remained for half a century, an old
hole of a room with a locked trunk in one corner and an
obsolete sewing machine in another. It was reached from
a marble-flagged gallery, running along its north side and
sharply turning immediately west of it to form a vestibule
in the southwest corner of the Palace. The only window
gave on an inner court on the south side. This window had
once been a glorious dreamway of stained glass, with a fire-
bird and a dazzled huntsman, but a football had recently
shattered the fabulous forest scene and now its new ordinary
pane was barred from the outside. On the west-side wall,
above a whitewashed closet door, hung a large photograph in
a frame of black velvet. The fleeting and faint but thousands
of times repeated action of the same sun that was accused
of sending messages from the tower, had gradually pati-

nated this picture which showed the romantic profile and broad bare shoulders of the forgotten actress Iris Acht, said to have been for several years, ending with her sudden death in 1888, the mistress of Thurgus. In the opposite, east-side wall a frivolous-looking door, similar in turquoise color-ation to the room's only other one (opening into the gallery) but securely hasped, had once led to the old rake's bed-chamber; it had now lost its crystal knob, and was flanked on the east-side wall by two banished engravings belonging to the room's period of decay. They were of the sort that is not really supposed to be looked at, pictures that exist merely as general notions of pictures to meet the humble ornamental needs of some corridor or waiting room: one was a shabby and lugubrious *Fête Flamande* after Teniers; the other had once hung in the nursery whose sleepy denizens had always taken it to depict foamy waves in the foreground instead of the blurry shapes of melancholy sheep that it now revealed.

The King sighed and began to undress. His camp bed and a bedtable had been placed, facing the window, in the north-east corner. East was the turquoise door; north, the door of the gallery; west, the door of the closet; south, the window. His black blazer and white trousers were taken away by his former valet's valet. The King sat down on the edge of the bed in his pajamas. The man returned with a pair of mo-rocco bed slippers, pulled them on his master's listless feet, and was off with the discarded pumps. The King's wander-ing gaze stopped at the casement which was half open. One could see part of the dimly lit court where under an enclosed poplar two soldiers on a stone bench were playing lansquenet. The summer night was starless and stirless, with distant spasms of silent lightning. Around the lantern that stood on the bench a batlike moth blindly flapped—until the punter knocked it down with his cap. The King yawned, and the illumined card players shivered and dissolved in the prism of his tears. His bored glance traveled from wall to wall. The gallery door stood slightly ajar, and one could hear the steps of the guard coming and going. Above the closet, Iris Acht squared her shoulders and looked away. A cricket cricked. The bedside light was just strong enough to put a bright gleam on the gilt key in the lock of the closet door. And all at once that spark on that key caused a wonderful conflagration to spread in the prisoner's mind.

We shall now go back from mid-August 1958 to a certain afternoon in May three decades earlier when he was a dark strong lad of thirteen with a silver ring on the forefinger of his sun-tanned hand. Queen Blenda, his mother, had recently left for Vienna and Rome. He had several dear playmates but none could compete with Oleg, Duke of Rahl. In those days growing boys of high-born families wore on festive occasions—of which we had so many during our long northern spring—sleeveless jerseys, white anklesocks with black buckle shoes, and very tight, very short shorts called *hotinguens*. I wish I could provide the reader with cut-out figures and parts of attire as given in paper-doll charts for children armed with scissors. It would brighten a little these dark evenings that are destroying my brain. Both lads were handsome, long-legged specimens of Varangian boyhood. At twelve, Oleg was the best center forward at the Ducal School. When stripped and shiny in the mist of the bath house, his bold virilia contrasted harshly with his girlish grace. He was a regular faunlet. On that particular afternoon a copious shower lacquered the spring foliage of the palace garden, and oh, how the Persian lilacs in riotous bloom tumbled and tossed behind the green-streaming, amethyst-blotched windowpanes! One would have to play indoors. Oleg was late. Would he come at all?

It occurred to the young Prince to disinter a set of precious toys (the gift of a foreign potentate who had recently been assassinated) which had amused Oleg and him during a previous Easter, and then had been laid aside as happens with those special, artistic playthings which allow their bubble of pleasure to yield all its tang at once before retreating into museum oblivion. What he particularly desired to rediscover now was an elaborate toy circus contained in a box as big as a croquet case. He craved for it; his eyes, his brain, and that in his brain which corresponded to the ball of his thumb, vividly remembered the brown boy acrobats with spangled nates, an elegant and melancholy clown with a ruff, and especially three pup-sized elephants of polished wood with such versatile joints that you could make the sleek jumbo stand upright on one foreleg or rear up solidly on the top of a small white barrel ringed with red. Less than a fortnight had passed since Oleg's last visit, when for the first time the two boys had been allowed to share the same bed, and the tingle of their misbehavior, and the foreglow of another such night, were now mixed in our young Prince with an embarrassment that suggested refuge in earlier, more innocent games.

His English tutor who, after a picnic in Mandevil Forest, was laid up with a sprained ankle, did not know where that circus might be; he advised looking for it in an old lumber room at the end of the West Gallery. Thither the Prince betook himself. That dusty black trunk? It looked grimly negative. The rain was more audible here owing to the proximity of a prolix gutter pipe. What about the closet?

Its gilt key turned reluctantly. All three shelves and the
space beneath were stuffed with disparate objects: a palette
with the dregs of many sunsets; a cupful of counters; an
ivory backscratcher; a thirty-twomo edition of *Timon of
Athens* translated into Zemblan by his uncle Conmal, the
Queen's brother; a seaside *situla* (toy pail); a sixty-five-
carat blue diamond accidentally added in his childhood,
from his late father's knickknackatory, to the pebbles and
shells in that pail; a finger of chalk; and a square board with
a design of interlaced figures for some long-forgotten
game. He was about to look elsewhere in the closet when
on trying to dislodge a piece of black velvet, one corner of
which had unaccountably got caught behind the shelf,
something gave, the shelf budged, proved removable, and revealed just under its farther edge, in the back of the closet, a
keyhole to which the same gilt key was found to fit.

Impatiently he cleared the other two shelves of all they
held (mainly old clothes and shoes), removed them as he
had done with the middle one, and unlocked the sliding
door at the back of the closet. The elephants were forgotten,
he stood on the threshold of a secret passage. Its deep darkness was total but something about its speluncar acoustics
foretold, clearing its throat hollowly, great things, and he
hurried to his own quarters to fetch a couple of flashlights
and a pedometer. As he was returning, Oleg arrived. He
carried a tulip. His soft blond locks had been cut since his
last visit to the palace, and the young Prince thought: Yes,
I knew he would be different. But when Oleg knitted his
golden brows and bent close to hear about the discovery, the
young Prince knew by the downy warmth of that crimson
ear and by the vivacious nod greeting the proposed investigation, that no change had occurred in his dear bedfellow.

As soon as Monsieur Beauchamp had sat down for a game of chess at the bedside of Mr. Campbell and had offered his raised fists to choose from, the young Prince took Oleg to the magical closet. The wary, silent, green-carpeted steps of an *escalier dérobé* led to a stone-paved underground passage. Strictly speaking it was "underground" only in brief spells when, after burrowing under the southwest vestibule next to the lumber room, it went under a series of terraces, under the avenue of birches in the royal park, and then under the three transverse streets, Academy Boulevard, Coriolanus Lane and Timon Alley, that still separated it from its final destination. Otherwise, in its angular and cryptic course it adapted itself to the various structures which it followed, here availing itself of a bulwark to fit in its side like a pencil in the pencil hold of a pocket diary, there running through the cellars of a great mansion too rich in dark passageways to notice the stealthy intrusion. Possibly, in the intervening years, certain arcane connections had been established between the abandoned passage and the outer world by the random repercussions of work in surrounding layers of masonry or by the blind pokings of time itself; for here and there magic apertures and penetrations, so narrow and deep as to drive one insane, could be deduced from a pool of sweet, foul ditch water, bespeaking a moat, or from a dusky odor of earth and turf, marking the proximity of a glacis slope overhead; and at one point, where the passage crept through the basement of a huge ducal villa, with hothouses famous for their collections of desert flora, a light spread of sand momentarily changed the sound of one's tread. Oleg walked in front: his shapely buttocks encased in tight indigo cotton moved alertly, and his own erect radiance, rather than his flambeau, seemed to illume with leaps of light the low ceiling and crowding walls. Behind him the young Prince's electric torch played on the ground and gave a coating of flour to the back of Oleg's bare thighs. The air was musty and cold. On and on went the fantastic burrow. It developed a slight ascending grade. The pedometer had tocked off 1,888 yards, when at last they reached the end. The magic key of the lumber room closet slipped with gratifying ease into the keyhole of a green door confronting them, and would have accomplished the act promised by its smooth entrance, had not a burst of strange sounds coming from behind the door caused our explorers to pause. Two terrible voices, a man's and a woman's, now rising to a passionate pitch, now sinking to raucous undertones, were exchanging insults in Gutnish as spoken by the fisher-folk of Western Zembla. An abominable threat made the woman shriek out in fright. Sudden silence ensued, presently broken by the man's murmuring some brief phrase of casual approval ("Perfect, my dear," or "Couldn't be better") that was more eerie than anything that had come before.

Without consulting each other, the young Prince and his friend veered in absurd panic and, with the pedometer beating wildly, raced back the way they had come. "Ouf!" said Oleg once the last shelf had been replaced. "You're all chalky behind," said the young Prince as they swung upstairs. They found Beauchamp and Campbell ending their game in a draw. It was near dinner time. The two lads were told to wash their hands. The recent thrill of adventure had been superseded already by another sort of excitement. They locked themselves up. The tap ran unheeded. Both were in a manly state and moaning like doves.

This detailed recollection, whose structure and maculation have taken some time to describe in this note, skimmed through the King's memory in one instant. Certain creatures of the past, and this was one of them, may lie dormant for thirty years as this one had, while their natural habitat undergoes calamitous alterations. Soon after the discovery of the secret passage he almost died of pneumonia. In his delirium he would strive one moment to follow a luminous disk probing an endless tunnel and try the next to clasp the melting haunches of his fair ingle. To recuperate he was sent for a couple of seasons to southern Europe. The death of Oleg at fifteen, in a toboggan accident, helped to obliterate the reality of their adventure. A national revolution was needed to make that secret passage real again.

Having satisfied himself that the guard's creaky steps had moved some distance away, the King opened the closet. It was empty now, save for the tiny volume of *Timon Afinsken* still lying in one corner, and for some old sport clothes and gymnasium shoes crammed into the bottom compartment. The footfalls were now coming back. He did not dare pursue his examination and relocked the closet door.

It was evident he would need a few moments of perfect security to perform with a minimum of noise a succession of small actions: enter the closet, lock it from the inside, remove the shelves, open the secret door, replace the shelves, slip into the yawning darkness, close the secret door and lock it. Say ninety seconds.

He stepped out into the gallery, and the guard, a rather handsome but incredibly stupid Extremist, immediately advanced towards him. "I have a certain urgent desire," said the King. "I want, Hal, to play the piano before going to bed." Hal (if that was his name) led the way to the music room where, as the King knew, Odon kept vigil over the shrouded harp. He was a fox-browed, burly Irishman, with a pink head now covered by the rakish cap of a Russki factory worker. The King sat down at the Bechstein and, as soon as they were left alone, explained briefly the situation while taking tinkling notes with one hand: "Never heard of any passage," muttered Odon with the annoyance of a chess player who is shown how he might have saved the game he has lost. Was His Majesty absolutely sure? His Majesty was. Did he suppose it took one out of the Palace? Definitely out of the Palace.

Anyway, Odon had to leave in a few moments, being due to act that night in *The Merman*, a fine old melodrama which had not been performed, he said, for at least three decades. "I'm quite satisfied with my own melodrama," remarked the King. "Alas," said Odon. Furrowing his forehead, he slowly got into his leathern coat. One could do nothing tonight. If he asked the commandant to be left on duty, it would only provoke suspicion, and the least suspicion might be fatal. Tomorrow he would find some opportunity to inspect that new avenue of escape, *if* it was that and not a dead end. Would Charlie (His Majesty) promise not to attempt anything until then? "But they are moving closer and closer," said the King alluding to the noise of rapping and ripping that came from the Picture Gallery. "Not really," said Odon, "one inch per hour, maybe two. I must be going now," he added indicating with a twitch of the eyelid the solemn and corpulent guard who was coming to relieve him.

Under the unshakable but quite erroneus belief that the crown jewels were concealed somewhere in the Palace, the new administration had engaged a couple of foreign experts (see note to line 681) to locate them. The good work had been going on for a month. The two Russians, after practically dismantling the Council Chamber and several other rooms of state, had transferred their activites to that part of the gallery where the huge oils of Eystein had fascinated several generations of Zemblan princes and princesses. While unable to catch a likeness, and therefore wisely limiting himself to a conventional style of complimentary portraiture, Eystein showed himself to be a prodigious master of the trompe l'oeil in the depiction of various objects surrounding his dignified dead models and making them look even deader by contrast to the fallen petal or the polished panel that he rendered with such love and skill. But in some of those portraits Eystein had also resorted to a weird form of trickery: among his decorations of wood or wool, gold or velvet, he would insert one which was really made of the material elsewhere imitated by paint. This device which was apparently meant to enhance the effect of his tactile and tonal values had, however, something ignoble about it and disclosed not only an essential flaw in Eystein's talent, but the basic fact that "reality" is neither the subject nor the object of true art which creates its own special reality having nothing to do with the average "reality" perceived by the communal eye. But to return to our technicians whose tapping is approaching along the gallery toward the bend where the King and Odon stand ready to part. At this spot hung a portrait representing a former Keeper of the Treasure, decrepit Count Kernel, who was painted with fingers resting lightly on an embossed and emblazoned box whose side facing the spectator consisted of an inset oblong made of real bronze, while upon the shaded top of the box, drawn in perspective, the artist had pictured a plate with the beautifully executed, twin-lobed, brainlike, halved kernel of a walnut.

"They are in for a surprise," murmured Odon in his mother tongue, while in a corner the fat guard was going through some dutiful, rather lonesome, rifle-butt-banging formalities.

The two Soviet professionals could be excused for assuming they would find a real receptacle behind the real metal. At the present moment they were about to decide whether to pry out the plaque or take down the picture; but we can anticipate a little and assure the reader that the receptacle, an oblong hole in the wall, was there all right; it contained nothing, however, except the broken bits of a nutshell.

Somewhere an iron curtain had gone up, baring a painted one, with nymphs and nenuphars. "I shall bring you your flute tomorrow," cried Odon meaningfully in the vernacular, and smiled, and waved, already bemisted, already receding into the remoteness of his Thespian world.

The fat guard led the King back to his room and turned him over to handsome Hal. It was half past nine. The King went to bed. The valet, a moody rascal, brought him his usual milk and cognac nightcap and took away his slippers and dressing gown. The man was practically out of the room when the King commanded him to put out the light, upon which an arm re-entered and a gloved hand found and turned the switch. Distant lightning still throbbed now and then in the window. The King finished his drink in the dark and replaced the empty tumbler on the night table where it knocked with a subdued ring against a steel flashlight prepared by the thoughtful authorities in case electricity failed as it lately did now and then.

He could not sleep. Turning his head he watched the line of light under the door. Presently it was gently opened and

his handsome young jailer peeped in. A bizarre little thought
danced through the King's mind; but all the youth wanted
was to warn his prisoner that he intended to join his companions in the adjacent court, and that the door would be
locked until he returned. If, however, the ex-King needed
anything, he could call from his window. "How long will
you be absent?" asked the King. *"Yeg ved ik* [I know
not]," answered the guard. "Good night, bad boy," said the
King.

He waited for the guard's silhouette to enter the light in
the courtyard where the other Thuleans welcomed him to
their game. Then, in secure darkness, the King rummaged
for some clothes on the floor of the closet and pulled on, over
his pajamas, what felt like skiing trousers and something that
smelled like an old sweater. Further gropings yielded a pair
of sneakers and a woolen headgear with flaps. He then went
through the actions mentally rehearsed before. As he was
removing the second shelf, an object fell with a miniature
thud; he guessed what it was and took it with him as a
talisman.

He dared not press the button of his torch until properly
engulfed, nor could he afford a noisy stumble, and therefore
negotiated the eighteen invisible steps in a more or less sitting position like a timid novice bum-scraping down the
lichened rocks of Mt. Kron. The dim light he discharged at
last was now his dearest companion, Oleg's ghost, the phantom of freedom. He experienced a blend of anguish and
exultation, a kind of amorous joy, the like of which he had
last known on the day of his coronation, when, as he walked
to his throne, a few bars of incredibly rich, deep, plenteous
music (whose authorship and physical source he was never
able to ascertain) struck his ear, and he inhaled the hair

oil of the pretty page who had bent to brush a rose petal off the footstool, and by the light of his torch the King now saw that he was hideously garbed in bright red.

The secret passage seemed to have grown more squalid. The intrusion of its surroundings was even more evident than on the day when two lads shivering in thin jerseys and shorts had explored it. The pool of opalescent ditch water had grown in length; along its edge walked a sick bat like a cripple with a broken umbrella. A remembered spread of colored sand bore the thirty-year-old patterned imprint of Oleg's shoe, as immortal as the tracks of an Egyptian child's tame gazelle made thirty centuries ago on blue Nilotic bricks drying in the sun. And, at the spot where the passage went through the foundations of a museum, there had somehow wandered down, to exile and disposal, a headless statue of Mercury, conductor of souls to the Lower World, and a cracked krater with two black figures shown dicing under a black palm.

The last bend of the passage, ending in the green door, contained an accumulation of loose boards across which the fugitive stepped not without stumbling. He unlocked the door and upon pulling it open was stopped by a heavy black drapery. As he began fumbling among its vertical folds for some sort of ingress, the weak light of his torch rolled its hopeless eye and went out. He dropped it: it fell into muffled nothingness. The King thrust both arms into the deep folds of the chocolate-smelling cloth and, despite the uncertainty and the danger of the moment, was, as it were, physically reminded by his own movement of the comical, at first controlled, then frantic undulations of a theatrical curtain through which a nervous actor tries vainly to pass. This grotesque sensation, at this diabolical instant, solved the mystery of the passage even before he wriggled at last through the drapery into the dimly lit, dimly cluttered *lumbarkamer* which had once been Iris Acht's dressing room in the Royal Theater. It still was what it had become after her death: a dusty hole of a room communicating with a kind of hall whither performers would sometimes wander during rehearsals. Pieces of mythological scenery leaning against the wall half concealed a large dusty velvet-framed photograph of King Thurgus—bushy mustache, pince-nez, medals —as he was at the time when the mile-long corridor provided an extravagant means for his trysts with Iris.

The scarlet-clothed fugitive blinked and made for the hall. It led to a number of dressing rooms. Somewhere beyond it a tempest of plaudits grew in volume before petering out. Other distant sounds marked the beginning of the intermission. Several costumed performers passed by the King, and in one of them he recognized Odon. He was wearing a velvet jacket with brass buttons, knickerbockers and striped stockings, the Sunday attire of Gutnish fishermen, and his fist still clutched the cardboard knife with which he had just dispatched his sweetheart. "Good God," he said on seeing the King.

Plucking a couple of cloaks from a heap of fantastic raiments, Odon pushed the King toward a staircase leading to the street. Simultaneously there was a commotion among a group of people smoking on the landing. An old intriguer who by dint of fawning on various Extremist officials had obtained the post of Scenic Director, suddenly pointed a vibrating finger at the King, but being afflicted with a bad stammer could not utter the words of indignant recognition which were making his dentures clack. The King tried to pull the front flap of his cap over his face—and almost lost his footing at the bottom of the narrow stairs. Outside it was raining. A puddle reflected his scarlet silhouette. Several vehicles stood in a transverse lane. It was there that Odon usually left his racing car. For one dreadful second he thought it was gone, but then recalled with exquisite relief that he had parked it that night in an adjacent alley. (See the interesting note to line 149.)

Lines 131-132:   I was the shadow of the waxwing slain by feigned remoteness in the windowpane.

The exquisite melody of the two lines opening the poem is picked up here. The repetition of that long-drawn note is saved from monotony by the subtle variation in line 132 where the assonance between its second word and the rhyme gives the ear a kind of languorous pleasure as would the echo of some half-remembered sorrowful song whose strain is more meaningful than its words. Today, when the "feigned remoteness" has indeed performed its dreadful duty, and the poem we have is the only "shadow" that remains, we cannot help reading into these lines something more than mirrorplay and mirage shimmer. We feel doom, in the image of Gradus, eating away the miles and miles of "feigned remoteness" between him and poor Shade. He, too, is to meet, in his urgent and blind flight, a reflection that will shatter him.

Although Gradus availed himself of all varieties of locomotion—rented cars, local trains, escalators, airplanes— somehow the eye of the mind sees him, and the muscles of the mind feel him, as always streaking across the sky with black traveling bag in one hand and loosely folded umbrella in the other, in a sustained glide high over sea and land. The force propelling him is the magic action of Shade's poem itself, the very mechanism and sweep of verse, the powerful iambic motor. Never before has the inexorable advance of fate received such a sensuous form (for other images of that transcendental tramp's approach see note to line 17).

Line 137: lemniscate

"A unicursal bicircular quartic" says my weary old dictionary. I cannot understand what this has to do with bicycling and suspect that Shade's phrase has no real meaning. As other poets before him, he seems to have fallen here under the spell of misleading euphony.

To take a striking example: what can be more resounding, more resplendent, more suggestive of choral and sculptured beauty, than the word *coramen?* In reality, however, it merely denotes the rude strap with which a Zemblan herdsman attaches his humble provisions and ragged blanket to the meekest of his cows when driving them up to the *vebodar* (upland pastures).

Line 143:   a clockwork toy

By a stroke of luck I have seen it! One evening in May or
June I dropped in to remind my friend about a collection of
pamphlets, by his grandfather, an eccentric clergyman, that
he had once said was stored in the basement. I found him
gloomily waiting for some people (members of his department, I believe, and their wives) who were coming for a
formal dinner. He willingly took me down into the basement but after rummaging among piles of dusty books and
magazines, said he would try to find them some other time.
It was then that I saw it on a shelf, between a candle-
stick and a handless alarm clock. He, thinking I might think
it had belonged to his dead daughter, hastily explained it
was as old as he. The boy was a little Negro of painted tin
with a keyhole in his side and no breadth to speak of, just
consisting of two more or less fused profiles, and his wheelbarrow was now all bent and broken. He said, brushing the
dust off his sleeves, that he kept it as a kind of *memento
mori*—he had had a strange fainting fit one day in his childhood while playing with that toy. We were interrupted by
Sybil's voice calling from above; but never mind, now the
rusty clockwork shall work again, for I have the key.

Line 149:   one foot upon a mountain

The Bera Range, a two-hundred-mile-long chain of rugged
mountains, not quite reaching the northern end of the
Zemblan peninsula (cut off basally by an impassable canal

from the mainland of madness), divides it into two parts, the flourishing eastern region of Onhava and other townships, such as Aros and Grindelwod, and the much narrower western strip with its quaint fishing hamlets and pleasant beach resorts. The two coasts are connected by two asphalted highways: the older one shirks difficulties by running first along the eastern slopes northward to Odevalla, Yeslove and Embla, and only then turning west at the northmost point of the peninsula; the newer one, an elaborate, twisting, marvelously graded road, traverses the range westward from just north of Onhava to Bregberg, and is termed in tourist booklets a "scenic drive." Several trails cross the mountains at various points and lead to passes none of which exceeds an altitude of five thousand feet; a few peaks rise some two thousand feet higher and retain their snow in midsummer; and from one of them, the highest and hardest, Mt. Glitterntin, one can distinguish on clear days, far out to the east, beyond the Gulf of Surprise, a dim iridescence which some say is Russia.

After escaping from the theater, our friends planned to follow the old highway for twenty miles northward, and then turn left on an unfrequented dirt road that would have brought them eventually to the main hideout of the Karlists, a baronial castle in a fir wood on the eastern slope of the Bera Range. But the vigilant stutterer had finally exploded in spasmodic speech; telephones had frantically worked; and the fugitives had hardly covered a dozen miles, when a confused blaze in the darkness before them, at the intersection of the old and new highways, revealed a roadblock that at least had the merit of canceling both routes at one stroke.

Odon spun the car around and at the first opportunity

swerved westward into the mountains. The narrow and
bumpy lane that engulfed them passed by a woodshed, arrived at a torrent, crossed it with a great clacking of boards,
and presently degenerated into a stump-cluttered cutting.
They were at the edge of Mandevil Forest. Thunder was
rumbling in the terrible brown sky.

For a few seconds both men stood looking upward. The
night and the trees concealed the acclivity. From this point a
good climber might reach Bregberg Pass by dawn—if he
managed to hit a regular trail after pushing through the
black wall of the forest. It was decided to part, Charlie proceeding toward the remote treasure in the sea cave, and
Odon remaining behind as a decoy. He would, he said, lead
them a merry chase, assume sensational disguises, and get
into touch with the rest of the gang. His mother was an
American, from New Wye in New England. She is said
to have been the first woman in the world to shoot wolves,
and, I believe, other animals, from an airplane.

A handshake, a flash of lightning. As the King waded into
the damp, dark bracken, its odor, its lacy resilience, and the
mixture of soft growth and steep ground reminded him of
the times he had picnicked hereabouts—in another part of
the forest but on the same mountainside, and higher up, as a
boy, on the boulderfield where Mr. Campbell had once
twisted an ankle and had to be carried down, smoking his
pipe, by two husky attendants. Rather dull memories, on the
whole. Wasn't there a hunting box nearby—just beyond
Silfhar Falls? Good capercaillie and woodcock shooting—a
sport much enjoyed by his late mother, Queen Blenda, a
tweedy and horsy queen. Now as then, the rain seethed in
the black trees, and if you paused you heard your heart
thumping, and the distant roar of the torrent. What is the

time, *kot or?* He pressed his repeater and, undismayed, it hissed and tinkled out ten twenty-one.

Anyone who has tried to struggle up a steep slope, on a dark night, through a tangle of inimical vegetation, knows what a formidable task our mountaineer had before him. For more than two hours he kept at it, stumbling against stumps, falling into ravines, clutching at invisible bushes, fighting off an army of conifers. He lost his cloak. He wondered if he had not better curl up in the undergrowth and wait for daybreak. All at once a pinhead light gleamed ahead and presently he found himself staggering up a slippery, recently mown meadow. A dog barked. A stone rolled underfoot. He realized he was near a mountainside *bore* (farmhouse). He also realized that he had toppled into a deep muddy ditch.

The gnarled farmer and his plump wife who, like personages in an old tedious tale offered the drenched fugitive a welcome shelter, mistook him for an eccentric camper who had got detached from his group. He was allowed to dry himself in a warm kitchen where he was given a fairy-tale meal of bread and cheese, and a bowl of mountain mead. His feelings (gratitude, exhaustion, pleasant warmth, drowsiness and so on) were too obvious to need description. A fire of larch roots crackled in the stove, and all the shadows of his lost kingdom gathered to play around his rocking chair as he dozed off between that blaze and the tremulous light of a little earthenware cresset, a beaked affair rather like a Roman lamp, hanging above a shelf where poor beady baubles and bits of nacre became microscopic soldiers swarming in desperate battle. He woke up with a crimp in the neck at the first full cowbell of dawn, found his host

outside, in a damp corner consigned to the humble needs of
nature, and bade the good *grunter* (mountain farmer)
show him the shortest way to the pass. "I'll rouse lazy Garh,"
said the farmer.

A rude staircase led up to a loft. The farmer placed his
gnarled hand on the gnarled balustrade and directed toward
the upper darkness a guttural call: "Garh! Garh!" Although
given to both sexes, the name is, strictly speaking, a mascu-
line one, and the King expected to see emerge from the loft
a bare-kneed mountain lad like a tawny angel. Instead
there appeared a disheveled young hussy wearing only a
man's shirt that came down to her pink shins and an over-
sized pair of brogues. A moment later, as in a transformation
act, she reappeared, her yellow hair still hanging lank and
loose, but the dirty shirt replaced by a dirty pullover, and
her legs sheathed in corduroy pants. She was told to conduct
the stranger to a spot from which he could easily reach the
pass. A sleepy and sullen expression blurred whatever appeal
her snub-nosed round face might have had for the local
shepherds; but she complied readily enough with her
father's wish. His wife was crooning an ancient song as she
busied herself with pot and pan.

Before leaving, the King asked his host, whose name was
Griff, to accept an old gold piece he chanced to have in his
pocket, the only money he possessed. Griff vigorously refused and, still remonstrating, started the laborious business
of unlocking and unbolting two or three heavy doors. The
King glanced at the old woman, received a wink of approval, and put the muted ducat on the mantelpiece, next to
a violet seashell against which was propped a color print
representing an elegant guardsman with his bare-shouldered

wife—Karl the Beloved, as he was twenty odd years before, and his young queen, an angry young virgin with coal-black hair and ice-blue eyes.

The stars had just faded. He followed the girl and a happy sheepdog up the overgrown trail that glistened with the ruby dew in the theatrical light of an alpine dawn. The very air seemed tinted and glazed. A sepulchral chill emanated from the sheer cliff along which the trail ascended; but on the opposite precipitous side, here and there between the tops of fir trees growing below, gossamer gleams of sunlight were beginning to weave patterns of warmth. At the next turning this warmth enveloped the fugitive, and a black butterfly came dancing down a pebbly rake. The path narrowed still more and gradually deteriorated amidst a jumble of boulders. The girl pointed to the slopes beyond it. He nodded. "Now go home," he said. "I shall rest here and then continue alone."

He sank down on the grass near a patch of matted elfinwood and inhaled the bright air. The panting dog lay down at his feet. Garh smiled for the first time. Zemblan mountain girls are as a rule mere mechanisms of haphazard lust, and Garh was no exception. As soon as she had settled beside him, she bent over and pulled over and off her tousled head the thick gray sweater, revealing her naked back and *blancmangé* breasts, and flooded her embarrassed companion with all the acridity of ungroomed womanhood. She was about to proceed with her stripping but he stopped her with a gesture and got up. He thanked her for all her kindness. He patted the innocent dog; and without turning once, with a springy step, the King started to walk up the turfy incline.

He was still chuckling over the wench's discomfiture when he came to the tremendous stones amassed around a small

lake which he had reached once or twice from the rocky
Kronberg side many years ago. Now he glimpsed the flash
of the pool through the aperture of a natural vault, a masterpiece of erosion. The vault was low and he bent his head to
step down toward the water. In its limpid tintarron he saw
his scarlet reflection but, oddly enough, owing to what
seemed to be at first blush an optical illusion, this reflection
was not at his feet but much further; moreover, it was accompanied by the ripple-warped reflection of a ledge that
jutted high above his present position. And finally, the
strain on the magic of the image caused it to snap as his
red-sweatered, red-capped doubleganger turned and vanished, whereas he, the observer, remained immobile. He
now advanced to the very lip of the water and was met
there by a genuine reflection, much larger and clearer than
the one that had deceived him. He skirted the pool. High
up in the deep-blue sky jutted the empty ledge whereon a
counterfeit king had just stood. A shiver of *alfear* (uncontrollable fear caused by elves) ran between his shoulder-
blades. He murmured a familiar prayer, crossed himself,
and resolutely proceeded toward the pass. At a high point
upon an adjacent ridge a *steinmann* (a heap of stones erected
as a memento of an ascent) had donned a cap of red wool in
his honor. He trudged on. But his heart was a conical ache
poking him from below in the throat, and after a while he
stopped again to take stock of conditions and decide whether
to scramble up the steep debris slope in front of him or to
strike off to the right along a strip of grass, gay with gentians,
that went winding between lichened rocks. He elected the
second route and in due course reached the pass.

Great fallen crags diversified the wayside. The *nippern*
(domed hills or "reeks") to the south were broken by a rock

and grass slope into light and shadow. Northward melted the green, gray, bluish mountains—Falkberg with its hood of snow, Mutraberg with the fan of its avalanche, Paberg (Mt. Peacock), and others,—separated by narrow dim valleys with intercalated cotton-wool bits of cloud that seemed placed between the receding sets of ridges to prevent their flanks from scraping against one another. Beyond them, in the final blue, loomed Mt. Glitterntin, a serrated edge of bright foil; and southward, a tender haze enveloped more distant ridges which led to one another in an endless array, through every grade of soft evanescence.

The pass had been reached, granite and gravity had been overcome; but the most dangerous stretch lay ahead. Westward a succession of heathered slopes led down to the shining sea. Up to this moment the mountain had stood between him and the gulf; now he was exposed to that arching blaze. He began the descent.

Three hours later he trod level ground. Two old women working in an orchard unbent in slow motion and stared after him. He had passed the pine groves of Boscobel and was approaching the quay of Blawick, when a black police car turned out of a transverse road and pulled up next to him: "The joke has gone too far," said the driver. "One hundred clowns are packed in Onhava jail, and the ex-King should be among them. Our local prison is much too small for more kings. The next masquerader will be shot at sight. What's your real name, Charlie?" "I'm British. I'm a tourist," said the King. "Well, anyway, take off that red *fufa*. And the cap. Give them here." He tossed the things in the back of the car and drove off.

The King walked on; the top of his blue pajamas tucked into his skiing pants might easily pass for a fancy shirt.

There was a pebble in his left shoe but he was too fagged out to do anything about it.

He recognized the seashore restaurant where many years earlier he had lunched incognito with two amusing, very amusing, sailors. Several heavily armed Extremists were drinking beer on the geranium-lined veranda, among the routine vacationists, some of whom were busy writing to distant friends. Through the geraniums, a gloved hand gave the King a picture postcard on which he found scribbled: *Proceed to R.C. Bon voyage!* Feigning a casual stroll, he reached the end of the embankment.

It was a lovely breezy afternoon with a western horizon like a luminous vacuum that sucked in one's eager heart. The King, now at the most critical point of his journey, looked about him, scrutinizing the few promenaders and trying to decide which of them might be police agents in disguise, ready to pounce upon him as soon as he vaulted the parapet and made for the Rippleson Caves. Only a single sail dyed a royal red marred with some human interest the marine expanse. Nitra and Indra (meaning "inner" and "outer"), two black islets that seemed to address each other in cloaked parley, were being photographed from the parapet by a Russian tourist, thickset, many-chinned, with a general's fleshy nape. His faded wife, wrapped up floatingly in a flowery *écharpe,* remarked in singsong Moscovan "Every time I see that kind of frightful disfigurement I can't help thinking of Nina's boy. War is an awful thing." "War?" queried her consort. "That must have been the explosion at the Glass Works in 1951—not war." They slowly walked past the King in the direction he had come from. On a sidewalk bench, facing the sea, a man with his crutches beside him was reading the Onhava *Post* which featured on the first page Odon in an Extremist uniform and Odon in the part of the Merman. Incredible as it may seem the palace guard had never realized that identity before. Now a goodly sum was offered for his capture. Rhythmically the waves lapped the shingle. The newspaper reader's face had been atrociously injured in the recently mentioned explosion, and all the art of plastic surgery had only resulted in a hideous tessellated texture with parts of pattern and parts of outline seeming to change, to fuse or to separate, like fluctuating cheeks and chins in a distortive mirror.

The short stretch of beach between the restaurant at the beginning of the promenade and the granite rocks at its end was almost empty: far to the left three fishermen were loading a rowboat with kelp-brown nets, and directly under the sidewalk, an elderly woman wearing a polka-dotted dress and having for headgear a cocked newspaper (Ex-KING SEEN—) sat knitting on the shingle with her back to the street. Her bandaged legs were stretched out on the sand; on one side of her lay a pair of carpet slippers and on the other a ball of red wool, the leading filament of which she would tug at every now and then with the immemorial elbow jerk of a Zemblan knitter to give a turn to her yarn clew and slacken the thread. Finally, on the sidewalk a little girl in a ballooning skirt was clumsily but energetically clattering about on roller skates. Could a dwarf in the police force pose as a pigtailed child?

Waiting for the Russian couple to recede, the King stopped beside the bench. The mosaic-faced man folded his newspaper, and one second before he spoke (in the neutral interval between smoke puff and detonation), the King knew it was Odon. "All one could do at short notice," said Odon, plucking at his cheek to display how the varicolored semitransparent film adhered to his face, altering its contours according to stress. "A polite person," he added, "does not, normally, examine too closely a poor fellow's disfigurement." "I was looking for *shpiks* [plainclothesmen]" said the King. "All day," said Odon, "they have been patrolling the quay. They are dining at present." "I'm thirsty and hungry," said the King. "There's some stuff in the boat. Let those Russians vanish. The child we can ignore." "What about that woman on the beach?" "That's young Baron Mandevil—chap who had that duel last year. Let's go now." "Couldn't we take him too?" "Wouldn't come—got a wife and a baby. Come on, Charlie, come on, Your Majesty." "He was my throne page on Coronation Day." Thus chatting, they reached the Rippleson Caves. I trust the reader has enjoyed this note.

Line 162:   With his pure tongue, etc.

This is a singularly roundabout way of describing a country girl's shy kiss; but the whole passage is very baroque. My own boyhood was too happy and healthy to contain anything remotely like the fainting fits experienced by Shade. It must have been with him a mild form of epilepsy, a derailment of the nerves at the same spot, on the same curve of the tracks, every day, for several weeks, until nature repaired the damage. Who can forget the good-natured faces, glossy with sweat, of copper-chested railway workers leaning upon their spades and following with their eyes the windows of the great express cautiously gliding by?

Line 167:   There was a time, etc.

The poet began Canto Two (on his fourteenth card) on July 5, his sixtieth birthday (see note to line 181, "today"). My slip—change to sixty-first.

Line 169:   survival after death

See note to line 549.

Line 171:   A great conspiracy

For almost a whole year after the King's escape the Extremists remained convinced that he and Odon had not left Zembla. The mistake can be only ascribed to the streak of stupidity that fatally runs through the most competent tyranny. Airborne machines and everything connected with them cast a veritable spell over the minds of our new rulers whom kind history had suddenly given a boxful of these zipping and zooming gadgets to play with. That an important fugitive would not perform by air the act of fleeing seemed to them inconceivable. Within minutes after the King and the actor had clattered down the backstairs of the Royal Theater, every wing in the sky and on the ground had been accounted for—such was the efficiency of the government. During the next weeks not one private or commercial plane was allowed to take off, and the inspection of transients became so rigorous and lengthy that international lines decided to cancel stopovers at Onhava. There were some casualties. A crimson balloon was enthusiastically shot down and the aeronaut (a well-known meteorologist) drowned in the Gulf of Surprise. A pilot from a Lapland base flying on a mission of mercy got lost in the fog and was so badly harassed by Zemblan fighters that he settled atop a mountain peak. Some excuse for all this could be found. The illusion of the King's presence in the wilds of Zembla was kept up by royalist plotters who decoyed entire regiments into searching the mountains and woods of our rugged peninsula. The government spent a ludicrous amount of energy on solemnly screening the hundreds of impostors packed in the country's jails. Most of them clowned their way back to freedom; a few, alas, fell. Then, in the spring of the following year, a stunning piece of news came from abroad. The Zemblan actor Odon was directing the making of a cinema picture in Paris!

It was now correctly conjectured that if Odon had fled, the King had fled too. At an extraordinary session of the Extremist government there was passed from hand to hand, in grim silence, a copy of a French newspaper with the headline: L'EX-ROI DE ZEMBLA EST-IL À PARIS? Vindictive exasperation rather than state strategy moved the secret organization of which Gradus was an obscure member to plot the destruction of the royal fugitive. Spiteful thugs! They may be compared to hoodlums who itch to torture the invulnerable gentleman whose testimony clapped them in prison for life. Such convicts have been known to go berserk at the thought that their elusive victim whose very testicles they crave to twist and tear with their talons, is sitting at a pergola feast on a sunny island or fondling some pretty young

creature between his knees in serene security—and laughing
at them! One supposes that no hell can be worse than the
helpless rage they experience as the awareness of that im-
placable sweet mirth reaches them and suffuses them, slowly
destroying their brutish brains. A group of especially de-
vout Extremists calling themselves the Shadows had got together and swore to hunt down the King and kill him wherever he might be. They were, in a sense, the shadow twins
of the Karlists and indeed several had cousins or even brothers among the followers of the King. No doubt, the origin of
either group could be traced to various reckless rituals in
student fraternities and military clubs, and their develop-
ment examined in terms of fads and anti-fads; but whereas
an objective historian associates a romantic and noble glamor
with Karlism, its shadow group must strike one as something definitely Gothic and nasty. The grotesque figure of
Gradus, a cross between bat and crab, was not much odder
than many other Shadows, such as, for example, Nodo,
Odon's epileptic half brother who cheated at cards, or a mad
Mandevil who had lost a leg in trying to make anti-matter.
Gradus had long been a member of all sorts of jejune leftist
organizations. He had never killed, though coming rather
close to it several times in his gray life. He insisted later that
when he found himself designated to track down and murder
the King, the choice was decided by a show of cards—but
let us not forget that it was Nodo who shuffled and dealt them
out. Perhaps our man's foreign origin secretly prompted a
nomination that would not cause any son of Zembla to incur
the dishonor of actual regicide. We can well imagine the
scene: the ghastly neon lights of the laboratory, in an annex
of the Glass Works, where the Shadows happened to hold
their meeting that night; the ace of spades lying on the tiled

floor; the vodka gulped down out of test tubes; the many hands clapping Gradus on his round back, and the dark exultation of the man as he received those rather treacherous congratulations. We place this fatidic moment at 0:05, July 2, 1959—which happens to be also the date upon which an innocent poet penned the first lines of his last poem.

Was Gradus really a suitable person for the job? Yes and no. One day in his early youth, when he worked as messenger boy for a large and depressing firm of cardboard box manufacturers, he quietly helped three companions to ambush a local lad whom they wished to beat up for winning a motorcycle at a fair. Young Gradus obtained an axe and directed the felling of a tree: it crashed improperly, though, not quite blocking the country lane down which their carefree prey used to ride in the growing dusk. The poor lad whizzing along toward the spot where those roughs crouched was a slim delicate-looking Lorrainer, and one must have been vile indeed to begrudge him his harmless enjoyment. Curiously enough, while they were lying in wait, our future regicide fell asleep in a ditch and thus missed the brief affray during which two of the attackers were knuckledusted and knocked out by the brave Lorrainer, and the third run over and crippled for life.

Gradus never became a real success in the glass business to which he turned again and again between his wine-selling and pamphlet-printing jobs. He started as a maker of Cartesian devils—imps of bottle glass bobbing up and down in methylate-filled tubes hawked during Catkin Week on the boulevards. He also worked as teazer, and later as flasher, at governmental factories—and was, I believe, more or less responsible for the remarkably ugly red-and-amber windows in the great public lavatory at rowdy but colorful Kalixhaven where the sailors are. He claimed to have improved the glitter and rattle of the so-called *feuilles-d'alarme* used by grape growers and orchardmen to scare the birds. I have staggered the notes referring to him in such a fashion that the first (see note to line 17 where some of his other activities are adumbrated) is the vaguest while those that follow become gradually clearer as gradual Gradus approaches in space and time.

Mere springs and coils produced the inward movements of our clockwork man. He might be termed a Puritan. One essential dislike, formidable in its simplicity, pervaded his dull soul: he disliked injustice and deception. He disliked their union—they were always together—with a wooden passion that neither had, nor needed, words to express itself. Such a dislike should have deserved praise had it not been a by-product of the man's hopeless stupidity. He called unjust and deceitful everything that surpassed his understanding. He worshiped general ideas and did so with pedantic aplomb. The generality was godly, the specific diabolical. If one person was poor and the other wealthy it did not matter what precisely had ruined one or made the other rich; the difference itself was unfair, and the poor man who did not denounce it was as wicked as the rich one who ignored it. People who knew too much, scientists, writers, mathematicians, crystalographers and so forth, were no better than kings or priests: they all held an unfair share of power of which others were cheated. A plain decent fellow should constantly be on the watch for some piece of clever knavery on the part of nature and neighbor.

The Zemblan Revolution provided Gradus with satisfactions but also produced frustrations. One highly irritating episode seems retrospectively most significant as belonging to an order of things that Gradus should have learned to expect but never did. An especially brilliant impersonator of the King, the tennis ace Julius Steinmann (son of the well-known philanthropist), had eluded for several months the police who had been driven to the limits of exasperation by his mimicking to perfection the voice of Charles the Beloved in a series of underground radio speeches deriding the government. When finally captured he was tried by a special commission, of which Gradus was member, and condemned to death. The firing squad bungled their job, and a little later the gallant young man was found recuperating from his wounds at a provincial hospital. When Gradus learned of this, he flew into one of his rare rages—not because the fact presupposed royalist machinations, but because the clean, honest, orderly course of death had been interfered with in an unclean, dishonest, disorderly manner. Without consulting anybody he rushed to the hospital, stormed in, located Julius in a crowded ward and managed to fire twice, both times missing, before the gun was wrested from him by a hefty male nurse. He rushed back to headquarters and returned with a dozen soldiers but his patient had disappeared.

Such things rankle—but what can Gradus do? The huddled fates engage in a great conspiracy against Gradus. One notes with pardonable glee that his likes are never granted the ultimate thrill of dispatching their victim themselves. Oh, surely, Gradus is active, capable, helpful, often indispensable. At the foot of the scaffold, on a raw and gray morning, it is Gradus who sweeps the night's powder snow off the narrow steps; but his long leathery face will not be the last one that the man who must mount those steps is to see in this world. It is Gradus who buys the cheap fiber valise that a luckier guy will plant, with a time bomb inside, under the bed of a former henchman. Nobody knows better than Gradus how to set a trap by means of a fake advertisement, but the rich old widow whom it hooks is courted and slain by another. When the fallen tyrant is tied, naked and howling, to a plank in the public square and killed piecemeal by the people who cut slices out, and eat them, and distribute his living body among themselves (as I read when young in a story about an Italian despot, which made of me a vegetarian for life), Gradus does not take part in the infernal sacrament: he points out the right instrument and directs the carving.

All this is as it should be; the world needs Gradus. But Gradus should not kill kings. Vinogradus should never, never provoke God. Leningradus should not aim his peashooter at people even in dreams, because if he does, a pair of colossally thick, abnormally hairy arms will hug him from behind and squeeze, squeeze, squeeze.

Line 172:   books and people

In a black pocketbook that I fortunately have with me I find, jotted down, here and there, among various extracts that had happened to please me (a footnote from Boswell's *Life of Dr. Johnson,* the inscriptions on the trees in Wordsmith's famous avenue, a quotation from St. Augustine, and so on), a few samples of John Shade's conversation which I had collected in order to refer to them in the presence of people whom my friendship with the poet might interest or annoy. His and my reader will, I trust, excuse me for breaking the orderly course of these comments and letting my illustrious friend speak for himself.

Book reviewers being mentioned, he said: "I have never acknowledged printed praise though sometimes I longed to embrace the glowing image of this or that paragon of discernment; and I have never bothered to lean out of my window and empty my skoramis on some poor hack's pate. I regard both the demolishment and the rave with like detachment." Kinbote: "I suppose you dismiss the first as the blabber of a blockhead and the second as a kind soul's friendly act?" Shade: "Exactly."

Speaking of the Head of the bloated Russian Department, Prof. Pnin, a regular martinet in regard to his underlings (happily, Prof. Botkin, who taught in another department, was not subordinated to that grotesque "perfectionist"): "How odd that Russian intellectuals should lack all sense of humor when they have such marvelous humorists as Gogol, Dostoevski, Chekhov, Zoshchenko, and those joint authors of genius Ilf and Petrov."

Talking of the vulgarity of a certain burly acquaintance of ours: "The man is as corny as a cook-out chef apron." Kinbote (laughing): "Wonderful!"

The subject of teaching Shakespeare at college level having been introduced: "First of all, dismiss ideas, and social background, and train the freshman to shiver, to get drunk on the poetry of *Hamlet* or *Lear,* to read with his spine and not with his skull." Kinbote: "You appreciate particularly the purple passages?" Shade: "Yes, my dear Charles, I roll upon them as a grateful mongrel on a spot of turf fouled by a Great Dane."

The respective impacts and penetrations of Marxism and

Freudism being talked of, I said: "The worst of two false doctrines is always that which is harder to eradicate." Shade: "No, Charlie, there are simpler criteria: Marxism needs a dictator, and a dictator needs a secret police, and that is the end of the world; but the Freudian, no matter how stupid, can still cast his vote at the poll, even if he is pleased to call it [smiling] *political pollination*."

Of students' papers: "I am generally very benevolent [said Shade]. But there are certain trifles I do not forgive." Kinbote: "For instance?" "Not having read the required book. Having read it like an idiot. Looking in it for symbols; example: 'The author uses the striking image *green leaves* because green is the symbol of happiness and frustration.' I am also in the habit of lowering a student's mark catastrophically if he uses 'simple' and 'sincere' in a commendatory sense; examples: 'Shelley's style is always very simple and good'; or 'Yeats is always sincere.' This is widespread, and when I hear a critic speaking of an author's sincerity I know that either the critic or the author is a fool." Kinbote: "But I am told this manner of thinking is taught in high school?" "That's where the broom should begin to sweep. A child should have thirty specialists to teach him thirty subjects, and not one harassed schoolmarm to show him a picture of a rice field and tell him this is China because she knows nothing about China, or anything else, and cannot tell the difference between longitude and latitude." Kinbote: "Yes. I agree."

Line 181: Today

Namely, July 5, 1959, 6th Sunday after Trinity. Shade began writing Canto Two "early in the morning" (thus noted at the top of Card 14). He continued (down to line 208) on and off throughout the day. Most of the evening and a part of the night were devoted to what his favorite eighteenth-century writers have termed "the Bustle and Vanity of the World." After the last guest had gone (on a bicycle), and the ashtrays had been emptied, all the windows were dark for a couple of hours; but then, at about 3 A.M., I saw from my upstairs bathroom that the poet had gone back to his desk in the lilac light of his den, and this nocturnal session brought the canto to line 230 (card 18). On another trip to the bathroom an hour and a half later, at sunrise, I found the light transferred to the bedroom, and smiled indulgently, for, according to my deductions, only two nights had passed since the three-thousand-nine-hundred-ninety-ninth time—but no matter. A few minutes later all was solid darkness again, and I went back to bed.

On July 5th, at noontime, in the other hemisphere, on the rain-swept tarmac of the Onhava airfield, Gradus, holding a French passport, walked towards a Russian commercial plane bound for Copenhagen, and this event synchronized with Shade's starting in the early morning (Atlantic seaboard time) to compose, or to set down after composing in bed, the opening lines of Canto Two. When almost twenty-four hours later he got to line 230, Gradus, after a refreshing night at the summer house of our consul in Copenhagen, an important Shadow, had entered, with the Shadow, a clothes store in order to conform to his description in later notes (to lines 286 and 408). Migraine again worse today.

As to my own activities, they were I am afraid most unsatisfactory from all points of view—emotional, creative, and social. That jinxy streak had started on the eve when I had been kind enough to offer a young friend—a candidate for my third ping-pong table who after a sensational series of traffic violations had been deprived of his driving license—to take him, in my powerful Kramler, all the way to his parents' estate, a little matter of two hundred miles. In the course of an all-night party, among crowds of strangers—young people, old people, cloyingly perfumed girls—in an atmosphere of fireworks, barbecue smoke, horseplay, jazz music, and auroral swimming, I lost all contact with the silly boy, was made to dance, was made to sing, got involved in the most boring bibble-babble imaginable with various relatives of the child, and finally, in some inconceivable manner, found myself transported to a different party on a different estate, where, after some indescribable parlor games, in which my beard was nearly snipped off, I had a fruit-and-rice breakfast and was taken by my anonymous host, a drunken old fool in tuxedo and riding breeches, on a stumbling round of his stables. Upon locating my car (off the road, in a pine grove), I tossed out of the driver's seat a pair of soggy swimming trunks and a girl's silver slipper. The brakes had aged overnight, and I soon ran out of gas on a desolate stretch of road. Six o'clock was being chimed by the clocks of Wordsmith College, when I reached Arcady, swearing to myself never to be caught like that again and innocently looking forward to the solace of a quiet evening with my poet. Only when I saw the beribboned flat carton I had placed on a chair in my hallway did I realize that I had almost missed his birthday.

Some time ago I had noticed that date on the jacket of one

of his books; had pondered the awful decrepitude of his breakfast attire; had playfully measured my arm against his; and had bought for him in Washington an utterly gorgeous silk dressing gown, a veritable dragon skin of oriental chromas, fit for a samurai; and this was what the carton contained.

Hurriedly I shed my clothes and, roaring my favorite hymn, took a shower. My versatile gardener, while administering to me a much-needed rubdown, informed me that the Shades were giving that night a big "buffet" dinner, and that Senator Blank (an outspoken statesman very much in the news and a cousin of John's) was expected.

Now there is nothing a lonesome man relishes more than an impromptu birthday party, and thinking—nay, feeling certain—that my unattended telephone had been ringing all day, I blithely dialed the Shades' number, and of course it was Sybil who answered.

"*Bon soir*, Sybil."

"Oh, hullo, Charles. Had a nice trip?"

"Well, to tell the truth—"

"Look, I know you want John but he is resting right now, and I'm frightfully busy. He'll call you back later, okay?"

"Later when—tonight?"

"No, tomorrow, I guess. There goes that doorbell. Bye-bye."

Strange. Why should Sybil have to listen to doorbells when, besides the maid and the cook, two white-coated hired boys were around? False pride prevented me from doing what I should have done—taken my royal gift under my arm and serenely marched over to that inhospitable house. Who knows—I might have been rewarded at the back door with a drop of kitchen sherry. I still hoped there had been a mistake, and Shade would telephone. It was a bitter wait, and the only effect that the bottle of champagne I drank all alone now at this window, now at that, had on me was a bad *crapula* (hangover).

From behind a drapery, from behind a box tree, through the golden veil of evening and through the black lacery of night, I kept watching that lawn, that drive, that fanlight, those jewel-bright windows. The sun had not yet set when, at a quarter past seven, I heard the first guest's car. Oh, I saw them all. I saw ancient Dr. Sutton, a snowy-headed, perfectly oval little gentleman arrive in a tottering Ford with his tall daughter, Mrs. Starr, a war widow. I saw a couple, later identified for me as Mr. Colt, a local lawyer, and his wife, whose blundering Cadillac half entered my driveway before retreating in a flurry of luminous nictitation. I saw a world-famous old writer, bent under the incubus of literary honors and his own prolific mediocrity, arrive in a taxi out of the dim times of yore when Shade and he had been joint editors of a little review. I saw Frank, the Shades' handyman, depart in the station wagon. I saw a retired professor of ornithology walk up from the highway where he had illegally parked his car. I saw, ensconced in their tiny Pulex, manned by her boy-handsome tousle-haired girl friend, the patroness of the arts who had sponsored Aunt Maud's last exhibition. I saw Frank return with the New Wye antiquarian, purblind Mr. Kaplun, and his wife, a dilapidated eagle. I saw a Korean graduate student in dinner jacket come on a bicycle, and the college president in baggy suit come on foot. I saw, in the performance of their ceremonial duties, in light and shadow, and from window to window, where like Martians the martinis and highballs cruised, the two white-coated youths from the hotel school, and realized that I knew well, quite well, the slighter of the two. And finally, at half past eight (when, I imagine, the lady of the house had begun to crack her finger joints as was her impatient wont) a long black limousine, officially glossy and rather funereal, glided into the aura of the drive, and while the fat Negro chauffeur hastened to open the car door, I saw, with pity, my poet emerge from his house, a white flower in his buttonhole and a grin of welcome on his liquor-flushed face.

Next morning, as soon as I saw Sybil drive away to fetch Ruby the maid who did not sleep in the house, I crossed over with the prettily and reproachfully wrapped up carton. In front of their garage, on the ground, I noticed a *buchmann*, a little pillar of library books which Sybil had obviously forgotten there. I bent towards them under the incubus of curiosity: they were mostly by Mr. Faulkner; and the next moment Sybil was back, her tires scrunching on the gravel right behind me. I added the books to my gift and placed the whole pile in her lap. That was nice of me—but what was that carton? Just a present for John. A present? Well, was it not his birthday yesterday? Yes, it was, but after all are not birthdays mere conventions? Conventions or not, but it was my birthday too—small difference of sixteen years, that's all. Oh my! Congratulations. And how did the party go? Well, you know what such parties are (here I reached in my pocket for another book—a book she did not expect). Yes, what are they? Oh, people whom you've known all your life and simply *must* invite once a year, men like Ben Kaplun and Dick Colt with whom we went to school, and that Washington cousin, and the fellow whose novels you and John think so phony. We did not ask you because we knew how tedious you find such affairs. This was my cue.

"Speaking of novels," I said, "you remember we decided

once, you, your husband and I, that Proust's rough masterpiece was a huge, ghoulish fairy tale, an asparagus dream,
totally unconnected with any possible people in any historical France, a sexual *travestissement* and a colossal farce, the
vocabulary of genius and its poetry, but no more, impossibly
rude hostesses, please let me speak, and even ruder guests,
mechanical Dostoevskian rows and Tolstoian nuances of
snobbishness repeated and expanded to an unsufferable
length, adorable seascapes, melting avenues, no, do not interrupt me, light and shade effects rivaling those of the
greatest English poets, a flora of metaphors, described—by
Cocteau, I think—as 'a mirage of suspended gardens,' and,
I have not yet finished, an absurd, rubber-and-wire romance between a blond young blackguard (the fictitious Marcel), and an improbable *jeune fille* who has a pasted-on bosom,
Vronski's (and Lyovin's) thick neck, and a cupid's buttocks
for cheeks; but—and now let me finish sweetly—we were
wrong, Sybil, we were wrong in denying our little *beau
ténébreux* the capacity of evoking 'human interest': it is
there, it is there—maybe a rather eighteenth-centuryish, or
even seventeenth-centuryish, brand, but it is there. Please,
dip or redip, spider, into this book [offering it], you will find
a pretty marker in it bought in France, I want John to keep
it. *Au revoir*, Sybil, I must go now. *I think my telephone is
ringing.*"

I am a very sly Zemblan. *Just in case*, I had brought with
me in my pocket the third and last volume of the *Biblio-
thèque de la Pléiade* edition, Paris, 1954, of Proust's work,
wherein I had marked certain passages on pages 269-271.
Mme. de Mortemart, having decided that Mme. de Valcourt
would *not* be among the "elected" at her soirée, intended to
send her a note on the next day saying "Dear Edith, I miss

you, last night I did not expect you too much (Edith would wonder: how could she at all, since she did not invite me?) because I know you are not overfond of this sort of parties which, if anything, bore you."

So much for John Shade's last birthday.

Lines 181-182:   waxwings . . . cicadas

The bird of lines 1-4 and 131 is again with us. It will re-appear in the ultimate line of the poem; and another cicada, leaving its envelope behind, will sing triumphantly at lines 236-244.

Line 189:   Starover Blue

See note to line 627. This reminds one of the Royal Game of the Goose, but played here with little airplanes of painted tin: a wild-goose game, rather (go to square 209).

Line 209:   gradual decay

Spacetime itself is decay; Gradus is flying west; he has reached gray-blue Copenhagen (see note to 181). After tomorrow (July 7) he will proceed to Paris. He has sped through this verse and is gone—presently to darken our pages again.

Lines 213-214:   A syllogism

This may please a boy. Later in life we learn that we *are* those "others."

Line 230:   a domestic ghost

Shade's former secretary, Jane Provost, whom I recently looked up in Chicago, told me about Hazel considerably more than her father did; he affected not to speak of his dead daughter, and since I did not foresee this work of inquiry and comment, I did not urge him to talk on the subject and unburden himself to me. True, in this canto he has unburdened himself pretty thoroughly, and his picture of Hazel is quite clear and complete; maybe a little too complete, architectonically, since the reader cannot help feeling that it has been expanded and elaborated to the detriment of certain other richer and rarer matters ousted by it. But a commentator's obligations cannot be shirked, however dull the information he must collect and convey. Hence this note.

It appears that in the beginning of 1950, long before the barn incident (see note to line 347), sixteen-year-old Hazel was involved in some appalling "psychokinetic" manifestations that lasted for nearly a month. Initially, one gathers, the poltergeist meant to impregnate the disturbance with the identity of Aunt Maud who had just died; the first object to perform was the basket in which she had once kept her half-paralyzed Skye terrier (the breed called in our country "weeping-willow dog"). Sybil had had the animal destroyed soon after its mistress's hospitalization, incurring the wrath of Hazel who was beside herself with distress. One morning this basket shot out of the "intact" sanctuary (see lines 90-98) and traveled along the corridor past the open door of the study, where Shade was at work; he saw it whizz by and spill its humble contents: a ragged coverlet, a rubber bone, and a partly discolored cushion. Next day the scene of action switched to the dining room where one of Aunt Maud's oils (*Cypress and Bat*) was found to be turned toward the wall. Other incidents followed, such as short flights accomplished by her scrapbook (see note to line 90) and, of course, all kinds of knockings, especially in the sanctuary, which would rouse Hazel from her, no doubt, peaceful sleep in the adjacent bedroom. But soon the poltergeist ran out of ideas in connection with Aunt Maud and became, as it were, more eclectic. All the banal motions that objects are limited to in such cases, were gone through in this one. Saucepans crashed in the kitchen; a snowball was found (perhaps, prematurely) in the icebox; once or twice Sybil saw a plate sail by like a discus and land safely on the sofa; lamps kept lighting up in various parts of the house; chairs waddled away to assemble in the impassable pantry; mysterious bits of string were found on the floor; invisible revelers staggered down the staircase in the middle of the night; and one winter morning Shade, upon rising and taking a look at the

weather, saw that the little table from his study upon which
he kept a Bible-like Webster open at M was standing in a
state of shock outdoors, on the snow (subliminally this may
have participated in the making of lines 5-12).

I imagine, that during that period the Shades, or at least
John Shade, experienced a sensation of odd instability as if
parts of the everyday, smoothly running world had got un-
screwed, and you became aware that one of your tires was
rolling beside you, or that your steering wheel had come off.
My poor friend could not help recalling the dramatic fits of
his early boyhood and wondering if this was not a new
genetic variant of the same theme, preserved through pro-
creation. Trying to hide from neighbors these horrible and
humiliating phenomena was not the least of Shade's worries.
He was terrified, and he was lacerated with pity. Although
never able to corner her, that flabby, feeble, clumsy and
solemn girl, who seemed more interested than frightened,
he and Sybil never doubted that in some extraordinary way
she was the agent of the disturbance which they saw as
representing (I now quote Jane P.) "an outward extension
or expulsion of insanity." They could not do much about it,
partly because they disliked modern voodoo-psychiatry, but
mainly because they were afraid of Hazel, and afraid to
hurt her. They had however a secret interview with old-
fashioned and learned Dr. Sutton, and this put them in better spirits. They were contemplating moving into another
house or, more exactly, loudly saying to each other, so as to
be overheard by anyone who might be listening, that they
were contemplating moving, when all at once the fiend was
gone, as happens with the *moskovett*, that bitter blast, that
colossus of cold air that blows on our eastern shores throughout March, and then one morning you hear the birds, and

the flags hang flaccid, and the outlines of the world are again in place. The phenomena ceased completely and were, if not forgotten, at least never referred to; but how curious it is that we do not perceive a mysterious sign of equation between the Hercules springing forth from a neurotic child's weak frame and the boisterous ghost of Aunt Maud; how curious that our rationality feels satisfied when we plump for the first explanation, though, actually, the scientific and the supernatural, the miracle of the muscle and the miracle of the mind, are *both* inexplicable as are all the ways of Our Lord.

Line 231: How ludicrous, etc.

A beautiful variant, with one curious gap, branches off at this point in the draft (dated July 6):

> Strange Other World where all our still-born dwell,
> And pets, revived, and invalids, grown well,
> And minds that died before arriving there:
> Poor old man Swift, poor —, poor Baudelaire

What might that dash stand for? Unless Shade gave prosodic value to the mute *e* in "Baudelaire," which I am quite certain he would never have done in English verse (cp. "Rabelais," line 501), the name required here must scan as a trochee. Among the names of celebrated poets, painters, philosophers, etc., known to have become insane or to have sunk into senile imbecility, we find many suitable ones. Was

Shade confronted by too much variety with nothing to help logic choose and so left a blank, relying upon the mysterious organic force that rescues poets to fill it in at its own convenience? Or was there something else—some obscure intuition, some prophetic scruple that prevented him from spelling out the name of an eminent man who happened to be an intimate friend of his? Was he perhaps playing safe because a reader in his household might have objected to that particular name being mentioned? And if it comes to that, *why* mention it at all in this tragical context? Dark, disturbing thoughts.

Line 238:   empty emerald case

This, I understand, is the semitransparent envelope left on a tree trunk by an adult cicada that has crawled up the trunk and emerged. Shade said that he had once questioned a class of three hundred students and only *three* knew what a cicada looked like. Ignorant settlers had dubbed it "locust," which is, of course, a grasshopper, and the same absurd mistake has been made by generations of translators of Lafontaine's *La Cigale et la Fourmi* (see lines 243-244). The *cigale*'s companion piece, the ant, is about to be embalmed in amber.

During our sunset rambles, of which there were so many, at least nine (according to my notes) in June, but dwindling to two in the first three weeks of July (they shall be resumed Elsewhere!), my friend had a rather coquettish way of pointing out with the tip of his cane various curious natural objects. He never tired of illustrating by means of these examples the extraordinary blend of Canadian Zone and Austral Zone that "obtained," as he put it, in that particular spot of Appalachia where at our altitude of about 1,500 feet northern species of birds, insects and plants commingled with southern representatives. As most literary celebrities, Shade did not seem to realize that a humble admirer who has cornered at last and has at last to himself the inaccessible man of genius, is considerably more interested in discussing with him literature and life than in being told that the "diana" (presumably a flower) occurs in New Wye together with the "atlantis" (presumably another flower), and things of that sort. I particularly remember one exasperating evening stroll (July 6) which my poet granted me, with majestic generosity, in compensation for a bad hurt (see, frequently see, note to line 181), in recompense for my small gift (which I do not think he ever used), and with the sanction of his wife who made it a point to accompany us part of the way to Dulwich Forest. By means of astute excursions into natural history Shade kept evading me, me, who was hysterically, intensely, uncontrollably curious to know what portion exactly of the Zemblan king's adventures he had completed in the course of the last four or five days. My usual shortcoming, pride, prevented me from pressing him with direct questions but I kept reverting to my own earlier themes—the escape from the palace, the adventures in the mountains—in order to force some confession from him. One would imagine that a poet, in the course of composing a long and difficult piece, would simply jump at the opportunity of talking about his triumphs and tribulations. But nothing of the sort! All I got in reply to my infinitely gentle and cautious interrogations were such phrases as: "Yep. It's coming along nicely," or

"Nope, I'm not talkin'," and finally he brushed me off with a rather offensive anecdote about King Alfred who, it was said, liked the stories of a Norwegian attendant he had but drove him away when engaged in other business: "Oh, there you are," rude Alfred would say to the gentle Norwegian who had come to weave a subtly different variant of some old Norse myth he had already related before: *"Oh there you are again!"* And thus it came to pass, my dears, that a fabulous exile, a God-inspired northern bard, is known today to English schoolboys by the trivial nickname: Ohthere.

However! On a later occasion my capricious and henpecked friend was much kinder (see note to line 802).

Line 240: That Englishman in Nice

The sea gulls of 1933 are all dead, of course. But by inserting a notice in *The London Times* one might procure the name of their benefactor—unless Shade invented him. When I visited Nice a quarter of a century later, there was, in lieu of that Englishman, a local character, an old bearded bum, tolerated or abetted as a tourist attraction, who stood like a statue of Verlaine with an unfastidious sea gull perched in profile on his matted hair, or took naps in the public sun, comfortably curled up with his back to the lulling roll of the sea, on a promenade bench, under which he had neatly arranged to dry, or ferment, multicolored gobbets of undeterminable victuals on a newspaper. Not many Englishmen walked there, anyway, though I noticed quite a few just east of Mentone, on the quay where in honor of

Queen Victoria a bulky monument, with difficulty embraced by the breeze, had been erected, but not yet unshrouded, to replace the one the Germans had taken away. Rather pathetically, the eager horn of her pet monoceros protruded through the shroud.

Line 246: . . . my dear

The poet addresses his wife. The passage devoted to her (lines 246-292) has its structural use as a transition to the theme of his daughter. I can, however, state that when dear Sybil's steps were heard upstairs, fierce and sharp, above our heads, everything was not always "all right"!

Line 247: Sybil

John Shade's wife, née Irondell (which comes not from a little valley yielding iron ore but from the French for "swallow"). She was a few months his senior. I understand she came of Canadian stock, as did Shade's maternal grandmother (a first cousin of Sybil's grandfather, if I am not greatly mistaken).

From the very first I tried to behave with the utmost courtesy toward my friend's wife, and from the very first she disliked and distrusted me. I was to learn later that when alluding to me in public she used to call me "an elephantine tick; a king-sized botfly; a macaco worm; the monstrous parasite of a genius." I pardon her—her and everybody.

Line 270:   My dark Vanessa

It is *so* like the heart of a scholar in search of a fond name to pile a butterfly genus upon an Orphic divinity on top of the inevitable allusion to *Van*homrigh, *E*sther! In this connection a couple of lines from one of Swift's poems (which in these backwoods I cannot locate) have stuck in my memory:

> When, lo! *Vanessa* in her bloom
> Advanced like *Atalanta*'s star

As to the Vanessa butterfly, it will reappear in lines 993-995 (to which see note). Shade used to say that its Old English name was The Red Admirable, later degraded to The Red Admiral. It is one of the few butterflies I happen to be familiar with. Zemblans call it *harvalda* (the heraldic one) possibly because a recognizable figure of it is borne in the escutcheon of the Dukes of Payn. In the autumn of certain years it used to occur rather commonly in the Palace Gardens and visit the Michaelmas daisies in company with a day-flying moth. I have seen The Red Admirable feasting on oozy plums and, once, on a dead rabbit. It is a most frolicsome fly. An almost tame specimen of it was the last natural object John Shade pointed out to me as he walked to his doom (see, see now, my note to lines 993-995).

I notice a whiff of Swift in some of my notes. I too am a desponder in my nature, an uneasy, peevish, and suspicious man, although I have my moments of volatility and *fou rire*.

Line 275:   We have been married forty years

John Shade and Sybil Swallow (see note to line 247) were married in 1919, exactly three decades before King Charles wed Disa, Duchess of Payn. Since the very beginning of his reign (1936-1958) representatives of the nation, salmon fishermen, non-union glaziers, military groups, worried relatives, and especially the Bishop of Yeslove, a sanguineous and saintly old man, had been doing their utmost to persuade him to give up his copious but sterile pleasures and take a wife. It was a matter not of morality but of succession. As in the case of some of his predecessors, rough alderkings who burned for boys, the clergy blandly ignored our young bachelor's pagan habits, but wanted him to do what an earlier and even more reluctant Charles had done: take a night off and lawfully engender an heir.

He saw nineteen-year-old Disa for the first time on the festive night of July the 5th, 1947, at a masked ball in his uncle's palace. She had come in male dress, as a Tirolese boy, a little knock-kneed but brave and lovely, and afterwards he drove her and her cousins (two guardsmen disguised as flowergirls) in his divine new convertible through the streets to see the tremendous birthday illumination, and the fackeltanz in the park, and the fireworks, and the pale upturned faces. He procrastinated for almost two years but was set upon by inhumanly eloquent advisers, and finally gave in. On the eve of his wedding he prayed most of the night locked up all alone in the cold vastness of the Onhava cathedral. Smug alderkings looked at him from the ruby-and-amethyst windows. Never had he so fervently asked God for guidance and strength (see further my note to lines 433-434).

After line 274 there is a false start in the draft:

> I like my name: Shade, *Ombre,* almost "man"
> In Spanish . . .

One regrets that the poet did not pursue this theme—and spare his reader the embarrassing intimacies that follow.

Line 286:   A jet's pink trail above the sunset fire

I, too, was wont to draw my poet's attention to the idyllic beauty of airplanes in the evening sky. Who could have guessed that on the very day (July 7) Shade penned this lambent line (the last one on his twenty-third card) Gradus, alias Degré, had flown from Copenhagen to Paris, thus completing the second lap of his sinister journey! Even in Arcady am I, says Death in the tombal scripture.

The activities of Gradus in Paris had been rather neatly planned by the Shadows. They were perfectly right in assuming that not only Odon but our former consul in Paris, the late Oswin Bretwit, would know where to find the King.

They decided to have Gradus try Bretwit first. That gentleman had a flat in Meudon where he dwelt alone, seldom going anywhere except the National Library (where he read
theosophic works and solved chess problems in old newspapers), and did not receive visitors. The Shadows' neat
plan sprung from a piece of luck. Suspecting that Gradus
lacked the mental equipment and mimic gifts necessary for
the impersonation of an enthusiastic Royalist, they suggested
he had better pose as a completely apolitical commissioner, a
neutral little man interested only in getting a good price for
various papers that private parties had asked him to take out
of Zembla and deliver to their rightful owners. Chance, in
one of its anti-Karlist moods, helped. One of the lesser Shadows whom we shall call Baron A. had a father-in-law called
Baron B., a harmless old codger long retired from the civil
service and quite incapable of understanding certain Renais-
sance aspects of the new regime. He had been, or thought he
had been (retrospective distance magnifies things), a close
friend of the late Minister of Foreign Affairs, Oswin Bretwit's father, and therefore was looking forward to the day
when he would be able to transmit to "young" Oswin (who,
he understood, was not exactly *persona grata* with the new
regime) a bundle of precious family papers that the dusty
baron had come across by chance in the files of a governmental office. All at once he was informed that now the day
had come: the documents would be immediately forwarded
to Paris. He was also allowed to prefix a brief note to them
which read:

Here are some precious papers belonging to your family. I
cannot do better than place them in the hands of the son of

the great man who was my fellow student in Heidelberg and my teacher in the diplomatic service. *Verba volant, scripta manent.*

The *scripta* in question were two hundred and thirteen long letters which had passed some seventy years ago between Zule Bretwit, Oswin's grand-uncle, Mayor of Odevalla, and a cousin of his, Ferz Bretwit, Mayor of Aros. This correspondence, a dismal exchange of bureaucratic platitudes and fustian jokes, was devoid of even such parochial interest as letters of this sort may possess in the eyes of a local historian—but of course there is no way of telling what will repel or attract a sentimental ancestralist—and this was what Oswin Bretwit had always been known to be by his former staff. I would like to take time out here to interrupt this dry commentary and pay a brief tribute to Oswin Bretwit.

Physically, he was a sickly bald-headed man resembling a pallid gland. His face was singularly featureless. He had café-au-lait eyes. One remembers him always as wearing a mourning band. But this insipid exterior belied the quality of the man. From beyond the shining corrugations of the ocean I salute here brave Bretwit! Let there appear for a moment his hand and mine firmly clasping each other across the water over the golden wake of an emblematic sun. Let no insurance firm or airline use this insigne on the glossy page of a magazine as an ad badge under the picture of a retired businessman stupefied and honored by the sight of the technicolored snack that the air hostess offers him with everything else she can give; rather, let this lofty handshake be regarded in our cynical age of frenzied heterosexualism as a last, but lasting, symbol of valor and self-abnegation. How fervently one had dreamed that a similar symbol but in verbal form might have imbued the poem of another dead friend; but this was not to be . . . Vainly does one look in *Pale Fire* (oh, pale, indeed!) for the warmth of my hand gripping yours, poor Shade!

But to return to the roofs of Paris. Courage was allied in Oswin Bretwit with integrity, kindness, dignity, and what can be euphemistically called endearing naïveté. When Gradus telephoned from the airport, and to whet his appetite read to him Baron B.'s message (minus the Latin tag), Bretwit's only thought was for the treat in store for him. Gradus had declined to say over the telephone what exactly the "precious papers" were, but it so happened that the ex-consul had been hoping lately to retrieve a valuable stamp collection that his father had bequeathed years ago to a now defunct cousin. The cousin had dwelt in the same house as Baron B., and with all these complicated and entrancing matters uppermost in his mind, the ex-consul, while awaiting his visitor, kept wondering not if the person from Zembla was a dangerous fraud, but whether he would bring all the albums at once or would do it gradually so as to see what he might get for his pains. Bretwit hoped the business would be completed that very night since on the following morning he was to be hospitalized and possibly operated upon (he was, and died under the knife).

If two secret agents belonging to rival factions meet in a battle of wits, and if one has none, the effect may be droll; it is dull if both are dolts. I defy anybody to find in the annals of plot and counterplot anything more inept and boring than the scene that occupies the rest of this conscientious note.

Gradus sat down, uncomfortably, on the edge of a sofa (upon which a tired king had reclined less than a year ago), dipped into his briefcase, handed to his host a bulky brown paper parcel and transferred his haunches to a chair near Bretwit's seat in order to watch in comfort his tussle with the string. In stunned silence Bretwit stared at what he finally unwrapped, and then said:

"Well, that's the end of a dream. This correspondence has been published in 1906 or 1907—no, 1906, after all—by Ferz Bretwit's widow—I may even have a copy of it somewhere among my books. Moreover, this is not a holograph but an apograph, made by a scribe for the printers—you will note that both mayors write the same hand."

"How interesting," said Gradus noting it.

"Naturally I appreciate the kind thought behind it," said Bretwit.

"We were sure you would," said pleased Gradus.

"Baron B. must be a little gaga," continued Bretwit, "but I repeat, his kind intention is touching. I suppose you want some money for bringing this treasure?"

"The pleasure it gives you should be our reward," answered Gradus. "But let me tell you frankly: we took a lot of pains in trying to do this properly, and I have come a long way. However, I want to offer you a little arrangement. You be nice to us and we'll be nice to you. I know your funds are somewhat—" (Small-fish gesture and wink).

"True enough," sighed Bretwit.

"If you go along with us it won't cost you a centime."

"Oh, I could pay *something*" (Pout and shrug).

"We don't need your money" (Traffic-stopper's palm). "But here's our plan. I have messages from other barons for other fugitives. In fact, I have letters for the most mysterious fugitive of all."

"What!" cried Bretwit in candid surprise. "They know at

home that His Majesty has left Zembla?" (I could have spanked the dear man.)

"Indeed, yes," said Gradus kneading his hands, and fairly panting with animal pleasure—a matter of instinct no doubt since the man certainly could not realize intelligently that the ex-consul's faux pas was nothing less than the first confirmation of the King's presence abroad: "Indeed," he repeated with a meaningful leer, "and I would be deeply obliged to you if you would recommend me to Mr. X."

At these words a false truth dawned upon Oswin Bretwit and he moaned to himself: Of course! How obtuse of me! He is one of us! The fingers of his left hand involuntarily started to twitch as if he were pulling a kikapoo puppet over it, while his eyes followed intently his interlocutor's low-class gesture of satisfaction. A Karlist agent, revealing himself to a superior, was expected to make a sign corresponding to the X (for Xavier) in the one-hand alphabet of deaf mutes: the hand held in horizontal position with the index curved rather flaccidly and the rest of the fingers bunched (many have criticized it for looking too droopy; it has now been replaced by a more virile combination). On the several occasions Bretwit had been given it, the manifestation had been preceded for him, during a moment of suspense—rather a gap in the texture of time than an actual delay—by something similar to what physicians call the aura, a strange sensation both tense and vaporous, a hot-cold ineffable exasperation pervading the entire nervous system before a seizure. And on this occasion too Bretwit felt the magic wine rise to his head.

"All right, I am ready. Give me the sign," he avidly said.

Gradus, deciding to risk it, glanced at the hand in Bretwit's lap: unperceived by its owner, it seemed to be prompting Gradus in a manual whisper. He tried to copy what it was doing its best to convey—mere rudiments of the required sign.

"No, no," said Bretwit with an indulgent smile for the awkward novice. "The other hand, my friend. His Majesty is left-handed, you know."

Gradus tried again—but, like an expelled puppet, the wild little prompter had disappeared. Sheepishly contemplating his five stubby strangers, Gradus went through the motions of an incompetent and half-paralyzed shadowgrapher and finally made an uncertain V-for-Victory sign. Bretwit's smile began to fade.

His smile gone, Bretwit (the name means Chess Intelligence) got up from his chair. In a larger room he would have paced up and down—not in this cluttered study. Gradus the Bungler buttoned all three buttons of his tight brown coat and shook his head several times.

"I think," he said crossly, "one must be fair. If I bring you these valuable papers, you must in return arrange an interview, or at least give me his address."

"I know who you are," cried Bretwit pointing. "You're a reporter! You are from that cheap Danish paper sticking out of your pocket" (Gradus mechanically fumbled at it and frowned). "I had hoped they had given up pestering me! The vulgar nuisance of it! Nothing is sacred to you, neither cancer, nor exile, nor the pride of a king" (alas, this is true not only of Gradus—he has colleagues in Arcady too).

Gradus sat staring at his new shoes—mahogany red with sieve-pitted caps. An ambulance screamed its impatient way through dark streets three stories below. Bretwit vented his irritation on the ancestral letters lying on the table. He snatched up the neat pile with its detached wrapping and flung it all in the wastepaper basket. The string dropped outside, at the feet of Gradus who picked it up and added it to the *scripta*.

"Please, go," said poor Bretwit. "I have a pain in my groin that is driving me mad. I have not slept for three nights. You journalists are an obstinate bunch but I am obstinate too. You will never learn from me anything about my king. Good-bye."

He waited on the landing for his visitor's steps to go down and reach the front door. It was opened and closed, and presently the automatic light on the stairs went out with the sound of a kick.

Line 287: humming as you pack

The card (his twenty-fourth) with this passage (lines 287-299) is marked July 7th, and under that date in my little agenda I find this scribble: Dr. AHLERT, 3.30 P.M. Feeling a bit nervous, as most people do at the prospect of seeing a doctor, I thought I would buy on my way to him something soothing to prevent an accelerated pulse from misleading credulous science. I found the drops I wanted, took the aromatic draught in the pharmacy, and was coming out when I noticed the Shades leaving a shop next door. She was carrying a new traveling grip. The dreadful thought that they might be going away on a summer vacation neutralized the medicine I had just swallowed. One gets so accustomed to another life's running alongside one's own that a sudden turn-off on the part of the parallel satellite causes in one a feeling of stupefaction, emptiness, and injustice. And what is more he had not yet finished "my" poem!

"Planning to travel?" I asked, smiling and pointing at the bag.

Sybil raised it by the ears like a rabbit and considered it with my eyes.

"Yes, at the end of the month," she said. "After John is through with his work."

(The poem!)

"And where, pray?" (turning to John).

Mr. Shade glanced at Mrs. Shade, and she replied for him in her usual brisk offhand fashion that they did not know for sure yet—it might be Wyoming or Utah or Montana, and perhaps they would rent somewhere a cabin at 6,000 or 7,000 feet.

"Among the lupines and the aspens," said the poet gravely. (Conjuring up the scene.)

I started to calculate aloud in meters the altitude that I thought much too high for John's heart but Sybil pulled him by the sleeve reminding him they had more shopping to do, and I was left with about 2,000 meters and a valerian-flavored burp.

But occasionally black-winged fate can display exquisite thoughtfulness! Ten minutes later Dr. A.—who treated Shade, too—was telling me in stolid detail that the Shades had rented a little ranch some friends of theirs, who were going elsewhere, had at Cedarn in Utana on the Idoming border. From the doctor's I flitted over to a travel agency, obtained maps and booklets, studied them, learned that on the mountainside above Cedarn there were two or three clusters of cabins, rushed my order to the Cedarn Post Office, and a few days later had rented for the month of August

what looked in the snapshots they sent me like a cross between a mujik's izba and Refuge Z, but it had a tiled bathroom and cost dearer than my Appalachian castle. Neither
the Shades nor I breathed a word about our summer address but I knew, and they did not, that it was the same. The
more I fumed at Sybil's evident intention to keep it concealed from me, the sweeter was the forevision of my sudden emergence in Tirolese garb from behind a boulder and
of John's sheepish but pleased grin. During the fortnight
that I had my demons fill my goetic mirror to overflow with
those pink and mauve cliffs and black junipers and winding
roads and sage brush changing to grass and lush blue flowers,
and death-pale aspens, and an endless sequence of green-
shorted Kinbotes meeting an anthology of poets and a
brocken of their wives, I must have made some awful mistake in my incantations, for the mountain slope is dry and
drear, and the Hurleys' tumble-down ranch, lifeless.

Line 293: She

Hazel Shade, the poet's daughter, born in 1934, died 1957
(see notes to lines 230 and 347).

Line 316: The Toothwort White haunted our woods in May

Frankly, I am not certain what this means. My dictionary
defines "toothwort" as "a kind of cress" and the noun "white"

as "any pure white breed of farm animal or a certain genus of lepidoptera." Little help is provided by the variant written in the margin:

In woods Virginia Whites occurred in May

Folklore characters, perhaps? Fairies? Or cabbage butterflies?

Line 319:   wood duck

A pretty conceit. The wood duck, a richly colored bird, emerald, amethyst, carnelian, with black and white markings, is incomparably more beautiful than the much-overrated swan, a serpentine goose with a dirty neck of yellowish plush and a frogman's black rubber flaps.

Incidentally, the popular nomenclature of American animals reflects the simple utilitarian minds of ignorant pioneers and has not yet acquired the patina of European faunal names.

Line 334:   Would never come for her

"Would he ever come for me?" I used to wonder waiting and waiting, in certain amber-and-rose crepuscules, for a ping-pong friend, or for old John Shade.

Line 347:   old barn

This barn, or rather shed, where "certain phenomena" occurred in October 1956 (a few months prior to Hazel Shade's death) had belonged to one Paul Hentzner, an eccentric farmer of German extraction, with old-fashioned hobbies such as taxidermy and herborizing. Through an odd trick of atavism, he was (according to Shade who liked to talk about him—the only time, incidentally, when my sweet old friend became a tiny bit of a bore!) a throwback to the "curious Germans" who three centuries ago had been the fathers of the first great naturalists. Although by academic standards an uneducated man, with no real knowledge of far things in space or time, he had about him a colorful and earthy something that pleased John Shade much better than the suburban refinements of the English Department. He who displayed such fastidious care in his choice of fellow ramblers liked to trudge with the gaunt solemn German, every other evening, up the wood path to Dulwich, and all around his acquaintance's fields. Delighting as he did in the right word, he esteemed Hentzner for knowing "the names of things"—though some of those names were no doubt local monstrosities, or Germanisms, or pure inventions on the old rascal's part.

Now he was walking with another companion. Limpidly do I remember one perfect evening when my friend sparkled with quips, and marrowskies, and anecdotes which I gallantly countered with tales of Zembla and harebreath escapes! As we were skirting Dulwich Forest, he interrupted me to indicate a natural grotto in the mossy rocks by the side of the path under the flowering dogwoods. This was the spot where the good farmer invariably stopped, and once, when they happened to be accompanied by his little boy, the latter, as he trotted beside them, pointed and remarked informatively: "Here Papa pisses." Another, less pointless, story awaited me at the top of the hill, where a square plot invaded with willow herb, milkweed and ironweed, and teeming with butterflies, contrasted sharply with the goldenrod all around it. After Hentzner's wife had left him (around 1950) taking with her their child, he sold his farmhouse (now replaced by a drive-in cinema) and went to live in town; but on summer nights he used to take a sleeping bag to the barn that stood at the far end of the land he still owned, and there one night he passed away.

That barn had stood on the weedy spot Shade was poking at with Aunt Maud's favorite cane. One Saturday evening a young student employee from the campus hotel and a local hoyden went into it for some purpose or other and were chatting or dozing there when they were frightened out of their wits by rattling sounds and flying lights causing them to flee in disorder. Nobody really cared what had routed them— whether it was an outraged ghost or a rejected swain. But the *Wordsmith Gazette* ("The oldest student newspaper in the USA") picked up the incident and started to worry the stuffing out of it like a mischievous pup. Several self-styled psychic researchers visited the place and the whole business was so blatantly turning into a rag, with the participation of the most notorious college pranksters, that Shade complained to the authorities with the result that the useless barn was demolished as constituting a fire hazard.

From Jane P. I obtained however a good deal of quite different, and much more pathetic information—which explained to me why my friend had thought fit to regale me with commonplace student mischief, but also made me regret that I prevented him from getting to the point he was confusely and self-consciously making (for as I have said in an earlier note, he never cared to refer to his dead child) by filling in a welcome pause with an extraordinary episode from the history of Onhava University. That episode took place in the year of grace 1876. But to return to Hazel Shade. She decided she wanted to investigate the "phenomena" herself for a paper ("on any subject") required in her psychology course by a cunning professor who was collecting data on "Autoneurynological Patterns among American university students." Her parents permitted her to make a nocturnal visit to the barn only under the condition that Jane P. —deemed a pillar of reliability—accompany her. Hardly had the girls settled down when an electric storm that was to last all night enveloped their refuge with such theatrical ululations and flashes as to make it impossible to attend to any indoor sounds or lights. Hazel did not give up, and a few days later asked Jane to come with her again, but Jane could not. She tells me she suggested that the White twins (nice fraternity boys accepted by the Shades) would come instead. But Hazel flatly refused this new arrangement, and after a row with her parents took her bull's-eye and notebook and set off alone. One can well imagine how the Shades dreaded a recrudescence of the poltergeist nuisance but the ever-sagacious Dr. Sutton affirmed—on what authority I cannot tell—that cases in which the same person was again involved in the same type of outbreaks after a lapse of six years were practically unknown.

Jane allowed me to copy out some of Hazel's notes from a typescript based on jottings made on the spot:

10:14 P. M. Investigation commenced.

10:23. Scrappy and scrabbly sounds.

10:25. A roundlet of pale light, the size of a small doily; flitted across the dark walls, the boarded windows, and the floor; changed its place; lingered here and there, dancing up and down; seemed to wait in teasing play for evadable pounce. Gone.

10:37. Back again.

The notes continue for several pages but for obvious reasons I must renounce to give them verbatim in this commentary. There were long pauses and "scratches and scrapings" again, and returns of the luminous circlet. She spoke to it. If asked something that it found deliciously silly ("Are you a will-o-the-wisp?") it would dash to and fro in ecstatic negation, and when it wanted to give a grave answer to a grave question ("Are you dead?") would slowly ascend with an air of gathering altitude for a weighty affirmative drop. For brief periods of time it responded to the alphabet she recited by staying put until the right letter was called whereupon it gave a small jump of approval. But these jumps would get more and more listless, and after a couple of words had been slowly spelled out, the roundlet went limp like a tired child and finally crawled into a chink; out of which it suddenly flew with extravagant brio and started to spin around the walls in its eagerness to resume the game. The jumble of broken words and meaningless syllables which she managed at last to collect came out in her dutiful notes as a short line of simple letter-groups. I transcribe:

pada ata lane pad not ogo old wart alan ther tale feur far rant lant tal told

In her *Remarks*, the recorder states she had to recite the alphabet, or at least begin to recite it (there is a merciful preponderance of a's) eighty times, but of these, seventeen yielded no results. Divisions based on such variable intervals cannot be but rather arbitrary; some of the balderdash may be recombined into other lexical units making no better sense (e.g., "war," "talant," "her," "arrant," etc.). The barn ghost seems to have expressed himself with the empasted difficulty of apoplexy or of a half-awakening from a half-dream slashed by a sword of light on the ceiling, a military disaster with cosmic consequences that cannot be phrased distinctly by the thick unwilling tongue. And in this case we too might wish to cut short a reader's or bedfellow's questions by sinking back into oblivion's bliss—had not a diabolical force urged us to seek a secret design in the abracadabra,

812 Some kind of link-and-bobolink, some kind
813 Of correlated pattern in the game.

I abhor such games; they make my temples throb with abominable pain—but I have braved it and pored endlessly, with a commentator's infinite patience and disgust, over the crippled syllables in Hazel's report to find the least allusion to the poor girl's fate. Not one hint did I find. Neither old Hentzner's specter, nor an ambushed scamp's toy flashlight, nor her own imaginative hysteria, express anything here that might be construed, however remotely, as containing a warning, or having some bearing on the circumstances of her soon-coming death.

Hazel's report might have been longer if—as she told Jane—a renewal of the "scrabbling" had not suddenly jarred

upon her tired nerves. The roundlet of light that until now
had been keeping its distance made a pugnacious dash at her
feet so that she nearly fell off the wooden block serving her
as a seat. She became overwhelmingly conscious that she was
alone in the company of an inexplicable and perhaps very
evil being, and with a shudder that all but dislocated her
shoulder blades she hastened to regain the heavenly shelter of
the starry night. A familiar footpath with soothing gestures
and other small tokens of consolation (lone cricket, lone
streetlight) led her home. She stopped and let forth a howl
of terror: a system of dark and pale patches coagulating into
a phantastic figure had risen from the garden bench which
the porch light just reached. I have no idea what the average
temperature of an October night in New Wye may be but
one is surprised that a father's anxiety should be great
enough in the present case to warrant conducting a vigil in
the open air in pajamas and the nondescript "bathrobe"
which my birthday present was to replace (see note to line
181).

There are always "three nights" in fairy tales, and in this
sad fairy tale there was a third one too. This time she wanted
her parents to witness the "talking light" with her. The
minutes of that third session in the barn have not been preserved but I offer the reader the following scene which I
feel cannot be too far removed from the truth:

THE HAUNTED BARN

Pitch-darkness. Father, Mother *and* Daughter *are heard
breathing gently in different corners. Three minutes pass.*

FATHER (*to Mother*)
Are you comfortable there?

MOTHER

Uh-huh. These potato sacks make a perfect——

DAUGHTER (*with steam-engine force*)

Sh-sh-sh!
*Fifteen minutes pass in silence. The eye begins to make out
here and there in the darkness bluish slits of night and one
star.*

MOTHER

That was Dad's tummy, I think——not a spook.

DAUGHTER (*mouthing it*)

Very funny!
*Another fifteen minutes elapse. Father, deep in workshop
thoughts, heaves a neutral sigh.*

DAUGHTER

Must we sigh all the time?
Fifteen minutes elapse.

MOTHER

If I start snoring let Spook pinch me.

DAUGHTER (*overemphasizing self-control*)

Mother! Please! Please, Mother!
*Father clears his throat but decides not to say anything.
Twelve more minutes elapse.*

MOTHER

Does anyone realize that there are still quite a few of those
creampuffs in the refrigerator?
That does it.

DAUGHTER (*exploding*)

Why must you *spoil* everything? Why must you *always* spoil everything? Why can't you leave people *alone?* Don't touch me!

FATHER

Now look, Hazel, Mother won't say another word, and we'll go on with this—but we've been sitting an hour here and it's getting late.

Two minutes pass. Life is hopeless, afterlife heartless. Hazel is heard quietly weeping in the dark. John Shade lights a lantern. Sybil lights a cigarette. Meeting adjourned.

The light never came back but it gleams again in a short poem "The Nature of Electricity," which John Shade had sent to the New York magazine *The Beau and the Butterfly,* some time in 1958, but which appeared only after his death:

> The dead, the gentle dead—who knows?—
> In tungsten filaments abide,
> And on my bedside table glows
> Another man's departed bride.
>
> And maybe Shakespeare floods a whole
> Town with innumerable lights,
> And Shelley's incandescent soul
> Lures the pale moths of starless nights.
>
> Streetlamps are numbered, and maybe
> Number nine-hundred-ninety-nine
> (So brightly beaming through a tree
> So green) is an old friend of mine.

> And when above the livid plain
> Forked lightning plays, therein may dwell
> The torments of a Tamerlane,
> The roar of tyrants torn in hell.

Science tells us, by the way, that the Earth would not merely fall apart, but vanish like a ghost, if Electricity were suddenly removed from the world.

Lines 347-348: She twisted words

One of the examples her father gives is odd. I am quite sure it was I who one day, when we were discussing "mirror words," observed (and I recall the poet's expression of stupefaction) that "spider" in reverse is "redips," and "T. S. Eliot," "toilest." But then it is also true that Hazel Shade resembled me in certain respects.

Lines 367-370: then—pen, again—explain

In speech John Shade, as a good American, rhymed "again" with "pen" and not with "explain." The adjacent position of these rhymes is curious.

Line 376: poem

I believe I can guess (in my bookless mountain cave) what poem is meant; but without looking it up I would not wish to name its author. Anyway, I deplore my friend's vicious thrusts at the most distinguished poets of his day.

Lines 376-377: was said in English Litt to be

This is replaced in the draft by the more significant—and more tuneful—variant:

the Head of our Department deemed

Although it may be taken to refer to the man (whoever he was) who occupied this post at the time Hazel Shade was a student, the reader cannot be blamed for applying it to Paul H., Jr., the fine administrator and inept scholar who since 1957 headed the English Department of Wordsmith College. We met now and then (see Forward and note to line 894) but not often. The Head of the Department to which I belonged was Prof. Nattochdag—"Netochka" as we called the dear man. Certainly the migraines that have lately tormented me to such a degree that I once had to leave in the midst of a concert at which I happened to be sitting beside Paul H., Jr., should not have been a stranger's business. They apparently were, very much so. He kept his eye on me, and immediately upon John Shade's demise circulated a mimeographed letter that began:

Several members of the Department of English are painfully concerned over the fate of a manuscript poem, or parts of a manuscript poem, left by the late John Shade. The manuscript fell into the hands of a person who not only is unqualified for the job of editing it, belonging as he does to another department, but is known to have a deranged mind. One wonders whether some legal action, etc.

"Legal action," of course, might be taken by somebody else too. But no matter; one's just anger is mitigated by the satisfaction of foreknowing that the *engagé* gentleman will be less worried about the fate of my friend's poem after reading the passage commented here. Southey liked a roasted rat for supper—which is especially comic in view of the rats that devoured his Bishop.

Line 384: book on Pope

The title of this work which can be found in any college library is *Supremely Blest,* a phrase borrowed from a Popian line, which I remember but cannot quote exactly. The book is concerned mainly with Pope's technique but also contains pithy observations on "the stylized morals of his age."

Lines 385-386: Jane Dean, Pete Dean

The transparent pseudonyms of two innocent people. I visited Jane Provost when passing through Chicago in August. I found her still unmarried. She showed me some amusing photos of her cousin Peter and his friends. She told me—and I have no reason to disbelieve her words—that Peter Provost (whom I desired very very much to meet, but he was, alas, selling automobiles in Detroit) might have exaggerated a wee bit, but certainly did not fib, when explaining that he had to keep a promise made to one of his dearest fraternity friends, a glorious young athlete whose "garland" will not, one hopes, be "briefer than a girl's." Such obligations are not to be treated lightly or disdainfully. Jane said she had tried to talk to the Shades after the tragedy, and later had written Sybil a long letter that was never acknowledged. I said, displaying a bit of the slang I had recently started to master: "You are telling me!"

Lines 403-404: it's eight fifteen (And here time forked)

From here to line 474 two themes alternate in a synchronous arrangement: television in the Shades' parlor and the replay, as it were, of Hazel's (already adumbrated) actions from the moment Peter met his blind date (406-407) and apologized for having to leave in a hurry (426-428) to Hazel's ride in the bus (445-447 and 457-459), ending with the watchman's finding her body (475-477). I have italicized the Hazel theme.

The whole thing strikes me as too labored and long, especially since the synchronization device has been already worked to death by Flaubert and Joyce. Otherwise the pattern is exquisite.

Line 408: A male hand

On July 10, the day John Shade wrote this, and perhaps
at the very minute he started to use his thirty-third index
card for lines 406-416, Gradus was driving in a hired car
from Geneva to Lex, where Odon was known to be resting,
after completing his motion picture, at the villa of an old
American friend, Joseph S. Lavender (the name hails from
the laundry, not from the laund). Our brilliant schemer had
been told that Joe Lavender collected photographs of the
artistic type called in French *ombrioles*. He had *not* been
told what exactly these were and dismissed them mentally as
"lampshades with landscapes." His cretinous plan was to
present himself as the agent of a Strasbourg art dealer
and then, over drinks with Lavender and his house guest,
endeavor to pick up clues to the King's whereabouts. He
did not reckon with the fact that Donald Odon with his
absolute sense of such things would have immediately deduced from the way Gradus displayed his empty palm before shaking hands or made a slight bow after every sip, and
other tricks of demeanor (which Gradus himself did not
notice in people but had acquired from them) that
wherever he had been born he had certainly lived for a considerable time in a low-class Zemblan environment and was
therefore a spy or worse. Gradus was also unaware that the
ombrioles Lavender collected (and I am sure Joe will not
resent this indiscretion) combined exquisite beauty with
highly indecent subject matter—nudities blending with fig
trees, oversize ardors, softly shaded hindercheeks, and also
a dapple of female charms.

From his Geneva hotel Gradus had tried to get Lavender
on the telephone but was told he could not be reached be-

fore noon. By noon Gradus was already under way and telephoned again, this time from Montreux. Lavender had been given the message and would Mr. Degré drop in around tea time. He luncheoned in a lakeside café, went for a stroll, asked the price of a small crystal giraffe in a souvenir shop, bought a newspaper, read it on a bench, and presently drove on. In the vicinity of Lex he lost his way among steep tortuous lanes. Upon stopping above a vineyard, at the rough entrance of an unfinished house, he was shown by the three index fingers of three masons the red roof of Lavender's villa high up in the ascending greenery on the opposite side of the road. He decided to leave the car and climb the stone steps of what looked like an easy short cut. While he was trudging up the walled walk with his eye on the rabbit foot of a poplar which now hid the red roof at the top of the climb, now disclosed it, the sun found a weak spot among the rain clouds and next moment a ragged blue hole in them grew a radiant rim. He felt the burden and the odor of his new brown suit bought in a Copenhagen store and already wrinkled. Puffing, consulting his wrist watch, and fanning himself with his trilby, also new, he reached at last the transverse continuation of the looping road he had left below. He crossed it, walked through a wicket and up a curving gravel path, and found himself in front of Lavender's villa. Its name, Libitina, was displayed in cursive script above one of the barred north windows, with its letters made of black wire and the dot over each of the three i's cleverly mimicked by the tarred head of a chalk-coated nail driven into the white façade. This device, and the north-facing window grates, Gradus had observed in Swiss villas before, but immunity to classical allusion deprived him of the pleasure he might have derived

from the tribute that Lavender's macabre joviality had paid
the Roman goddess of corpses and tombs. Another matter
engaged his attention: from a corner casement came the
sounds of a piano, a tumult of vigorous music which for some
odd reason, as he was to tell me later, suggested to him a
possibility he had not considered and caused his hand to fly
to his hip pocket as he prepared to meet not Lavender and
not Odon but that gifted hymnist, Charles the Beloved. The
music stopped as Gradus, confused by the whimsical shape
of the house, hesitated before a glassed-in porch. An elderly
footman in green appeared from a green side door and led
him to another entrance. With a show of carelessness not
improved by laborious repetition, Gradus asked him, first in
mediocre French, then in worse English, and finally in fair
German, if there were many guests staying in the house; but
the man only smiled and bowed him into the music room.
The musician had vanished. A harplike din still came from
the grand piano upon which a pair of beach sandals stood
as on the brink of a lily pond. From a window seat a gaunt
jet-glittering lady stiffly arose and introduced herself as the
governess of Mr. Lavender's nephew. Gradus mentioned his
eagerness to see Lavender's sensational collection: this aptly
defined its pictures of love-making in orchards, but the governess (whom the King had always called to her pleased
face Mademoiselle Belle instead of Mademoiselle Baud)
hastened to confess her total ignorance of her employer's
hobbies and treasures and suggested the visitor's taking a
look at the garden: "Gordon will show you his favorite
flowers" she said, and called into the next room "Gordon!"
Rather reluctantly there came out a slender but strong-
looking lad of fourteen or fifteen dyed a nectarine hue by
the sun. He had nothing on save a leopard-spotted loincloth.

His closely cropped hair was a tint lighter than his skin. His lovely bestial face wore an expression both sullen and sly. Our preoccupied plotter did not register any of these details and merely experienced a general impression of indecency. "Gordon is a musical prodigy," said Miss Baud, and the boy winced. "Gordon, will you show the garden to this gentleman?" The boy acquiesced, adding he would take a dip if nobody minded. He put on his sandals and led the way out. Through light and shade walked the strange pair: the graceful boy wreathed about the loins with ivy and the seedy killer in his cheap brown suit with a folded newspaper sticking out of his left-hand coat pocket.

"That's the Grotto," said Gordon. "I once spent the night here with a friend." Gradus let his indifferent glance enter the mossy recess where one could glimpse a collapsible mattress with a dark stain on its orange nylon. The boy applied avid lips to a pipe of spring water and wiped his wet hands on his black bathing trunks. Gradus consulted his watch. They strolled on. "You have not seen anything yet," said Gordon.

Although the house possessed at least half-a-dozen water closets, Mr. Lavender in fond memory of his grandfather's Delaware farm, had installed a rustic privy under the tallest poplar of his splendid garden, and for chosen guests, whose sense of humor could stand it, he would unhook from the comfortable neighborhood of the billiard room fireplace a heart-shaped, prettily embroidered bolster to take with them to the throne.

The door was open and across its inner side a boy's hand had scrawled in charcoal: *The King was here.*

"That's a fine visiting card," remarked Gradus with a forced laugh. "By the way, where is he now, that king?"

"Who knows," said the boy striking his flanks clothed in white tennis shorts, "that was last year. I guess he was heading for the Côte d'Azur, but I am not sure."

Dear Gordon lied, which was nice of him. He knew perfectly well that his big friend was no longer in Europe; but dear Gordon should not have brought up the Riviera matter which happened to be true and the mention of which caused Gradus, who knew that Queen Disa had a palazzo there, to mentally slap his brow.

They had now reached the swimming pool. Gradus, in deep thought, sank down on a canvas stool. He should wire headquarters at once. No need to prolong this visit. On the other hand, a sudden departure might look suspicious. The stool creaked under him and he looked around for another seat. The young woodwose had now closed his eyes and was stretched out supine on the pool's marble margin; his Tarzan brief had been cast aside on the turf. Gradus spat in disgust and walked back towards the house. Simultaneously the elderly footman came running down the steps of the terrace to tell him in three languages that he was wanted on the telephone. Mr. Lavender could not make it after all but would like to talk to Mr. Degré. After an exchange of civilities there was a pause and Lavender asked: "Sure you aren't a mucking snooper from that French rag?" "A what?" said Gradus, pronouncing the last word as "vot." "A mucking snooping son of a bitch?" Gradus hung up.

He retrieved his car and drove up to a higher level on the hillside. From the same road bay, on a misty and luminous September day, with the diagonal of the first silver filament crossing the space between two balusters, the King had surveyed the twinkling ripples of Lake Geneva and had noted their antiphonal response, the flashing of tinfoil scares in the hillside vineyards. Gradus as he stood there, and moodily looked down at the red tiles of Lavender's villa snuggling among its protective trees, could make out, with some help from his betters, a part of the lawn and a segment of the pool, and even distinguish a pair of sandals on its marble rim—all that remained of Narcissus. One assumes he wondered if he should not hang around for a bit to make sure he had not been bamboozled. From far below mounted the clink and tinkle of distant masonry work, and a sudden train passed between gardens, and a heraldic butterfly *volant en arrière,* sable, a bend gules, traversed the stone parapet, and John Shade took a fresh card.

Line 413:   a nymph came pirouetting

In the draft there is the lighter and more musical:

⁴¹³ A nymphet pirouetted

Lines 417-421:   I went upstairs, etc.

The draft yields an interesting variant:

⁴¹⁷ I fled upstairs at the first quawk of jazz
And read a galley proof: "Such verses as
'See the blind beggar dance, the cripple sing,

> The sot a hero, lunatic a king'
> Smack of their heartless age." Then came your call

This is, of course, from Pope's *Essay on Man*. One knows not what to wonder at more: Pope's not finding a monosyllable to replace "hero" (for example, "man") so as to accommodate the definite article before the next word, or Shade's replacing an admirable passage by the much flabbier final text. Or was he afraid of offending an authentic king? In pondering the near past I have never been able to ascertain retrospectively if he really had "guessed my secret," as he once observed (see note to line 991).

Line 426: Just behind (one oozy footstep) Frost

The reference is, of course, to Robert Frost (b. 1874). The line displays one of those combinations of pun and metaphor at which our poet excels. In the temperature charts of poetry high is low, and low high, so that the degree at which perfect crystallization occurs is above that of tepid facility. This is what our modest poet says, in effect, respecting the atmosphere of his own fame.

Frost is the author of one of the greatest short poems in the English language, a poem that every American boy knows by heart, about the wintry woods, and the dreary dusk, and the little horsebells of gentle remonstration in the dull darkening air, and that prodigious and poignant end —two closing lines identical in every syllable, but one personal and physical, and the other metaphysical and universal. I dare not quote from memory lest I displace one small precious word.

With all his excellent gifts, John Shade could never make *his* snowflakes settle that way.

Line 431: March night . . . headlights from afar approached

Note how delicately at this point the television theme happens to merge with the girl's theme (see line 440, *more* headlights in the fog . . .).

Lines 433-434: To the . . . sea Which we had visited in thirty-three

In 1933, Prince Charles was eighteen and Disa, Duchess of Payn, five. The allusion is to Nice (see also line 240) where the Shades spent the first part of that year; but here again, as in regard to so many fascinating facets of my friend's past life, I am not in the possession of particulars (who is to blame, dear S.S?) and not in the position to say whether or not, in the course of possible excursions along the coast, they ever reached Cap Turc and glimpsed from an oleander-lined lane, usually open to tourists, the Italianate villa built by Queen Disa's grandfather in 1908, and called then *Villa Paradiso,* or in Zemblan *Villa Paradisa,* later to forego the first half of its name in honor of his favorite granddaughter. There she spent the first fifteen summers of her life; thither did she return in 1953, "for reasons of health" (as impressed on the nation) but really, a banished queen; and there she still dwells.

When the Zemblan Revolution broke out (May 1, 1958), she wrote the King a wild letter in governess English, urging him to come and stay with her until the situation cleared up. The letter was intercepted by the Onhava police, translated into crude Zemblan by a Hindu member of the Extremist party, and then read aloud to the royal captive in a would-be ironic voice by the preposterous commandant of the palace. There happened to be in that letter one—only one, thank God—sentimental sentence: "I want you to know that no matter how much you hurt me, you cannot hurt my love," and this sentence (if we re-English it from the Zemblan) came out as: "I desire you and love when you flog me." He interrupted the commandant, calling him a buffoon and a rogue, and insulting everybody around so dreadfully that the Extremists had to decide fast whether to shoot him at once or let him have the original of the letter.

Eventually he managed to inform her that he was confined to the palace. Valiant Disa hurriedly left the Riviera and made a romantic but fortunately ineffectual attempt to return to Zembla. Had she been permitted to land, she would have been forthwith incarcerated, which would have reacted on the King's flight, doubling the difficulties of escape. A message from the Karlists containing these simple considerations checked her progress in Stockholm, and she flew back to her perch in a mood of frustration and fury (mainly, I think, because the message had been conveyed to her by a cousin of hers, good old Curdy Buff, whom she loathed). Several weeks passed and she was soon in a state of even worse agitation owing to rumors that her husband might be condemned to death. She left Cap Turc again. She had traveled to Brussels and chartered a plane to fly north, when another message, this time from Odon, came, saying that the King and he were out of Zembla, and that she should quietly regain Villa Disa and await there further news. In the autumn of the same year she was informed by Lavender that a man respresenting her husband would be coming to discuss with her certain business matters concerning property she and her husband jointly owned abroad. She was in the act of writing on the terrace under the jacaranda a disconsolate letter to Lavender when the tall, sheared and bearded visitor with the bouquet of flowers-of-the-gods who had been watching her from afar advanced through the garlands of shade. She looked up—and of course no dark spectacles and no make-up could for a moment fool her.

Since her final departure from Zembla he had visited her twice, the last time two years before, and during that lapse of time her pale-skin, dark-hair beauty had acquired a new, mature and melancholy glow. In Zembla, where most females are freckled blondes, we have the saying: *belwif ivurkumpf wid snew ebanumf*, "A beautiful woman should be like a compass rose of ivory with four parts of ebony." And this was the trim scheme nature had followed in Disa's case. There was something else, something I was to realize only when I read *Pale Fire*, or rather reread it after the first bitter hot mist of disappointment had cleared before my eyes. I am thinking of lines 261-267 in which Shade describes his wife. At the moment of his painting that poetical portrait, the sitter was twice the age of Queen Disa. I do not wish to be vulgar in dealing with these delicate matters but the fact remains that sixty-year-old Shade is lending here a well-conserved coeval the ethereal and eternal aspect she retains, or should retain, in his kind noble heart. Now the curious thing about it is that Disa at thirty, when last seen in September 1958, bore a singular resemblance not, of course, to Mrs. Shade as she was when I met her, but to the idealized and stylized picture painted by the poet in those lines of *Pale Fire*. Actually it was idealized and stylized only in regard to the older woman; in regard to Queen Disa, as she was that afternoon on that blue terrace, it represented a plain unretouched likeness. I trust the reader appreciates the strangeness of this, because if he does not, there is no sense in writing poems, or notes to poems, or anything at all.

She seemed also calmer than before; her self-control had improved. During the previous meetings, and throughout their marital life in Zembla, there had been, on her part, dreadful outbursts of temper. When in the first years of marriage he had wished to cope with those blazes and blasts, trying to make her take a rational view of her misfortune, he had found them very annoying; but gradually he learned to take advantage of them and welcomed them as giving him the opportunity of getting rid of her presence for lengthening periods of time by not calling her back after a sequence of doors had slammed ever more distantly, or by leaving the palace himself for some rural hideout.

In the beginning of their calamitous marriage he had strenuously tried to possess her but to no avail. He informed her he had never made love before (which was perfectly true insofar as the implied object could only mean one thing to her), upon which he was forced to endure the ridicule of having her dutiful purity involuntarily enact the ways of a courtesan with a client too young or too old; he said something to that effect (mainly to relieve the ordeal), and she made an atrocious scene. He farced himself with aphrodisiacs, but the anterior characters of her unfortunate sex kept fatally putting him off. One night when he tried tiger tea, and hopes rose high, he made the mistake of begging her to comply with an expedient which she made the mistake of denouncing as unnatural and disgusting. Finally he told her that an old riding accident was incapacitating him but that a cruise with his pals and a lot of sea bathing would be sure to restore his strength.

She had recently lost both parents and had no real friend to turn to for explanation and advice when the inevitable rumors reached her; these she was too proud to discuss with her ladies in waiting but she read books, found out all about our manly Zemblan customs, and concealed her naïve distress under a great show of sarcastic sophistication. He congratulated her on her attitude, solemnly swearing that he had given up, or at least would give up, the practices of his youth; but everywhere along the road powerful temptations stood at attention. He succumbed to them from time to time, then every other day, then several times daily—especially during the robust regime of Harfar Baron of Shalksbore, a phenomenally endowed young brute (whose family name, "knave's farm," is the most probable derivation of "Shakespeare"). Curdy Buff—as Harfar was nicknamed by his admirers—had a huge escort of acrobats and bareback riders, and the whole affair rather got out of hand so that Disa, upon unexpectedly returning from a trip to Sweden, found the Palace transformed into a circus. He again promised, again fell, and despite the utmost discretion was again caught. At last she removed to the Riviera leaving him to amuse himself with a band of Eton-collared, sweet-voiced minions imported from England.

What had the sentiments he entertained in regard to Disa ever amounted to? Friendly indifference and bleak respect. Not even in the first bloom of their marriage had he felt any tenderness or any excitement. Of pity, of heartache, there could be no question. He was, had always been, casual and heartless. But the heart of his dreaming self, both before and after the rupture, made extraordinary amends.

He dreamed of her more often, and with incomparably more poignancy, than his surface-life feelings for her warranted; these dreams occurred when he least thought of her, and worries in no way connected with her assumed her image in the subliminal world as a battle or a reform becomes a bird of wonder in a tale for children. These heart-rending dreams transformed the drab prose of his feelings for her into strong and strange poetry, subsiding undulations of which would flash and disturb him throughout the day, bringing back the pang and the richness—and then only the pang, and then only its glancing reflection—but not affecting at all his attitude towards the real Disa.

Her image, as she entered and re-entered his sleep, rising apprehensively from a distant sofa or going in search of the messenger who, they said, had just passed through the draperies, took into account changes of fashion; but the Disa wearing the dress he had seen on her the summer of the Glass Works explosion, or last Sunday, or in any other antechamber of time, forever remained exactly as she looked on the day he had first told her he did not love her. That happened during a hopeless trip to Italy, in a lakeside hotel garden—roses, black araucarias, rusty, greenish hydrangeas—one cloudless evening with the mountains of the far shore swimming in a sunset haze and the lake all peach syrup regularly rippled with pale blue, and the captions of a newspaper spread flat on the foul bottom near the stone bank perfectly readable through the shallow diaphanous filth, and because, upon hearing him out, she sank down on the lawn in an impossible posture, examining a grass culm and frowning, he had taken his words back at once; but the shock had fatally starred the mirror, and thenceforth in his dreams her image was infected with the memory of that confession as with some disease or the secret aftereffects of a surgical operation too intimate to be mentioned.

The gist, rather than the actual plot of the dream, was a constant refutation of his not loving her. His dream-love for her exceeded in emotional tone, in spiritual passion and depth, anything he had experienced in his surface existence. This love was like an endless wringing of hands, like a blundering of the soul through an infinite maze of hopelessness and remorse. They were, in a sense, amorous dreams, for they were permeated with tenderness, with a longing to sink his head onto her lap and sob away the monstrous past. They brimmed with the awful awareness of her being so young and so helpless. They were purer than his life. What carnal aura there was in them came not from her but from those with whom he betrayed her—prickly-chinned Phrynia, pretty Timandra with that boom under her apron—and even so the sexual scum remained some-where far above the sunken treasure and was quite unim-portant. He would see her being accosted by a misty relative so distant as to be practically featureless. She would quickly hide what she held and extend her arched hand to be kissed. He knew she had just come across a telltale object—a

riding boot in his bed—establishing beyond any doubt his
unfaithfulness. Sweat beaded her pale, naked forehead—
but she had to listen to the prattle of a chance visitor or
direct the movements of a workman with a ladder who was
nodding his head and looking up as he carried it in his arms
to the broken window. One might bear—a strong merciless
dreamer might bear—the knowledge of her grief and pride
but none could bear the sight of her automatic smile as she
turned from the agony of the disclosure to the polite triviali-
ties required of her. She would be canceling an illumination, or discussing hospital cots with the head nurse, or
merely ordering breakfast for two in the sea cave—and
through the everyday plainness of the talk, through the play
of the charming gestures with which she always accompanied
certain readymade phrases, he, the groaning dreamer, perceived the disarray of her soul and was aware that an odious,
undeserved, humiliating disaster had befallen her, and that
only obligations of etiquette and her staunch kindness to a
guiltless third party gave her the force to smile. As one
watched the light on her face, one foresaw it would fade in a
moment, to be replaced—as soon as the visitor left—by that
impossible little frown the dreamer could never forget. He
would help her again to her feet on the same lakeside lawn,
with parts of the lake fitting themselves into the spaces between the rising balusters, and presently he and she would be
walking side by side along an anonymous alley, and he would
feel she was looking at him out of the corner of a faint smile
but when he forced himself to confront that questioning glim-
mer, she was no longer there. Everything had changed, everybody was happy. And he absolutely had to find her at once to
tell her that he adored her, but the large audience before him
separated him from the door, and the notes reaching him

through a succession of hands said that she was not available; that she was inaugurating a fire; that she had married an American businessman; that she had become a character in a novel; that she was dead.

No such qualms disturbed him as he sat now on the terrace of her villa and recounted his lucky escape from the Palace. She enjoyed his description of the underground link with the theater and tried to visualize the jolly scramble across the mountains; but the part concerning Garh displeased her as if, paradoxically, she would have preferred him to have gone through a bit of wholesome houghmagandy with the wench. She told him sharply to skip such interludes, and he made her a droll little bow. But when he began to discuss the political situation (two Soviet generals had just been attached to the Extremist government as Foreign Advisers), a familiar vacant expression appeared in her eyes. Now that he was safely out of the country, the entire blue bulk of Zembla, from Embla Point to Emblem Bay, could sink in the sea for all she cared. That he had lost weight was of more concern to her than that he had lost a kingdom. Perfunctorily she inquired about the crown jewels; he revealed to her their unusual hiding place, and she melted in girlish mirth as she had not done for years and years. "I do have some business matters to discuss," he said. "And there are papers you have to sign." Up in the trellis a telephone climbed with the roses. One of her former ladies in waiting, the languid and elegant Fleur de Fyler (now fortyish and faded), still wearing pearls in her raven hair and the traditional white mantilla, brought certain documents from Disa's boudoir. Upon hearing the King's mellow voice behind the laurels, Fleur recognized it

before she could be misled by his excellent disguise. Two
footmen, handsome young strangers of a marked Latin type,
appeared with the tea and caught Fleur in mid-curtsey. A
sudden breeze groped among the glycines. Defiler of flowers.
He asked Fleur as she turned to go with the *Disa* orchids if
she still played the viola. She shook her head several times
not wishing to speak without addressing him and not daring
to do so while the servants might be within earshot.

They were alone again. Disa quickly found the papers he
needed. Having finished with that, they talked for a while
about nice trivial things, such as the motion picture, based
on a Zemblan legend, that Odon hoped to make in Paris or
Rome. How would he represent, they wondered, the
narstran, a hellish hall where the souls of murderers were
tortured under a constant drizzle of drake venom coming
down from the foggy vault? By and large the interview was
proceeding in a most satisfactory manner—though her
fingers trembled a little when her hand touched the elbow
rest of his chair. Careful now.

"What are your plans?" she inquired. "Why can't you stay
here as long as you want? Please do. I'll be going to Rome
soon, you'll have the whole house to yourself. Imagine, you
can bed here as many as forty guests, forty Arabian thieves."
(Influence of the huge terracotta vases in the garden.)

He answered he would be going to America some time
next month and had business in Paris tomorrow.

Why America? What would he do there?

Teach. Examine literary masterpieces with brilliant and
charming young people. A hobby he could now freely indulge.

"And, of course, I don't know," she mumbled looking

away, "I don't know but perhaps if you'd have nothing against it, I might visit New York—I mean, just for a week or two, and not this year but the next."

He complimented her on her silver-spangled jacket. She persevered: "Well?" "And your hairdo is most becoming." "Oh, what does it matter," she wailed, "what on earth does anything matter!" "I must be on my way," he whispered with a smile and got up. "Kiss me," she said, and was like a limp, shivering ragdoll in his arms for a moment.

He walked to the gate. At the turn of the path he glanced back and saw in the distance her white figure with the listless grace of ineffable grief bending over the garden table, and suddenly a fragile bridge was suspended between waking indifference and dream-love. But she moved, and he saw it was not she at all but only poor Fleur de Fyler collecting the documents left among the tea things. (See note to line 80.)

When in the course of an evening stroll in May or June, 1959, I offered Shade all this marvelous material, he looked at me quizzically and said: "That's all very well, Charles. But there are just two questions. How can you know that all this intimate stuff about your rather appalling king is true? And if true, how can one hope to print such personal things about people who, presumably, are still alive?"

"My dear John," I replied gently and urgently, "do not worry about trifles. Once transmuted by you into poetry, the stuff *will* be true, and the people *will* come alive. A poet's purified truth can cause no pain, no offense. True art is above false honor."

"Sure, sure," said Shade. "One can harness words like performing fleas and make them drive other fleas. Oh, sure."

"And moreover," I continued as we walked down the

road right into a vast sunset, "as soon as your poem is
ready, as soon as the glory of Zembla merges with the glory
of your verse, I intend to divulge to you an ultimate truth,
an extraordinary secret, that will put your mind completely
at rest."

Line 469: his gun

Gradus, as he drove back to Geneva, wondered when he
would be able to use it, that gun. The afternoon was un-
bearably hot. The lake had developed a scaling of silver and
a touch of reflected thunderhead. As many old glaziers, he
could deduce rather accurately water temperature from certain indices of brilliancy and motion, and now judged it to be
at least 23°. As soon as he got back to his hotel he made a
long-distance call to headquarters. It proved a terrible experience. Under the assumption that it would attract less attention than a BIC language, the conspirators conducted telephone conversations in English—broken English, to be exact, with one tense, no articles, and two pronunciations, both
wrong. Furthermore, by their following the crafty system
(invented in the chief BIC country) of using two different
sets of code words—headquarters, for instance, saying
"bureau" for "king," and Gradus saying "letter," they
enormously increased the difficulty of communication. Each
side, finally, had forgotten the meaning of certain phrases
pertaining to the other's vocabulary so that in result, their
tangled and expensive talk combined charades with an ob-
stacle race in the dark. Headquarters thought it understood

that letters from the King divulging his whereabouts could be obtained by breaking into Villa Disa and rifling the Queen's bureau; Gradus, who had said nothing of the sort, but had merely tried to convey the results of his Lex visit, was chagrined to learn that instead of looking for the King in Nice he was expected to wait for a consignment of canned salmon in Geneva. One thing, though, came out clearly: next time he should not telephone, but wire or write.

Line 470: Negro

We were talking one day about Prejudice. Earlier, at lunch in the Faculty Club, Prof. H.'s guest, a decrepit emeritus from Boston—whom his host described with deep respect as "a true Patrician, a real blue-blooded Brahmin" (the Brahmin's grandsire sold braces in Belfast)—had happened to say quite naturally and debonairly, in allusion to the origins of a not very engaging new man in the College Library, "one of the Chosen People, I understand" (enunciated with a small snort of comfortable relish); upon which Assistant Professor Misha Gordon, a red-haired musician, had roundly remarked that "of course, God might choose His people but man should choose his expressions."

As we strolled back, my friend and I, to our adjacent castles, under the sort of light April rain that in one of his lyrical poems he calls:

A rapid pencil sketch of Spring

Shade said that more than anything on earth he loathed Vulgarity and Brutality, and that one found these two ideally united in racial prejudice. He said that, as a man of letters, he could not help preferring "is a Jew" to "is Jewish" and "is a Negro" to "is colored"; but immediately added that this way of alluding to two kinds of bias in one breath was a good example of careless, or demagogic, lumping (much exploited by Left-Wingers) since it erased the distinction between two historical hells: diabolical persecution and the barbarous traditions of slavery. On the other hand (he admitted) the tears of all ill-treated human beings, throughout the hopelessness of all time, mathematically equaled each other; and perhaps (he thought) one did not err too much in tracing a family likeness (tensing of simian nostrils, sickening dulling of eyes) between the jasmine-belt lyncher and the mystical anti-Semite when under the influence of their pet obsessions. I said that a young Negro gardener (see note to line 998) whom I had recently hired —soon after the dismissal of an unforgettable roomer (see Foreword)—invariably used the word "colored." As a dealer in old and new words (observed Shade) he strongly objected to that epithet not only because it was artistically misleading, but also because its sense depended too much upon application and applier. Many competent Negroes (he agreed) considered it to be the only dignified word, emotionally neutral and ethically inoffensive; their endorsement obliged decent non-Negroes to follow their lead, and poets do not like to be led; but the genteel adore endorsements and now use "colored man" for "Negro" as they do "nude" for "naked" or "perspiration" for "sweat"; although of course (he conceded) there might be times when the poet welcomed the dimple of a marble haunch in "nude" or an appropriate beadiness in "perspiration." One also heard it used (he continued) by the prejudiced as a jocular euphemism in a darky anecdote when something funny is said or done by "the colored gentleman" (a sudden brother here of "the Hebrew gentleman" in Victorian novelettes).

I had not quite understood his *artistic* objection to "colored." He explained it thus: Figures in the first scientific works on flowers, birds, butterflies and so forth were hand-painted by diligent aquarellists. In defective or premature publications the figures on some plates remained blank. The juxtaposition of the phrases "a white" and "a colored man" always reminded my poet, so imperiously as to dispel their accepted sense, of those outlines one longed to fill with their lawful colors—the green and purple of an exotic plant, the solid blue of a plumage, the geranium bar of a scalloped wing. "And moreover [he said] we, whites, are not white at all, we are mauve at birth, then tea-rose, and later all kinds of repulsive colors."

Line 475: A watchman, Father Time

The reader should notice the nice response to line 312.

Line 490: Exe

Exe obviously stands for Exton, a factory town on the south shore of Omega Lake. It has a rather famous natural

history museum with many showcases containing birds collected and mounted by Samuel Shade.

Line 493:   She took her poor young life

The following note is not an apology of suicide—it is the
simple and sober description of a spiritual situation.

The more lucid and overwhelming one's belief in Providence, the greater the temptation to get it over with, this
business of life, but the greater too one's fear of the terrible
sin implicit in self-destruction. Let us first consider the
temptation. As more thoroughly discussed elsewhere in this
commentary (see note to line 550), a serious conception of
any form of afterlife inevitably and necessarily presupposes some degree of belief in Providence; and, conversely,
deep Christian faith presupposes some belief in some sort of
spiritual survival. The vision of that survival need not be a
rational one, i.e., need not present the precise features of
personal fancies or the general atmosphere of a subtropi-
cal Oriental park. In fact, a good Zemblan Christian is
taught that true faith is not there to supply pictures or maps,
but that it should quietly content itself with a warm haze of
pleasurable anticipation. To take a homely example: little
Christopher's family is about to migrate to a distant colony
where his father has been assigned to a lifetime post. Little
Christopher, a frail lad of nine or ten, relies completely (so
completely, in fact, as to blot out the very awareness of this
reliance) on his elders' arranging all the details of departure, passage and arrival. He cannot imagine, nor does he

try to imagine, the particular aspects of the new place awaiting him but he is dimly and comfortably convinced that it will be even better than his homestead, with the big oak, and the mountain, and his pony, and the park, and the stable, and Grimm, the old groom, who has a way of fondling him whenever nobody is around.

Something of this simple trust we too should have. With this divine mist of utter dependence permeating one's being, no wonder one is tempted, no wonder one weighs on one's palm with a dreamy smile the compact firearm in its case of suede leather hardly bigger than a castlegate key or a boy's seamed purse, no wonder one peers over the parapet into an inviting abyss.

I am choosing these images rather casually. There are purists who maintain that a gentleman should use a brace of pistols, one for each temple, or a bare botkin (note the correct spelling), and that ladies should either swallow a lethal dose or drown with clumsy Ophelia. Humbler humans have preferred sundry forms of suffocation, and minor poets have even tried such fancy releases as vein tapping in the quadruped tub of a drafty boardinghouse bathroom. All this is uncertain and messy. Of the not very many ways known of shedding one's body, falling, falling, falling is the supreme method, but you have to select your sill or ledge very carefully so as not to hurt yourself or others. Jumping from a high bridge is not recommended even if you cannot swim, for wind and water abound in weird contingencies, and tragedy ought not to culminate in a record dive or a policeman's promotion. If you rent a cell in the luminous waffle, room 1915 or 1959, in a tall business center hotel browing the star dust, and pull up the window, and gently —not fall, not jump—but roll out as you should for air comfort, there is always the chance of knocking clean through into your own hell a pacific noctambulator walking his dog; in this respect a back room might be safer, especially if giving on the roof of an old tenacious normal house far below where a cat may be trusted to flash out of the way. Another popular take-off is a mountaintop with a sheer drop of say 500 meters but you must find it, because you will be surprised how easy it is to miscalculate your deflection offset, and have some hidden projection, some fool of a crag, rush forth to catch you, causing you to bounce off it into the brush, thwarted, mangled and unnecessarily alive. The ideal drop is from an aircraft, your muscles relaxed, your pilot puzzled, your packed parachute shuffled off, cast off, shrugged off—farewell, *shootka* (little chute)! Down you go, but all the while you feel suspended and buoyed as you somersault in slow motion like a somnolent tumbler pigeon, and sprawl supine on the eiderdown of the air, or lazily turn to embrace your pillow, enjoying every last instant of soft, deep, death-padded life, with the earth's green seesaw now above, now below, and the voluptuous crucifixion, as you stretch yourself in the growing rush, in the nearing swish, and then your loved body's obliteration in the Lap of the Lord. If I were a poet I would certainly make an ode to the sweet urge to close one's eyes and surrender utterly unto the perfect safety of wooed death. Ecstatically one forefeels the vastness of the Divine Embrace enfolding one's liberated spirit, the warm bath of physical dissolution, the universal unknown engulfing the minuscule unknown that had been the only real part of one's temporary personality.

When the soul adores Him Who guides it through mortal life, when it distinguishes His sign at every turn of the trail, painted on the boulder and notched in the fir trunk, when every page in the book of one's personal fate bears His watermark, how can one doubt that He will also preserve us through all eternity?

So what can stop one from effecting the transition? What can help us to resist the intolerable temptation? What can prevent us from yielding to the burning desire for merging in God?

We who burrow in filth every day may be forgiven perhaps the one sin that ends all sins.

Line 501: L'if

The yew in French. It is curious that the Zemblan word for the weeping willow is also "*if*" (the yew is *tas*).

Line 502: The grand potato

An execrable pun, deliberately placed in this epigraphic position to stress lack of respect for Death. I remember from my schoolroom days Rabelais' *soi-disant* "last words" among other bright bits in some French manual: *Je m'en vais chercher le grand peut-être.*

Line 502:   IPH

Good taste and the law of libel prevent me from disclos-
ing the real name of the respectable institute of higher
philosophy at which our poet pokes a good deal of fanciful
fun in this canto. Its terminal initials, HP, provide its
students with the abbreviation Hi-Phi, and Shade neatly
parodies this in his IPH, or If, combinations. It is situated,
most picturesquely, in a southwestern state that must re-
main anonymous here.

I am also obliged to observe that I strongly disapprove of
the flippancy with which our poet treats, in this canto, certain aspects of spiritual hope which religion alone can fulfill
(see also note to 549).

Line 549:   While snubbing gods including the big G

Here indeed is the Gist of the matter. And this, I think,
not only the institute (see line 517) but our poet himself
missed. For a Christian, no Beyond is acceptable or imaginable without the participation of God in our eternal destiny,
and this in turn implies a condign punishment for every
sin, great and small. My little diary happens to contain a
few jottings referring to a conversation the poet and I had
on June 23 "on my terrace after a game of chess, a draw." I
transcribe them here only because they cast a fascinating
light on his attitude toward the subject.

I had mentioned—I do not recall in what connection—
certain differences between my Church and his. It should be

noted that our Zemblan brand of Protestantism is rather
closely related to the "higher" churches of the Anglican
Communion, but has some magnificent peculiarities of its
own. The Reformation with us had been headed by a composer of genius; our liturgy is penetrated with rich music;
our boy choirs are the sweetest in the world. Sybil Shade
came from a Catholic family but since early girlhood developed, as she told me herself, "a religion of her own"—
which is generally synonymous, at the best, with a half-
hearted attachment to some half-heathen sect or, at the
worst, with tepid atheism. She had weaned her husband not
only from the Episcopal Church of his fathers, but from all
forms of sacramental worship.

We happened to start speaking of the general present-day
nebulation of the notion of "sin," of its confusion with the
much more carnally colored idea of "crime," and I alluded
briefly to my childhood contacts with certain rituals of our
church. Confession with us is auricular and is conducted in a
richly ornamented recess, the confessionist holding a lighted
taper and standing with it beside the priest's high-backed
seat which is shaped almost exactly as the coronation chair
of a Scottish king. Little polite boy that I was, I always
feared to stain his purple-black sleeve with the scalding
tears of wax that kept dripping onto my knuckles, forming
there tight little crusts, and I was fascinated by the illumed
concavity of his ear resembling a seashell or a glossy orchid,
a convoluted receptacle that seemed much too large for the
disposal of my peccadilloes.

SHADE: All the seven deadly sins are peccadilloes but
without three of them, Pride, Lust and Sloth, poetry might
never have been born.

KINBOTE: Is it fair to base objections upon obsolete terminology?

SHADE: All religions are based upon obsolete terminology.

KINBOTE: What we term Original Sin can never grow obsolete.

SHADE: I know nothing about that. In fact when I was small I thought it meant Cain killing Abel. Personally, I am with the old snuff-takers: *L'homme est né bon.*

KINBOTE: Yet disobeying the Divine Will is a fundamental definition of Sin.

SHADE: I cannot disobey something which I do not know and the reality of which I have the right to deny.

KINBOTE: Tut-tut. Do you also deny that there are sins?

SHADE: I can name only two: murder, and the deliberate infliction of pain.

KINBOTE: Then a man spending his life in absolute solitude could not be a sinner?

SHADE: He could torture animals. He could poison the springs on his island. He could denounce an innocent man in a posthumous manifesto.

KINBOTE: And so the password is——?

SHADE: Pity.

KINBOTE: But who instilled it in us, John? Who is the Judge of life, and the Designer of death?

SHADE: Life is a great surprise. I do not see why death should not be an even greater one.

KINBOTE: Now I have caught you, John: once we deny a Higher Intelligence that plans and administrates our individual hereafters we are bound to accept the unspeakably dreadful notion of Chance reaching into eternity. Consider the situation. Throughout eternity our poor ghosts are exposed to nameless vicissitudes. There is no appeal, no advice, no support, no protection, nothing. Poor Kinbote's ghost, poor Shade's shade, may have blundered, may have taken the wrong turn somewhere—oh, from sheer absent-mindedness, or simply through ignorance of a trivial rule in the preposterous game of nature—if there be any rules.

SHADE: There are rules in chess problems: interdiction of dual solutions, for instance.

KINBOTE: I had in mind diabolical rules likely to be broken by the other party as soon as we come to understand them. That is why goetic magic does not always work. The demons in their prismatic malice betray the agreement between us and them, and we are again in the chaos of chance. Even if we temper Chance with Necessity and allow godless determinism, the mechanism of cause and effect, to provide our souls after death with the dubious solace of metastatistics, we still have to reckon with the individual mishap, the thousand and second highway accident of those scheduled for Independence Day in Hades. No-no, if we want to be serious about the hereafter let us not begin by degrading it to the level of a science-fiction yarn or a spiritualistic case history. The idea of one's soul plunging into limitless and chaotic afterlife with no Providence to direct her—

SHADE: There is always a psychopompos around the corner, isn't there?

KINBOTE: Not around *that* corner, John. With no Providence the soul must rely on the dust of its husk, on the experience gathered in the course of corporeal confinement, and cling childishly to small-town principles, local by-laws and a personality consisting mainly of the shadows of its own prison bars. Such an idea is not to be entertained one instant by the religious mind. How much more intelligent it is—even from a proud infidel's point of view!—to accept God's Presence—a faint phosphorescence at first, a pale light in the dimness of bodily life, and a dazzling radiance after it? I too, I too, my dear John, have been assailed in my time by religious doubts. The church helped me to fight them off. It also helped me not to ask too much, not to demand too clear an image of what is unimaginable. St. Augustine said—

SHADE: Why must one *always* quote St. Augustine to me?

KINBOTE: As St. Augustine said, "One can know what God is not; one cannot know what He is." I think I know what He is not: He is not despair, He is not terror, He is not the earth in one's rattling throat, not the black hum in one's ears fading to nothing in nothing. I know also that the world could not have occurred fortuitously and that somehow Mind is involved as a main factor in the making of the universe. In trying to find the right name for that Universal Mind, or First Cause, or the Absolute, or Nature, I submit that the Name of God has priority.

Line 550: debris

I wish to say something about an earlier note (to line 12). Conscience and scholarship have debated the question, and I now think that the two lines given in that note are distorted and tainted by wistful thinking. It is the *only* time in the course of the writing of these difficult comments, that I have tarried, in my distress and disappointment, on the brink of falsification. I must ask the reader to ignore those two lines (which, I am afraid, do not even scan properly). I could strike them out before publication but that would mean reworking the entire note, or at least a considerable part of it, and I have no time for such stupidities.

Lines 557-558: How to locate in blackness, with a gasp, Terra the Fair, an orbicle of jasp

The loveliest couplet in this canto.

Line 579: the other

Far from me be it to hint at the existence of some other woman in my friend's life. Serenely he played the part of exemplary husband assigned to him by his small-town admirers and was, besides, mortally afraid of his wife. More than once did I stop the gossipmongers who linked his name with that of one of his students (see Foreword). Of late, American novelists, most of whom are members of a United English Department that, with one thing and another, must be more soaked in literary talent, Freudian fancies, and ignoble heterosexual lust than all the rest of the world, have driven the topic to extinction; therefore I could not face the tedium of introducing that young lady here. Anyway, I hardly knew her. One evening I invited her to a little party with the Shades for the express purpose of refuting those rumors; and that reminds me I should say something about the curious rituals of invitation and counterinvitation in bleak New Wye.

Upon referring to my little diary, I see that during the five-month period of my intercourse with the Shades I was invited to their table exactly three times. Initiation took place on Saturday, March the 14th, when I dined at their house with the following people: Nattochdag (whom I saw every day in his office); Professor Gordon of the Music Department (who completely dominated the conversation); the Head of the Russian Department (a farcical pedant of whom the less said the better); and three or four interchangeable women (of whom one—Mrs. Gordon, I think) was enceinte, and another, a perfect stranger, steadily talked to me, or rather *into* me, from eight to eleven owing to an unfortunate afterdinner distribution of available seats. My next treat, a smaller but by no means cozier *souper* on Saturday, May 23, was attended by Milton Stone (a new librarian, with whom Shade discussed till midnight the classification of certain Wordsmithiana); good old Nattochdag (whom I continued to see every day); and an undeodorized Frenchwoman (who gave me a complete picture of language-teaching conditions at the University of California). The date of my third and last meal at the Shades is not entered in my little book but I know it was one morning in June when I brought over a beautiful plan I had drawn of the King's Palace in Onhava with all sorts of heraldic niceties, and a touch of gold paint that I had some trouble in ob-

taining, and was graciously urged to stay for an impromptu
lunch. I should add that, despite my protests, at all three
meals my vegetarian limitations of fare were not taken into
account, and I was exposed to animal matter in, or around,
some of the contaminated greens I might have deigned to
taste. I revanched myself rather neatly. Of a dozen or so in-
vitations that I extended, the Shades accepted just three.
Every one of these meals was built around some vegetable
that I subjected to as many exquisite metamorphoses as
Parmentier had his pet tuber undergo. Every time I had but
one additional guest to entertain Mrs. Shade (who, if you
please—thinning my voice to a feminine pitch—was allergic
to artichokes, avocado pears, African acorns—in fact
to everything beginning with an "a"). I find nothing more
conducive to the blunting of one's appetite than to have
none but elderly persons sitting around one at table, foul-
ing their napkins with the disintegration of their make-up,
and surreptitiously trying, behind noncommittal smiles, to
dislodge the red-hot torture point of a raspberry seed from
between false gum and dead gum. So I had young people,
students: the first time, the son of a padishah; the second
time, my gardener; and the third time, that girl in the black
leotard, with that long white face and eyelids painted a
ghoulish green; but she came very late, and the Shades left
very early—in fact, I doubt if the confrontation lasted
more than ten minutes, whereupon I had the task of entertaining the young lady with phonograph records far into
the night when at last she rang up somebody to accompany
her to a "diner" in Dulwich.

Line 584: The mother and the child

Es ist die Mutter mit ihrem Kind (see note to line 664).

Line 596: Points at the puddle in his basement room

We all know those dreams in which something Stygian soaks through and Lethe leaks in the dreary terms of defective plumbing. Following this line, there is a false start preserved in the draft—and I hope the reader will feel something of the chill that ran down my long and supple spine when I discovered this variant:

> Should the dead murderer try to embrace
> His outraged victim whom he now must face?
> Do objects have a soul? Or perish must
> Alike great temples and Tanagra dust?

The last syllable of "Tanagra" and the first three letters of "dust" form the name of the murderer whose *shargar* (puny ghost) the radiant spirit of our poet was soon to face. "Simple chance!" the pedestrian reader may cry. But let him try to see, as I have tried to see, how many such combinations are possible and plausible. "Lenin*grad* *us*ed to be Petrograd?" "A prig *rad* (obs. past tense of read) *us?*"

This variant is so prodigious that only scholarly discipline and a scrupulous regard for the truth prevented me from inserting it here, and deleting four lines elsewhere (for example, the weak lines 627-630) so as to preserve the length of the poem.

Shade composed these lines on Tuesday, July 14th. What was Gradus doing that day? Nothing. Combinational fate rests on its laurels. We saw him last on the late afternoon of July 10th when he returned from Lex to his hotel in Geneva, and there we left him.

For the next four days Gradus remained fretting in Geneva. The amusing paradox with these men of action is that they constantly have to endure long stretches of otiosity that they are unable to fill with anything, lacking as they do the resources of an adventurous mind. As many people of little culture, Gradus was a voracious reader of newspapers, pamphlets, chance leaflets and the multilingual literature that comes with nose drops and digestive tablets; but this summed up his concessions to intellectual curiosity, and since his eyesight was not too good, and the consumability of local news not unlimited, he had to rely a great deal on the torpor of sidewalk cafés and on the makeshift of sleep.

How much happier the wide-awake indolents, the monarchs among men, the rich monstrous brains deriving intense enjoyment and rapturous pangs from the balustrade of a terrace at nightfall, from the lights and the lake below, from the distant mountain shapes melting into the dark apricot of the afterglow, from the black conifers outlined against the pale ink of the zenith, and from the garnet and green flounces of the water along the silent, sad, forbidden shoreline. Oh my sweet Boscobel! And the tender and terrible memories, and the shame, and the glory, and the maddening intimations, and the star that no party member can ever reach.

On Wednesday morning, still without news, Gradus telegraphed headquarters saying that he thought it unwise to wait any longer and that he would be staying at Hotel Lazuli, Nice.

Lines 597-608:   the thoughts we should roll-call, etc.

This passage should be associated in the reader's mind with the extraordinary variant given in the preceding note, for only a week later Tana*gra dust* and "our royal hands" were to come together, in real life, in real death.

Had he not fled, our Charles II might have been executed; this would have certainly happened had he been apprehended between the palace and the Rippleson Caves; but he sensed those thick fingers of fate only seldom during his flight; he sensed them feeling for him (as those of a grim old shepherd checking a daughter's virginity) when he was slipping, that night, on the damp ferny flank of Mt. Mandevil (see note to line 149), and next day, at a more eerie altitude, in the heady blue, where the mountaineer becomes aware of a phantom companion. Many times that night our King cast himself upon the ground with the desperate resolution of resting there till dawn that he might shift with less torment what hazard soever he ran. (I am thinking of yet another Charles, another long dark man above two yards high.) But it was all rather physical, or neurotic, and I know perfectly well that my King, if caught and condemned and led away to be shot, would have behaved as he does in lines 606-608: thus he would look about him with insolent composure, and thus he would

> Taunt our inferiors, cheerfully deride
> The dedicated imbeciles and spit
> Into their eyes just for the fun of it

Let me close this important note with a rather anti-Darwinian aphorism: The one who kills is *always* his victim's inferior.

Line 603: Listen to distant cocks crow

One will recall the admirable image in a recent poem by Edsel Ford:

> And often when the cock crew, shaking fire
> Out of the morning and the misty mow

A mow (in Zemblan *muwan*) is the field next to a barn.

Lines 609-614: Nor can one help, etc.

This passage is different in the draft:

609 Nor can one help the exile caught by death
    In a chance inn exposed to the hot breath
    Of this America, this humid night:
    Through slatted blinds the stripes of colored light
    Grope for his bed—magicians from the past
    With philtered gems—and life is ebbing fast.

This describes rather well the "chance inn," a log cabin, with a tiled bathroom, where I am trying to coordinate these notes. At first I was greatly bothered by the blare of diabolical radio music from what I thought was some kind of amusement park across the road—it turned out to be camping tourists—and I was thinking of moving to another place, when they forestalled me. Now it is quieter, except for an irritating wind rattling through the withered aspens, and Cedarn is again a ghost town, and there are no summer fools or spies to stare at me, and my little blue-jeaned fisherman no longer stands on his stone in the stream, and perhaps it is better so.

Line 615: two tongues

English and Zemblan, English and Russian, English and Lettish, English and Estonian, English and Lithuanian, English and Russian, English and Ukrainian, English and Polish, English and Czech, English and Russian, English and Hungarian, English and Rumanian, English and Albanian, English and Bulgarian, English and Serbo-Croatian, English and Russian, American and European.

Line 619:   tuber's eye

The pun sprouts (see line 502).

Line 627:   The great Starover Blue

Presumably, permission from Prof. Blue was obtained but even so the plunging of a real person, no matter how sportive and willing, into an invented milieu where he is made to perform in accordance with the invention, strikes one as a singularly tasteless device, especially since other real-life characters, except members of the family, of course, are pseudonymized in the poem.

This name, no doubt, is most tempting. The star over the blue eminently suits an astronomer though actually neither his first nor second name bears any relation to the celestial vault: the first was given him in memory of his grandfather, a Russian *starover* (accented, incidentally, on the ultima), that is, Old Believer (member of a schismatic sect), named Sinyavin, from *siniy*, Russ. "blue." This Sinyavin migrated from Saratov to Seattle and begot a son who eventually changed his name to Blue and married Stella Lazurchik, an Americanized Kashube. So it goes. Honest Starover Blue will probably be surprised by the epithet bestowed upon him by a jesting Shade. The writer feels moved to pay here a small tribute to the amiable old freak, adored by everybody on the campus and nicknamed by the students Colonel Starbottle, evidently because of his exceptionally convivial habits. After all, there were other great men in our poet's en-

tourage—for example, that distinguished Zemblan scholar
Oscar Nattochdag.

Line 629:   The fate of beasts

Above this the poet wrote and struck out:

The madman's fate

The ultimate destiny of madmen's souls has been probed
by many Zemblan theologians who generally hold the view
that even the most demented mind still contains within its
diseased mass a sane basic particle that survives death and
suddenly expands, bursts out as it were, in peals of healthy
and triumphant laughter when the world of timorous fools
and trim blockheads has fallen away far behind. Personally,
I have not known any lunatics; but have heard of several
amusing cases in New Wye ("Even in Arcady am I," says
Dementia, chained to her gray column). There was for instance a student who went berserk. There was an old tre-
mendously trustworthy college porter who one day, in the
Projection Room, showed a squeamish coed something of
which she had no doubt seen better samples; but my favorite
case is that of an Exton railway employee whose delusion
was described to me by Mrs. H., of all people. There was a
big Summer School party at the Hurleys', to which one of my
second ping-pong table partners, a pal of the Hurley boys
had taken me because I knew my poet was to recite there
something and I was beside myself with apprehension be-

237

lieving it might be my Zembla (it proved to be an obscure
poem by one of his obscure friends—my Shade was very kind
to the unsuccessful). The reader will understand if I say
that, at my altitude, I can never feel "lost" in a crowd, but it
is also true that I did not know many people at the H.'s. As I
circulated, with a smile on my face and a cocktail in my
hand, through the crush, I espied at last the top of my poet's
head and the bright brown chignon of Mrs. H. above the
backs of two adjacent chairs. At the moment I advanced behind them I heard him object to some remark she had just
made:

"That is the wrong word," he said. "One should not apply
it to a person who deliberately peels off a drab and unhappy
past and replaces it with a brilliant invention. That's merely
turning a new leaf with the left hand."

I patted my friend on the head and bowed slightly to
Eberthella H. The poet looked at me with glazed eyes. She
said:

"You must help us, Mr. Kinbote: I maintain that what's
his name, old—the old man, you know, at the Exton railway
station, who thought he was God and began redirecting the
trains, was technically a loony, but John calls him a fellow
poet."

"We all are, in a sense, poets, Madam," I replied, and
offered a lighted match to my friend who had his pipe in his
teeth and was beating himself with both hands on various
parts of his torso.

I am not sure this trivial variant has been worth com-
menting; indeed, the whole passage about the activities of
the IPH would be quite Hudibrastic had its pedestrian
verse been one foot shorter.

Line 662: Who rides so late in the night and the wind

This line, and indeed the whole passage (lines 653-664), allude to the well-known poem by Goethe about the erlking, hoary enchanter of the elf-haunted alderwood, who falls in love with the delicate little boy of a belated traveler. One cannot sufficiently admire the ingenious way in which Shade manages to transfer something of the broken rhythm of the ballad (a trisyllabic meter at heart) into his iambic verse:

662 Who rídes so láte in the níght and the wínd
663 . . . .
664 . . . . Ít is the fáther wíth his chíld

Goethe's two lines opening the poem come out most exactly and beautifully, with the bonus of an unexpected rhyme (also in French: *vent-enfant*), in my own language:

Ret wóren ok spóz on nátt ut vétt?
Éto est vótchez ut míd ik détt.

Another fabulous ruler, the last king of Zembla, kept repeating these haunting lines to himself both in Zemblan and German, as a chance accompaniment of drumming fatigue and anxiety, while he climbed through the bracken belt of the dark mountains he had to traverse in his bid for freedom.

Lines 671-672: The Untamed Seahorse

See Browning's *My Last Duchess*.

See it and condemn the fashionable device of entitling a collection of essays or a volume of poetry—or a long poem, alas—with a phrase lifted from a more or less celebrated poetical work of the past. Such titles possess a specious glamor acceptable maybe in the names of vintage wines and plump courtesans but only degrading in regard to the talent that substitutes the easy allusiveness of literacy for original fancy and shifts onto a bust's shoulders the responsibility for ornateness since anybody can flip through a *Midsummer-Night's Dream* or *Romeo and Juliet,* or, perhaps, the *Sonnets* and take his pick.

Line 678: into French

Two of these translations appeared in the August number of the *Nouvelle Revue Canadienne* which reached College Town bookshops in the last week of July, that is at a time of sadness and mental confusion when good taste forbade me to show Sybil Shade some of the critical notes I made in my pocket diary.

In her version of Donne's famous Holy Sonnet X composed in his widowery:

> Death be not proud, though some have calléd thee
> Mighty and dreadful, for, thou art not so

one deplores the superfluous ejaculation in the second line introduced there only to coagulate the caesura:

> *Ne soit pas fière, Mort! Quoique certains te disent*
> *Et puissante et terrible, ah, Mort, tu ne l'es pas*

and while the enclosed rhyme "so-overthrow" (lines 2-3) is fortunate in finding an easy counterpart in *pas-bas*, one objects to the enclosing *disent-prise* rhymes (1-4) which in a *French* sonnet of *circa* 1617 would be an impossible infringement of the visual rule.

I have no space here to list a number of other blurrings and blunders in this Canadian version of the Dean of St. Paul's denouncement of Death, that slave—not only to "fate" and "chance"—but also to *us* ("kings and desperate men").

The other poem, Andrew Marvell's "The Nymph on the Death of her Fawn," seems to be, technically, even tougher to stuff into French verse. If in the Donne translation, Miss Irondell was perfectly justified in matching English pentameters with French Alexandrines, I doubt that here she should have preferred *l'impair* and accommodated with nine syllables what Marvell fits into eight. In the lines:

> And, quite regardless of my smart,
> Left me his fawn but took his heart

which come out as:

> *Et se moquant bien de ma douleur*
> *Me laissa son faon, mais pris son coeur*

one regrets that the translator, even with the help of an ampler prosodic womb, did not manage to fold in the long legs of her French fawn, and render "quite regardless of" by "*sans le moindre égard pour*" or something of the sort.

Further on, the couplet

> Thy love was far more better than
> The love of false and cruel man

though translated literally:

> *Que ton amour était fort meilleur*
> *Qu'amour d'homme cruel et trompeur*

is not as pure idiomatically as might seem at first glance. And finally, the lovely closule:

> Had it lived long it would have been
> Lilies without, roses within

contains in our lady's French not only a solecism but also that kind of illegal run-on which a translator is guilty of, when passing a stop sign:

> *Il aurait été, s'il eut longtemps*
> *Vécu, lys dehors, roses dedans.*

How magnificently those two lines can be mimed and rhymed in our magic Zemblan ("the tongue of the mirror," as the great Conmal has termed it)!

> *Id wodo bin, war id lev lan,*
> *Indran iz lil ut roz nitran.*

Line 680: Lolita

Major hurricanes are given feminine names in America.
The feminine gender is suggested not so much by the sex
of furies and harridans as by a general professional application. Thus any machine is a she to its fond user, and any
fire (even a "pale" one!) is she to the fireman, as water is
she to the passionate plumber. Why our poet chose to give
his 1958 hurricane a little-used Spanish name (sometimes
given to parrots) instead of Linda or Lois, is not clear.

Line 681: gloomy Russians spied

There is really nothing metaphysical, or racial, about this
gloom. It is merely the outward sign of congested nationalism
and a provincial's sense of inferiority—that dreadful blend
so typical of Zemblans under the Extremist rule and of Russians under the Soviet regime. Ideas in modern Russia are
machine-cut blocks coming in solid colors; the nuance is out-
lawed, the interval walled up, the curve grossly stepped.

However, not all Russians are gloomy, and the two young
experts from Moscow whom our new government engaged
to locate the Zemblan crown jewels turned out to be positively rollicking. The Extremists were right in believing that
Baron Bland, the Keeper of the Treasure, had succeeded in
hiding those jewels before he jumped or fell from the North
Tower; but they did not know he had had a helper and were
wrong in thinking the jewels must be looked for in the
palace which the gentle white-haired Bland had never left

except to die. I may add, with pardonable satisfaction, that they were, and still are, cached in a totally different—and quite unexpected—corner of Zembla.

In an earlier note (to line 130) the reader has already glimpsed those two treasure hunters at work. After the King's escape and the belated discovery of the secret passage, they continued their elaborate excavations until the palace was all honeycombed and partly demolished, an entire wall of one room collapsing one night, to yield, in a niche whose presence nobody had suspected, an ancient salt cellar of bronze and King Wigbert's drinking horn; but you will never find our crown, necklace and scepter.

All this is the rule of a supernal game, all this is the immutable fable of fate, and should not be construed as reflecting on the efficiency of the two Soviet experts—who, anyway, were to be marvelously successful on a later occasion with another job (see note to line 747). Their names (probably fictitious) were Andronnikov and Niagarin. One has seldom seen, at least among waxworks, a pair of more pleasant, presentable chaps. Everybody admired their clean-shaven jaws, elementary facial expressions, wavy hair, and perfect teeth. Tall handsome Andronnikov seldom smiled but the crinkly little rays of his orbital flesh bespoke infinite humor while the twin furrows descending from the sides of his shapely nostrils evoked glamorous associations with flying aces and sagebrush heroes. Niagarin, on the other hand, was of comparatively short stature, had somewhat more rounded, albeit quite manly features, and every now and then would flash a big boyish smile remindful of scoutmasters with something to hide, or those gentlemen who cheat in television quizzes. It was delightful to watch the two splendid Sovietchiks running about in the yard and kicking a chalk-dusty, thumping-tight soccer ball (looking so large and bald in such surroundings). Andronnikov could tap-play it on his toe up and down a dozen times before punting it rocket straight into the melancholy, surprised, bleached, harmless heavens; and Niagarin could imitate to perfection the mannerisms of a certain stupendous Dynamo goalkeeper. They used to hand out to the kitchen boys Russian caramels with plums or cherries depicted on the rich luscious six-cornered wrappers that enclosed a jacket of thinner paper with the mauve mummy inside; and lustful country girls were known to creep up along the *drungen* (bramble-choked footpaths) to the very foot of the bulwark when the two silhouetted against the now flushed sky sang beautiful sentimental military duets at eventide on the rampart. Niagarin had a soulful tenor voice, and Andronnikov a hearty baritone, and both wore elegant jackboots of soft black leather, and the sky turned away showing its ethereal vertebrae.

Niagarin who had lived in Canada spoke English and French; Andronnikov had some German. The little Zemblan they knew was pronounced with that comical Russian accent that gives vowels a kind of didactic plenitude of sound. They were considered models of dash by the Extremist guards, and my dear Odonello once earned a harsh reprimand from the commandant by not having withstood the temptation to imitate their walk: both moved with an identical little swagger, and both were conspicuously bandy-legged.

When I was a child, Russia enjoyed quite a vogue at the court of Zembla but that was a different Russia—a Russia that hated tyrants and Philistines, injustice and cruelty, the Russia of ladies and gentlemen and liberal aspirations. We may add that Charles the Beloved could boast of some Russian blood. In medieval times two of his ancestors had married Novgorod princesses. Queen Yaruga (reigned 1799-1800) his great-great-granddam, was half Russian; and most historians believe that Yaruga's only child Igor was not the son of Uran the Last (reigned 1798-1799) but the fruit of her amours with the Russian adventurer Hodinski, her *goliart* (court jester) and a poet of genius, said to have forged in his spare time a famous old Russian *chanson de geste,* generally attributed to an anonymous bard of the twelfth century.

Line 682: Lang

A modern Fra Pandolf no doubt. I do not remember seeing any such painting around the house. Or did Shade have in mind a photographic portrait? There was one such portrait on the piano, and another in Shade's study. How much fairer it would have been to Shade's and his friend's reader if the lady had deigned answer some of my urgent queries.

Line 691: the attack

John Shade's heart attack (Oct. 17, 1958) practically coincided with the disguised king's arrival in America where he descended by parachute from a chartered plane piloted by Colonel Montacute, in a field of hay-feverish, rank-flowering weeds, near Baltimore whose oriole is not an oriole. It had all been perfectly timed, and he was still wrestling with the unfamiliar French contraption when the Rolls-Royce from Sylvia O'Donnell's manor turned toward his green silks from a road and approached along the *mowntrop*, its fat wheels bouncing disapprovingly and its black shining body slowly gliding along. Fain would I elucidate this business of parachuting but (it being a matter of mere sentimental tradition rather than a useful manner of transportation) this is not strictly necessary in these notes to *Pale Fire*. While Kingsley, the British chauffeur, an old and absolutely faithful retainer, was doing his best to cram the bulky and ill-folded parachute into the boot, I relaxed on a shooting stick he had supplied me with, sipping a delightful Scotch and water from the car bar and glancing (amid an ovation of crickets and that vortex of yellow and maroon butterflies that so pleased Chateaubriand on *his* arrival in America) at an article in *The New York Times* in which Sylvia had vigorously and messily marked out in red pencil a communication from New Wye which told of the "distinguished poet's" hospitalization. I had been looking forward to meeting my favorite American poet who, as I felt sure at the moment, would die long before the Spring Term, but the disappointment was little more than a mental shrug of accepted regret, and discarding the newspaper, I looked around me with enchantment and physical wellbeing despite the congestion in my nose. Beyond the field the great green steps of turf ascended to the multicolored coppices; one could see above them the white brow of the manor; clouds melted into the blue. Suddenly I sneezed, and sneezed again. Kingsley offered me another drink but I declined it, and democratically joined him in the front seat. My hostess was in bed, suffering from the aftereffects of a special injection that she had been given in anticipation of a journey to a special place in Africa. In answer to my "Well, how are you?" she murmured that the Andes had been simply marvelous, and then in a slightly less indolent tone of voice inquired about a notorious actress with whom her son was said to be living in sin. Odon, I said, had promised me he would not marry her. She inquired if I had had a good hop and dingled a bronze bell. Good old Sylvia! She had in common with Fleur de Fyler a vagueness of manner, a languor of demeanor which was partly natural and partly cultivated as a convenient alibi for when she was drunk, and in some wonderful way she managed to combine that indolence with volubility reminding one of a slow-speaking ventriloquist who is interrupted by his garrulous doll. Changeless Sylvia! During three decades I had seen from time to time, from palace to palace, that same flat nut-colored bobbed hair, those childish pale-blue eyes, the vacant smile, the stylish long legs, the willowy hesitating movements.

A tray with fruit and drinks was brought in by a *jeune beauté*, as dear Marcel would have put it, nor could one help recalling another author, Gide the Lucid, who praises in his African notes so warmly the satiny skin of black imps.

"You nearly lost the opportunity to meet our brightest star," said Sylvia who was Wordsmith University's main trustee (and, in point of fact, had been solely responsible for arranging my amusing lectureship there). "I have just called up the college—yes, take that footstool—and he is much better. Try this mascana fruit, I got it especially for you, but the boy is strictly hetero, and, generally speaking, Your Majesty will have to be quite careful from now on. I'm sure you'll like it up there though I wish I could figure out why anybody should be so keen on teaching Zemblan. I think Disa ought to come too. I have rented for you what they say is their best house, and it is near the Shades."

She knew them very slightly but had heard many endearing stories about the poet from Billy Reading, "one of the very few American college presidents who know Latin." And let me add here how much I was honored a fortnight later to meet in Washington that limp-looking, absent-minded, shabbily dressed splendid American gentleman whose mind was a library and not a debating hall. Next Monday Sylvia flew away but I stayed on for a while, resting from my adventures, musing, reading, taking notes, and riding a lot in the lovely countryside with two charming ladies and their shy little groom. I have often felt when leaving a place that I had enjoyed, somewhat like a tight cork that is drawn out for the sweet dark wine to be drained, and then you are off to new vineyards and conquests. I spent a couple of pleasant months visiting the libraries of New York and Washington, flew to Florida for Christmas, and when ready to start for my new Arcady deemed it nice and dutiful to send the poet a polite note congratulating him on his restored health and jokingly "warning" him that beginning with February he would have a very ardent admirer of his for neighbor. I never received any answer, and my civility was never recalled later so I suppose it got lost among the many "fan" letters that literary celebrities receive, although one might have expected Sylvia or somebody to have told the Shades of my arrival.

The poet's recovery turned out indeed to be very speedy and would have to be called miraculous had there been anything organically wrong with his heart. There was not; a poet's nerves can play the queerest tricks but they also can quickly recapture the rhythm of health, and soon John Shade, in his chair at the head of an oval table, was again speaking of his favorite Pope to eight pious young men, a crippled extramural woman and three coeds, one of them a tutorial dream. He had been told not to curtail his customary exercise, such as walks, but I must admit I experienced myself palpitations and cold sweats at the sight of that precious old man wielding rude garden tools or squirming up the college hall stairs as a Japanese fish up a cataract. Incidentally: the reader should not take too seriously or too literally the passage about the alert doctor (an alert doctor, who as I well know once confused neuralgia with cerebral sclerosis). As I gathered from Shade himself, no emergency incision was performed; the heart was not compressed by hand; and if it stopped pumping at all, the pause must have been very brief and so to speak superficial. All this of course cannot detract from the great epic beauty of the passage. (Lines 691-697)

Line 697: Conclusive destination

Gradus landed at the Côte d'Azur airport in the early afternoon of July 15, 1959. Despite his worries he could not help being impressed by the torrent of magnificent trucks, agile motor bicycles and cosmopolitan private cars on the Promenade. He remembered and disliked the torrid heat and the blinding blue of the sea. Hotel Lazuli, where before World War Two he had spent a week with a consumptive Bosnian terrorist, when it was a squalid, running-water place frequented by young Germans, was now a squalid, running-water place frequented by old Frenchmen. It was situated in a transverse street, between two thoroughfares parallel to the quay, and the ceaseless roar of crisscross traffic mingling with the grinding and banging of construction work proceeding under the auspices of a crane opposite the hotel (which had been surrounded by a stagnant calm two decades earlier) was a delightful surprise for Gradus, who always liked a little noise to keep his mind off things. ("*Ça distrait,*" as he said to the apologetic hostlerwife and her sister).

After scrupulously washing his hands, he went out again, a tremor of excitement running like fever down his crooked spine. At one of the tables of a sidewalk café on the corner of his street and the Promenade, a man in a bottle-green jacket, sitting in the company of an obvious whore, clapped both palms to his face, emitted the sound of a muffled sneeze, and kept masking himself with his hands as he pretended to wait for the second installment. Gradus walked along the north side of the embankment. After stopping for a minute before the display of a souvenir shop, he went inside, asked the price of a little hippopotamus made of violet glass, and purchased a map of Nice and its environs. As he walked on to the taxi stand in rue Gambetta, he happened to notice two young tourists in loud shirts stained with sweat, their faces and necks a bright pink from the heat and imprudent solarization; they carried carefully folded over their arms the silk-lined doublebreasted coats of their widetrousered dark suits and did not look at our sleuth who despite his being exceptionally unobservant felt the undulation of something faintly familiar as they brushed past. They knew nothing of his presence abroad or of his interesting job; in point of fact, only a few minutes ago had their, and his, superior discovered that Gradus was in Nice and not in Geneva. Neither had Gradus been informed that he would be assisted in his quest by the Soviet sportsmen, Andronnikov and Niagarin, whom he had casually met once or twice on the Onhava Palace grounds when re-paning a broken window and checking for the new government the rare Rippleson panes in one of the ex-royal hothouses; and next moment he had lost the thread end of recognition as he settled down with the prudent wriggle of a short-legged person in the back seat of an old Cadillac and asked to be taken to a restaurant between Pellos and Cap Turc. It is hard to say what our man's hopes and intentions were. Did he want just to peep through the myrtles and oleanders at an imagined swimming pool? Did he expect to hear the continuation of Gordon's bravura piece played now in another rendition, by two larger and stronger hands? Would he have crept, pistol in hand, to where a sun-bathing giant lay spread-eagled, a spread eagle of hair on his chest? We do not know, nor did Gradus perhaps know himself; anyway, he was spared an unnecessary journey. Modern taximen are as talkative as were the barbers of old, and even before the old Cadillac had rolled out of town, our unfortunate killer knew that his driver's brother had worked in the gardens of Villa Disa but that at present nobody lived there, the Queen having gone to Italy for the rest of July.

At his hotel the beaming proprietress handed him a telegram. It chided him in Danish for leaving Geneva and told him to undertake nothing until further notice. It also advised him to forget his work and amuse himself. But what (save dreams of blood) could be his amusements? He was not interested in sightseeing or seasiding. He had long stopped drinking. He did not go to concerts. He did not gamble. Sexual impulses had greatly bothered him at one time but that was over. After his wife, a beader in Radugovitra, had left him (with a gypsy lover), he had lived in sin with his mother-in-law until she was removed, blind and dropsical, to an asylum for decayed widows. Since then he had tried several times to castrate himself, had been laid up at the Glassman Hospital with a severe infection, and now, at forty-four, was quite cured of the lust that Nature, the grand cheat, puts into us to inveigle us into propagation. No wonder the advice to amuse himself infuriated him. I think I shall break this note here.

Lines 704-707: A system, etc.

The fitting-in of the threefold "cells interlinked" is most skillfully managed, and one derives logical satisfaction from the "system" and "stem" interplay.

Lines 727-728: No, Mr. Shade . . . just half a shade

Another fine example of our poet's special brand of combinational magic. The subtle pun here turns on two additional meanings of "shade" besides the obvious synonym of "nuance." The doctor is made to suggest that not only did Shade retain in his trance half of his identity but that he was also half a ghost. Knowing the particular medical man who treated my friend at the time, I venture to add that he is far too stodgy to have displayed any such wit.

Lines 734-735: probably . . . wobble . . . limp blimp . . . unstable

A third burst of contrapuntal pyrotechnics. The poet's plan is to display in the very texture of his text the intricacies of the "game" in which he seeks the key to life and death (see lines 808-829).

Line 741: the outer glare

On the morning of July 16 (while Shade was working on the 698-746 section of his poem) dull Gradus, dreading another day of enforced inactivity in sardonically sparkling, stimulatingly noisy Nice, decided that until hunger drove him out he would not budge from a leathern armchair in the simulacrum of a lobby among the brown smells of his dingy hotel. Unhurriedly he went through a heap of old magazines on a nearby table. There he sat, a little monument of taciturnity, sighing, puffing out his cheeks, licking his thumb before turning a page, gaping at the pictures, and moving his lips as he climbed down the columns of printed matter. Having replaced everything in a neat pile, he sank

back in his chair closing and opening his gabled hands in
various constructions of tedium—when a man who had occupied a seat next to him got up and walked into the outer
glare leaving his paper behind. Gradus pulled it into his lap,
spread it out—and froze over a strange piece of local news
that caught his eye: burglars had broken into Villa Disa and
ransacked a bureau, taking from a jewel box a number of
valuable old medals.

Here was something to brood upon. Had this vaguely unpleasant incident some bearing on his quest? Should he do
something about it? Cable headquarters? Hard to word suc-
cinctly a simple fact without having it look like a crypto-
gram. Airmail a clipping? He was in his room working on the
newspaper with a safety razor blade when there was a bright
rap-rap at the door. Gradus admitted an unexpected visitor
—one of the greater Shadows, whom he had thought to be
onhava-onhava ("far, far away"), in wild, misty, almost
legendary Zembla! What stunning conjuring tricks our magical mechanical age plays with old mother space and old
father time!

He was a merry, perhaps overmerry, fellow, in a green
velvet jacket. Nobody liked him, but he certainly had a
keen mind. His name, Izumrudov, sounded rather Russian
but actually meant "of the Umruds," an Eskimo tribe
sometimes seen paddling their umyaks (hide-lined boats)
on the emerald waters of our northern shores. Grinning, he
said friend Gradus must get together his travel documents,
including a health certificate, and take the earliest available
jet to New York. Bowing, he congratulated him on having
indicated with such phenomenal acumen the right place
and the right way. Yes, after a thorough perlustration of the
loot that Andron and Niagarushka had obtained from the

Queen's rosewood writing desk (mostly bills, and treasured snapshots, and those silly medals) a letter from the King did turn up giving his address which was of all places— Our man, who interrupted the herald of success to say he had *never*—was bidden not to display so much modesty. A slip of paper was now produced on which Izumrudov, shaking with laughter (death is hilarious), wrote out for Gradus their client's alias, the name of the university where he taught, and that of the town where it was situated. No, the slip was not for keeps. He could keep it only while memorizing it. This brand of paper (used by macaroon makers) was not only digestible but delicious. The gay green vision withdrew—to resume his whoring no doubt. How one hates such men!

Lines 747-748: a story in the magazine about a Mrs. Z.

Anybody having access to a good library could, no doubt, easily trace that story to its source and find the name of the lady; but such humdrum potterings are beneath true scholarship.

Line 768: address

At this point my reader may be amused by my allusion to John Shade in a letter (of which I fortunately preserved a carbon copy) that I wrote to a correspondent living in southern France on April 2, 1959:

My dear, you are absurd. I do not give you, and will not give you or anybody, my home address not because I fear you might look me up, as you are pleased to conjecture: *all* my mail goes to my office address. The suburban houses here have open letter boxes out in the street, and anybody can cram them with advertisements or purloin letters addressed to me (not out of mere curiosity, mind you, but from other, more sinister, motives). I send this by air and urgently repeat the address Sylvia gave you: Dr. C. Kinbote, KINBOTE (*not* "Charles X. Kingbot, Esq.," as you, or Sylvia, wrote; *please*, be more careful—and more intelligent), Wordsmith University, New Wye, Appalachia, USA.

I am not cross with you but I have all sorts of worries, and my nerves are on edge. I believed—believed deeply and candidly—in the affection of a person who lived here, under my roof, but have been hurt and betrayed, as never happened in the days of my forefathers, who could have the offender tortured, though of course I do not wish to have anybody tortured.

It has been dreadfully cold here, but thank God now a regular northern winter has turned into a southern spring.

Do not try to explain to me what your lawyer tells you but have him explain it to my lawyer, and *he* will explain it to me.

My work at the university is pleasant, and I have a most charming neighbor—now do not sigh and raise your eyebrows, my dear—he is a very old gentleman—the old gentleman in fact who was responsible for that bit about the ginkgo tree in your green album (see again—I mean the reader should see again—the note to line 49).

It might be safer if you did not write me *too* often, my dear.

Line 782:   your poem

An image of Mont Blanc's "blue-shaded buttresses and sun-creamed domes" is fleetingly glimpsed through the cloud of that particular poem which I wish I could quote but do not have at hand. The "white mountain" of the lady's dream, caused by a misprint to tally with Shade's "white fountain," makes a thematic appearance here, blurred as it were by the lady's grotesque pronunciation.

Line 802:   mountain

The passage 797 (second part of line)-809, on the poet's sixty-fifth card, was composed between the sunset of July 18 and the dawn of July 19. That morning I had prayed in two different churches (on either side, as it were, of my Zemblan denomination, not represented in New Wye) and had strolled home in an elevated state of mind. There was no cloud in the wistful sky, and the very earth seemed to be sighing after our Lord Jesus Christ. On such sunny, sad mornings I always feel in my bones that there is a chance yet of my not being excluded from Heaven, and that salvation may be granted to me despite the frozen mud and horror in my heart. As I was ascending with bowed head the gravel path to my poor rented house, I heard with absolute distinction, as if he were standing at my shoulder and speaking loudly, as to a slightly deaf man, Shade's voice say: "Come tonight, Charlie." I looked around me in awe and wonder: I was quite alone. I at once telephoned. The Shades were out, said the cheeky ancillula, an obnoxious little fan who came to cook for them on Sundays and no doubt dreamt of getting the old poet to cuddle her some wifeless day. I retelephoned two hours later; got, as usual, Sybil; insisted on talking to my friend (my "messages" were never transmitted), obtained him, and asked him as calmly as possible what he had been doing around noon when I had heard him like a big bird in my garden. He could not quite remember, said wait a minute, he had been playing golf with Paul (whoever that was), or at least watching Paul play with another colleague. I cried that I must see him in the evening and all at once, with no reason at all, burst into tears, flooding the telephone and gasping for breath, a paroxysm which had not happened to me since Bob left me on March 30. There was a flurry of confabulation between the Shades, and then John said: "Charles, listen. Let's go for a good ramble tonight, I'll meet you at eight." It was my second good ramble since July 6 (that unsatisfactory nature talk); the third one, on July 21, was to be exceedingly brief.

Where was I? Yes, trudging along again as in the old days with John, in the woods of Arcady, under a salmon sky.

"Well," I said gaily, "what were you writing about last night, John? Your study window was simply blazing."

"Mountains," he answered.

The Bera Range, an erection of veined stone and shaggy firs, rose before me in all its power and pride. The splendid news made my heart pound, and I felt that I could now, in my turn, afford to be generous. I begged my friend not to impart to me anything more if he did not wish it. He said yes, he did not, and began bewailing the difficulties of his self-imposed task. He calculated that during the last twenty-four hours his brain had put in, roughly, a thousand minutes of work, and had produced fifty lines (say, 797-847) or one syllable every two minutes. He had finished his Third, penultimate, Canto, and had started on Canto Four, his last (see Foreword, see Foreword, at once), and would I mind very much if we started to go home—though it was only around nine—so that he could plunge back into his chaos and drag out of it, with all its wet stars, his cosmos?

How could I say no? That mountain air had gone to my head: he was reassembling my Zembla!

Line 803: a misprint

Translators of Shade's poem are bound to have trouble with the transformation, at one stroke, of "mountain" into "fountain": it cannot be rendered in French or German, or Russian, or Zemblan; so the translator will have to put into one of those footnotes that are the rogue's galleries of words. However! There exists to my knowledge one absolutely extraordinary, unbelievably elegant case, where not only two, but *three* words are involved. The story itself is trivial enough (and probably apocryphal). A newspaper account of a Russian tsar's coronation had, instead of *korona* (crown), the misprint *vorona* (crow), and when next day this was apologetically "corrected," it got misprinted a second time as *korova* (cow). The artistic correlation between the crown-crow-cow series and the Russian *korona-vorona-korova* series is something that would have, I am sure, enraptured my poet. I have seen nothing like it on lexical playfields and the odds against the double coincidence defy computation.

Line 810: a web of sense

One of the five cabins of which this motor court consists is occupied by the owner, a blear-eyed, seventy-year-old man whose twisted limp reminds me of Shade. He runs a small gas station nearby, sells worms to fishermen, and usually does not bother me, but the other day he suggested I "grab any old book" from a shelf in his room. Not wishing to offend him, I cocked my head at them, to one side, and then to the other, but they were all dog-eared paperback mystery stories and did not rate more than a sigh and a smile. He said wait a minute—and took from a bedside recess a battered clothbound treasure. "A great book by a great guy," the Letters of Franklin Lane. "Used to see a lot of him in Rainier Park when I was a young ranger up there. You take it for a couple of days. You won't regret it!"

I did not. Here is a passage that curiously echoes Shade's tone at the end of Canto Three. It comes from a manuscript fragment written by Lane on May 17, 1921, on the eve of his death, after a major operation: "And if I had passed into that other land, whom would I have sought? . . . Aristotle! — Ah, there would be a man to talk with! What satisfaction to see him take, like reins from between his fingers, the long ribbon of man's life and trace it through the mystifying maze of all the wonderful adventure. . . . The crooked made straight. The Daedalian plan simplified by a look from above—smeared out as it were by the splotch of some master thumb that made the whole involuted, boggling thing one beautiful straight line."

Line 819:   Playing a game of worlds

My illustrious friend showed a childish predilection for all sorts of word games and especially for so-called word golf. He would interrupt the flow of a prismatic conversation to indulge in this particular pastime, and naturally it would have been boorish of me to refuse playing with him. Some of my records are: hate-love in three, lass-male in four, and live-dead in five (with "lend" in the middle).

Line 822:   killing a Balkan king

Fervently would I wish to report that the reading in the draft was:

killing a Zemblan king

—but alas, it is not so: the card with the draft has not been preserved by Shade.

Line 830:   Sybil, it is

This elaborate rhyme comes as an apotheosis crowning the entire canto and synthesizing the contrapuntal aspects of its "accidents and possibilities."

Lines 835-838:   Now I shall spy, etc.

The canto, begun on July 19th, on card sixty-eight, opens with a typical Shadism: the cunning working-in of several inter-echoing phrases into a jumble of enjambments. Actually, the promise made in these four lines will not be really kept except for the repetition of their incantatory rhythm in lines 915 and 923-924 (leading to the savage attack in 925-930). The poet like a fiery rooster seems to flap his wings in a preparatory burst of would-be inspiration, but the sun does not rise. Instead of the wild poetry promised here, we get a jest or two, a bit of satire, and at the end of the canto, a wonderful radiance of tenderness and repose.

Lines 841-872:   two methods of composing

Really three if we count the all-important method of relying on the flash and flute of the subliminal world and its "mute command" (line 871).

Line 873:   My best time

As my dear friend was beginning with this line his July 20 batch of cards (card seventy-one to card seventy-six, ending with line 948), Gradus, at the Orly airport, was walking aboard a jetliner, fastening his seat belt, reading a newspaper, rising, soaring, desecrating the sky.

Lines 887-888: Since my biographer may be too staid or know too little

Too staid? Know too little? Had my poor friend precognized *who* that would be, he would have been spared those conjectures. As a matter of fact I had the pleasure and the honor of witnessing (one March morning) the performance he describes in the next lines. I was going to Washington and just before starting remembered he had said he wanted me to look up something in the Library of Congress. I hear so clearly in my mind's ear Sybil's cool voice saying: "But John cannot see you, he is in his bath"; and John's raucous roar coming from the bathroom: "Let him in, Sybil, he won't rape me!" But neither he nor I could recall what that something was.

Line 894: a king

Pictures of the King had not infrequently appeared in America during the first months of the Zemblan Revolution. Every now and then some busybody on the campus with a retentive memory, or one of the clubwomen who were always after Shade and his eccentric friend, used to ask me with the inane meaningfulness adopted in such cases if anybody had told me how much I resembled that unfortunate monarch. I would counter with something on the lines of "all Chinese look alike" and change the subject. One day, however, in the lounge of the Faculty Club where I lolled surrounded by a number of my colleagues, I had to put up with a particularly embarrassing onset. A visiting German lecturer from Oxford kept exclaiming, aloud and under his breath, that the resemblance was "absolutely unheard of," and when I negligently observed that all bearded Zemblans resembled one another—and that, in fact, the name Zembla is a corruption not of the Russian *zemlya*, but of Semblerland, a land of reflections, of "resemblers"—my tormentor said: "Ah, yes, but King Charles wore no beard, and yet it is his very face! I had [he added] the honor of being seated within a few yards of the royal box at a Sport Festival in Onhava which I visited with my wife, who is Swedish, in 1956. We have a photograph of him at home, and her sister knew very well the mother of one of his pages, an interesting woman. Don't you see [almost tugging at Shade's lapel] the astounding similarity of features—of the upper part of the face, and the eyes, yes, the eyes, and the nose bridge?"

"Nay, sir" [said Shade, refolding a leg and slightly rolling in his armchair as wont to do when about to deliver a pronouncement] "there is no resemblance at all. I have seen the King in newsreels, and there is no resemblance. Resemblances are the shadows of differences. Different people see different similarities and similar differences."

Good Netochka, who had been looking singularly uncomfortable during this exchange, remarked in his gentle voice how sad it was to think that such a "sympathetic ruler" had probably perished in prison.

A professor of physics now joined in. He was a so-called Pink, who believed in what so-called Pinks believe in (Progressive Education, the Integrity of anyone spying for Russia, Fall-outs occasioned solely by US-made bombs, the existence in the near past of a McCarthy Era, Soviet achievements including *Dr. Zhivago,* and so forth): "Your regrets are groundless" [said he]. "That sorry ruler is known to have escaped disguised as a nun; but whatever happens, or has happened to him, cannot interest the Zemblan people. History has denounced him, and that is his epitaph."

Shade: "True, sir. In due time history will have denounced everybody. The King may be dead, or he may be as much alive as you and Kinbote, but let us respect facts. I have it from him [pointing to me] that the widely circulated stuff about the nun is a vulgar pro-Extremist fabrication. The Extremists and their friends invented a lot of nonsense to conceal their discomfiture; but the truth is that the King walked out of the palace, and crossed the mountains, and left the country, not in the black garb of a pale spinster but dressed as an athlete in scarlet wool."

"Strange, strange," said the German visitor, who by some quirk of alderwood ancestry had been alone to catch the eerie note that had throbbed by and was gone.

Shade [smiling and massaging my knee]: "Kings do not die—they only disappear, eh, Charles?"

"Who said that?" asked sharply, as if coming out of a trance, the ignorant, and always suspicious, Head of the English Department.

"Take my own case," continued my dear friend ignoring

Mr. H. "I have been said to resemble at least four people: Samuel Johnson; the lovingly reconstructed ancestor of man in the Exton Museum; and two local characters, one being the slapdash disheveled hag who ladles out the mash in the Levin Hall cafeteria."

"The third in the witch row," I precised quaintly, and everybody laughed.

"I would rather say," remarked Mr. Pardon—American History—"that she looks like Judge Goldsworth" ("One of us," interposed Shade inclining his head), "especially when he is real mad at the whole world after a good dinner."

"I hear," hastily began Netochka, "that the Goldsworths are having a wonderful time—"

"What a pity I cannot prove my point," muttered the tenacious German visitor. "If only there was a picture here. Couldn't there be somewhere—"

"Sure," said young Emerald and left his seat.

Professor Pardon now spoke to me: "I was under the impression that you were born in Russia, and that your name was a kind of anagram of Botkin or Botkine?"

Kinbote: "You are confusing me with some refugee from Nova Zembla" [sarcastically stressing the "Nova"].

"Didn't you tell me, Charles, that *kinbote* means regicide in your language?" asked my dear Shade.

"Yes, a king's destroyer," I said (longing to explain that a king who sinks his identity in the mirror of exile is in a sense just that).

Shade [addressing the German visitor]: "Professor Kinbote is the author of a remarkable book on surnames. I believe [to me] there exists an English translation?"

"Oxford, 1956," I replied.

"You do know Russian, though?" said Pardon. "I think I heard you, the other day, talking to—what's his name—oh, my goodness" [laboriously composing his lips].

Shade: "Sir, we all find it difficult to *attack* that name" [laughing].

Professor Hurley: "Think of the French word for 'tire': *punoo*."

Shade: "Why, sir, I am afraid you have only punctured the difficulty" [laughing uproariously].

"Flatman," quipped I. "Yes," I went on, turning to Pardon, "I certainly do speak Russian. You see, it was the fashionable language *par excellence*, much more so than French, among the nobles of Zembla at least, and at its court. Today, of course, all this has changed. It is now the lower classes who are forcibly taught to speak Russian."

"Aren't we, too, trying to teach Russian in our schools?" said Pink.

In the meantime, at the other end of the room, young Emerald had been communing with the bookshelves. At this point he returned with the T-Z volume of an illustrated encyclopedia.

"Well," said he, "here he is, that king. But look, he is young and handsome" ("Oh, that won't do," wailed the German visitor.) "Young, handsome, and wearing a fancy uniform," continued Emerald. "Quite the fancy pansy, in fact."

"And you," I said quietly, "are a foul-minded pup in a cheap green jacket."

"But what have I said?" the young instructor inquired of the company, spreading out his palms like a disciple in Leonardo's *Last Supper*.

"Now, now," said Shade. "I'm sure, Charles, our young

friend never intended to insult your sovereign and name-
sake."

"He could not, even if he had wished," I observed placidly,
turning it all into a joke.

Gerald Emerald extended his hand—which at the moment of writing still remains in that position.

Lines 895-899:   The more I weigh . . . or this dewlap

Instead of these facile and revolting lines, the draft gives:

895 I have a certain liking, I admit,
     For Parody, that last resort of wit:
     "In nature's strife when fortitude prevails
     The victim falters and the victor fails."
899 Yes, reader, Pope

Line 920:   little hairs stand on end

Alfred Housman (1859-1936), whose collection *The Shrop-
shire Lad* vies with the *In Memoriam* of Alfred Tennyson
(1809-1892) in representing, perhaps (no, delete this craven
"perhaps"), the highest achievement of English poetry in a
hundred years, says somewhere (in a foreword?) exactly
the opposite: The bristling of thrilled little hairs obstructed
his barbering; but since both Alfreds certainly used an Ordinary Razor, and John Shade an ancient Gillette, the

discrepancy may have been due to the use of different instruments.

Line 922:   held up by Our Cream

This is not quite exact. In the advertisement to which it refers, the whiskers are held up by a bubbly foam, not by a creamy substance.

After this line, instead of lines 923-930, we find the following, lightly deleted, variant:

> All artists have been born in what they call
> A sorry age; mine is the worst of all:
> An age that thinks spacebombs and spaceships take
> A genius with a foreign name to make,
> When any jackass can rig up the stuff;
> An age in which a pack of rogues can bluff
> The selenographer; a comic age
> That sees in Dr. Schweitzer a great sage.

Having struck this out, the poet tried another theme, but these lines he also canceled:

> England where poets flew the highest, now
> Wants them to plod and Pegasus to plough;
> Now the prosemongers of the Grubby Group,
> The Message Man, the owlish Nincompoop
> And all the Social Novels of our age
> Leave but a pinch of coal dust on the page.

Line 929:   Freud

In my mind's eye I see again the poet literally collapsing
on his lawn, beating the grass with his fist, and shaking
and howling with laughter, and myself, Dr. Kinbote, a torrent of tears streaming down my beard, as I try to read co-
herently certain tidbits from a book I had filched from a
classroom: a learned work on psychoanalysis, used in American colleges, repeat, used in American colleges. Alas, I find
only two items preserved in my notebook:

> By picking the nose in spite of all commands to the contrary,
> or when a youth is all the time sticking his finger through his
> buttonhole . . . the analytic teacher knows that the appetite
> of the lustful one knows no limit in his phantasies.
>
> (Quoted by Prof. C. from Dr. Oskar Pfister, *The
> Psychoanalytical Method*, 1917, N.Y., p. 79)

> The little cap of red velvet in the German version of Little
> Red Riding Hood is a symbol of menstruation.
>
> (Quoted by Prof. C. from Erich Fromm, *The
> Forgotten Language*, 1951, N.Y., p. 240.)

Do those clowns really *believe* what they teach?

Line 934:   big trucks

I must say I do not remember hearing very often "big
trucks" passing in our vicinity. Loud cars, yes—but not
trucks.

Line 937:   Old Zembla

I am a weary and sad commentator today.

Parallel to the left-hand side of this card (his seventy-sixth) the poet has written, on the eve of his death, a line (from Pope's Second Epistle of the *Essay on Man*) that he may have intended to cite in a footnote:

At Greenland, Zembla, or the Lord knows where

So this is all treacherous old Shade could say about Zembla —*my* Zembla? While shaving his stubble off? Strange, strange . . .

Lines 939-940:   Man's life, etc.

If I correctly understand the sense of this succinct observation, our poet suggests here that human life is but a series of footnotes to a vast obscure unfinished masterpiece.

Line 949:   And all the time

Thus, some time in the morning of July 21, the last day of his life, John Shade began his last batch of cards (seventy-seven to eighty). Two silent time zones had now merged to form the standard time of one man's fate; and it is not impossible that the poet in New Wye and the thug in New York awoke that morning at the same crushed beat of their Timekeeper's stopwatch.

Line 949:   and all the time

And all the time he was coming nearer.

A formidable thunderstorm had greeted Gradus in New York on the night of his arrival from Paris (Monday, July 20). The tropical rainfall flooded basements and subway tracks. Kaleidoscopic reflections played in the riverlike streets. Vinogradus had never seen such a display of lightning, neither had Jacques d'Argus—or Jack Grey, for that matter (let us not forget Jack Grey!). He put up in a third-class Broadway hotel and slept soundly, lying belly up *on* the bedclothes, in striped pajamas—the kind that Zemblans call *rusker sirsusker* ("Russian seersucker suit")—and retaining as usual his socks: not since July 11, when he had visited a Finnish bathouse in Switzerland, had he seen his bare feet.

It was now July 21. At eight in the morning New York roused Gradus with a bang and a roar. As usual he started his blurry daily existence by blowing his nose. Then he took out of its nightbox of cardboard and inserted into his Comus-mask mouth an exceptionally large and fierce-looking set of teeth: the only bad flaw really in his otherwise harmless appearance. This done, he fished out of his briefcase two petit-beurres he had saved and an even older but still quite palatable small, softish, near-ham sandwich, vaguely associated with the train journey from Nice to Paris last Satur-

day night: not so much thriftiness on his part (the Shadows
had advanced him a handsome sum, anyway), but an animal
attachment to the habits of his frugal youth. After breakfast-
ing in bed on these delicacies, he began preparations for
the most important day in his life. He had shaved yesterday
—that was out of the way. His trusty pajamas he stuffed not
into his traveling bag but into the briefcase, dressed, un-
clipped from the inside of his coat a cameo-pink, inter-
dentally clogged pocket comb, drew it through his bristly
hair, carefully donned his trilby, washed both hands with
the nice, modern liquid soap in the nice, modern, almost
odorless lavatory across the corridor, micturated, rinsed one
hand, and feeling clean and neat, went out for a stroll.

He had never visited New York before; but as many
near-cretins, he was above novelty. On the previous night he
had counted the mounting rows of lighted windows in several
skyscrapers, and now, after checking the height of a few
more buildings, he felt that he knew all there was to know.
He had a brimming cup and half a saucerful of coffee at a
crowded and wet counter and spent the rest of the smoke-
blue morning moving from bench to bench and from paper
to paper in the westside alleys of Central Park.

He began with the day's copy of *The New York Times*.
His lips moving like wrestling worms, he read about all
kinds of things. Hrushchov (whom they spelled "Khrush-
chev") had abruptly put off a visit to Scandinavia and was
to visit Zembla instead (here I tune in: *"Vï nazïvaete sebya
zemblerami,* you call yourselves Zemblans, *a ya vas nazïvayu
zemlyakami,* and I call you fellow countrymen!" Laughter
and applause). The United States was about to launch its
first atom-driven merchant ship (just to annoy the Ruskers,
of course. J.G.). Last night, in Newark, an apartment house

at 555 South Street was hit by a thunderbolt that smashed a
TV set and injured two people watching an actress lost in a
violent studio storm (those tormented spirits are terrible!
C.X.K. *teste* J.S.). The Rachel Jewelry Company in Brook-
lyn advertised in agate type for a jewelry polisher who
"must have experience on costume jewelry" (oh, Degré
had!). The Helman brothers said they had assisted in the
negotiations for the placement of a sizable note: $11,000,-
000, Decker Glass Manufacturing Company, Inc., note due
July 1, 1979," and Gradus, grown young again, reread this
twice, with the background gray thought, perhaps, that he
would be sixty-four four days after that (no comment). On
another bench he found a Monday issue of the same newspaper. During a visit to a museum in Whitehorse (Gradus
kicked at a pigeon that came too near), the Queen of
England walked to a corner of the White Animals Room,
removed her right glove and, with her back turned to several
evidently observant people, rubbed her forehead and one
of her eyes. A pro-Red revolt had erupted in Iraq. Asked
about the Soviet exhibition at the New York Coliseum, Carl
Sandburg, a poet, replied, and I quote: "They make their
appeal on the highest of intellectual levels." A hack re-
viewer of new books for tourists, reviewing his own tour
through Norway, said that the fjords were too famous to
need (his) description, and that all Scandinavians loved
flowers. And at a picnic for international children a Zemblan
moppet cried to her Japanese friend: *Ufgut, ufgut, velkam
ut Semblerland!* (Adieu, adieu, till we meet in Zembla!)
I confess it has been a wonderful game—this looking up in
the WUL of various ephemerides over the shadow of a
padded shoulder.

Jacques d'Argus looked for a twentieth time at his

watch. He strolled like a pigeon with his hands behind him. He had his mahogany shoes shined—and appreciated the way the dirty but pretty boy clacked taut his rag. In a restaurant on Broadway he consumed a large portion of pinkish pork with sauerkraut, a double helping of elastic French fries, and the half of an overripe melon. From my rented cloudlet I contemplate him with quiet surprise: here he is, this creature ready to commit a monstrous act—and coarsely enjoying a coarse meal! We must assume, I think, that the forward projection of what imagination he had, stopped at the act, on the brink of all its possible consequences; ghost consequences, comparable to the ghost toes of an amputee or to the fanning out of additional squares which a chess knight (that skip-space piece), standing on a marginal file, "feels" in phantom extensions beyond the board, but which have no effect whatever on his real moves, on the real play.

He strolled back and paid the equivalent of three thousand Zemblan crowns for his short but nice stay at Beverland Hotel. With the illusion of practical foresight he transferred his fiber suitcase and—after a moment of hesitation—his raincoat to the anonymous security of a station locker—where, I suppose, they are still lying as snug as my gemmed scepter, ruby necklace, and diamond-studded crown in—no matter, where. On his fateful journey he took only the battered black briefcase we know: it contained a clean nylon shirt, a dirty pajama, a safety razor, a third petit-beurre, an empty cardboard box, a thick illustrated paper he had not quite finished with in the park, a glass eye he once made for his old mistress, and a dozen syndicalist brochures, each in several copies, printed with his own hands many years ago.

He had to check in at the airport at 2 P.M. The night before, when making his reservation, he had not been able to get a seat on the earlier flight to New Wye because of some convention there. He had fiddled with railway schedules, but these had evidently been arranged by a practical joker since the only available direct train (dubbed the Square Wheel by our jolted and jerked students) left at 5:13 A.M., dawdled at flag stations, and took eleven hours to cover the four hundred miles to Exton; you could try to cheat it by going via Washington but then you had to wait there at least three hours for a sleepy local. Buses were out so far as Gradus was concerned since he always got roadsick in them unless he drugged himself with Fahrmamine pills, and that might affect his aim. Come to think of it, he was not feeling too steady anyway.

Gradus is now much nearer to us in space and time than he was in the preceding cantos. He has short upright black hair. We can fill in the bleak oblong of his face with most of its elements such as thick eyebrows and a wart on the chin. He has a ruddy but unhealthy complexion. We see, fairly in focus, the structure of his somewhat mesmeric organs of vision. We see his melancholy nose with its crooked ridge and grooved tip. We see the mineral blue of his jaw and the gravelly pointillé of his suppressed mustache.

We know already some of his gestures, we know the chimpanzee slouch of his broad body and short hindlegs. We have heard enough about his creased suit. We can at last describe his tie, an Easter gift from a dressy butcher, his brother-in-law in Onhava: imitation silk, color chocolate brown, barred with red, the end tucked into the shirt between the second and third buttons, a Zemblan fashion of the nineteen thirties—and a father-waistcoat substitute ac-

cording to the learned. Repulsive black hairs coat the back
of his honest rude hands, the scrupulously clean hands of an
ultra-unionized artisan, with a perceptible deformation of
both thumbs, typical of bobêche-makers. We see, rather suddenly, his humid flesh. We can even make out (as, head-on
but quite safely, phantom-like, we pass through him,
through the shimmering propeller of his flying machine,
through the delegates waving and grinning at us) his ma-
genta and mulberry insides, and the strange, not so good sea
swell undulating in his entrails.

We can now go further and describe, to a doctor or to
anybody else willing to listen to us, the condition of this
primate's soul. He could read, write and reckon, he was endowed with a modicum of self-awareness (with which he
did not know what to do), some duration consciousness, and
a good memory for faces, names, dates and the like. Spirit-
ually he did not exist. Morally he was a dummy pursuing another dummy. The fact that his weapon was a real one, and
his quarry a highly developed human being, this fact belonged to *our* world of events; in his, it had no meaning. I
grant you that the idea of destroying "the king" did hold for
him *some* degree of pleasure, and therefore we should add
to the list of his personal parts the capacity of forming notions, mainly general notions, as I have mentioned in another note which I will not bother to look up. There might
be (I am allowing a lot) a slight, very slight, sensual satisfaction, not more I would say than what a petty hedonist
enjoys at the moment when, retaining his breath, before a
magnifying mirror, his thumbnails pressing with deadly ac-
curacy on both sides of a full stop, he expulses totally the
eely, semitransparent plug of a comedo—and exhales an Ah

of relief. Gradus would not have killed anybody had he not derived pleasure not only from the imagined act (insofar as he was capable of imagining a palpable future) but also from having been given an important, responsible assignment (which happened to require he should kill) by a group of people sharing his notion of justice, but he would not have taken that job if in killing he had not found something like that rather disgusting anticomedoist's little thrill.

I have considered in my earlier note (I now see it is the note to line 171) the particular dislikes, and hence the motives, of our "automatic man," as I phrased it at a time when he did not have as much body, did not offend the senses as violently as now; was, in a word, further removed from our sunny, green, grass-fragrant Arcady. But Our Lord has fashioned man so marvelously that no amount of motive hunting and rational inquiry can ever *really* explain how and why anybody is capable of destroying a fellow creature (this argument necessitates, I know, a temporary granting to Gradus of the status of man), unless he is defending the life of his son, or his own, or the achievement of a lifetime; so that in final judgment of the Gradus versus the Crown case I would submit that if his human incompleteness be deemed insufficient to explain his idiotic journey across the Atlantic just to empty the magazine of his gun, we may concede, doctor, that our half-man was also half mad.

Aboard the small and uncomfortable plane flying into the sun he found himself wedged among several belated delegates to the New Wye Linguistic Conference, all of them lapel-labeled, and representing the same foreign language, but none being able to speak it, so that conversation was conducted (across our hunched-up killer and on all sides of his immobile face) in rather ordinary Anglo-American. During this ordeal, poor Gradus kept wondering what caused another discomfort which kept troubling him on and off throughout the flight, and which was worse than the babble of the monolinguists. He could not settle what to attribute it to—pork, cabbage, fried potatoes or melon—for upon re-tasting them one by one in spasmodic retrospect he found little to choose between their different but equally sickening flavors. My own opinion, which I would like the doctor to confirm, is that the French sandwich was engaged in an intestinal internecine war with the "French" fries.

Upon arriving after five at the New Wye airport he drank two papercupfuls of nice cold milk from a dispenser and acquired a map at the desk. With broad blunt finger tapping the configuration of the campus that resembled a writhing stomach, he asked the clerk what hotel was nearest to the university. A car, he was told, would take him to the Campus Hotel which was a few minutes' walk from the Main Hall (now Shade Hall). During the ride he suddenly became aware of such urgent qualms that he was forced to visit the washroom as soon as he got to the solidly booked hotel. There his misery resolved itself in a scalding torrent of indigestion. Hardly had he refastened his trousers and checked the bulge of his hip pocket than a renewal of stabs and queaks caused him to strip his thighs again which he did with such awkward precipitation that his small Browning was all but sent flying into the depths of the toilet.

He was still groaning and grinding his dentures when he and his briefcase re-offended the sun. It shone with all sorts of speckled effects through the trees, and College Town was gay with summer students and visiting linguists, among

whom Gradus might have easily passed for a salesman hawk-
ing Basic-English primers for American schoolchildren or
those wonderful new translating machines that can do it so
much faster than a man or an animal.

A grave disappointment awaited him at Main Hall: it
had closed for the day. Three students lying on the grass suggested he try the Library, and all three pointed to it across
the lawn. Thither trudged our thug.

"I don't know where he lives," said the girl at the desk.
"But I know he is here right now. You'll find him, I'm sure,
in North West Three where we have the Icelandic Collection. You go south [waving her pencil] and turn west,
and then west again where you see a sort of, a sort of [pencil
making a circular wiggle—round table? round bookshelf?]
— No, wait a minute, you better just keep going west till
you hit the Florence Houghton Room, and there you cross
over to the north side of the building. You cannot miss it"
[returning pencil to ear].

Not being a mariner or a fugitive king, he promptly got
lost and after vainly progressing through a labyrinth of
stacks, asked about the Icelandic Collection of a stern-
looking mother librarian who was checking cards in a steel
cabinet on a landing. Her slow and detailed directions
promptly led him back to the main desk.

"Please, I cannot find," he said, slowly shaking his head.

"Didn't you—" the girl began, and suddenly pointed
up: "Oh, there he is!"

Along the open gallery that ran above the hall, parallel
to its short side, a tall bearded man was crossing over at a
military quick march from east to west. He vanished behind
a bookcase but not before Gradus had recognized the great

rugged frame, the erect carriage, the high-bridged nose, the straight brow, and the energetic arm swing, of Charles Xavier the Beloved.

Our pursuer made for the nearest stairs—and soon found himself among the bewitched hush of Rare Books. The room was beautiful and had no doors; in fact, some moments passed before he could discover the draped entrance he himself had just used. The awful perplexities of his quest blending with the renewal of impossible pangs in his belly, he dashed back—ran three steps down and nine steps up, and burst into a circular room where a bald-headed suntanned professor in a Hawaiian shirt sat at a round table reading with an ironic expression on his face a Russian book. He paid no attention to Gradus who traversed the room, stepped over a fat little white dog without awakening it, clattered down a helical staircase and found himself in Vault P. Here, a well-lit, pipe-lined, white-washed passage led him to the sudden paradise of a water closet for plumbers or lost scholars where, cursing, he hurriedly transferred his automatic from its precarious dangle-pouch to his coat and relieved himself of another portion of the liquid hell inside him. He started to climb up again, and noticed in the temple light of the stacks an employee, a slim Hindu boy, with a call card in his hand. I had never spoken to that lad but had felt more than once his blue-brown gaze upon me, and no doubt my academic pseudonym was familiar to him but some sensitive cell in him, some chord of intuition, reacted to the harshness of the killer's interrogation and, as if protecting me from a cloudy danger, he smiled and said: "I do not know him, sir."

Gradus returned to the Main Desk.

"Too bad," said the girl, "I just saw him leave."

"*Bozhe moy, Bozhe moy,*" muttered Gradus, who sometimes at moments of stress used Russian ejaculations.

"You'll find him in the directory," she said pushing it
towards him, and dismissing the sick man's existence to attend to the wants of Mr. Gerald Emerald who was taking
out a fat bestseller in a cellophane jacket.

Moaning and shifting from one foot to the other, Gradus
started leafing through the college directory but when he
found the address, he was faced with the problem of getting
there.

"Dulwich Road," he cried to the girl. "Near? Far? Very
far, probably?"

"Are you by any chance Professor Pnin's new assistant?"
asked Emerald.

"No," said the girl. "This man is looking for Dr. Kinbote,
I think. You are looking for Dr. Kinbote, aren't you?"

"Yes, and I can't any more," said Gradus.

"I thought so," said the girl. "Doesn't he live somewhere
near Mr. Shade, Gerry?"

"Oh, definitely," said Gerry, and turned to the killer: "I
can drive you there if you like. It is on my way."

Did they talk in the car, these two characters, the man in
green and the man in brown? Who can say? They did not.
After all, the drive took only a few minutes (it took me, at
the wheel of my powerful Kramler, four and a half).

"I think I'll drop you here," said Mr. Emerald. "It's that
house up there."

One finds it hard to decide what Gradus alias Grey
wanted more at that minute: discharge his gun or rid himself of the inexhaustible lava in his bowels. As he began
hurriedly fumbling at the car door, unfastidious Emerald
leaned, close to him, across him, almost merging with him,

to help him open it—and then, slamming it shut again, whizzed on to some tryst in the valley. My reader will, I hope, appreciate all the minute particulars I have taken such trouble to present to him after a long talk I had with the killer; he will appreciate them even more if I tell him that, according to the legend spread later by the police, Jack Grey had been given a lift, all the way from Roanoke, or somewhere, by a lonesome trucker! One can only hope that an impartial search will turn up the trilby forgotten in the Library—or in Mr. Emerald's car.

Line 957: Night Rote

I remember one little poem from *Night Rote* (meaning "the nocturnal sound of the sea") that happened to be my first contact with the American poet Shade. A young lecturer on American Literature, a brilliant and charming boy from Boston, showed me that slim and lovely volume in Onhava, in my student days. The following lines opening this poem, which is entitled "Art," pleased me by their catchy lilt and jarred upon the religious sentiments instilled in me by our very "high" Zemblan church.

> From mammoth hunts and Odysseys
> And Oriental charms
> To the Italian goddesses
> With Flemish babes in arms.

Line 962:   Help me, Will. Pale Fire.

Paraphrased, this evidently means: Let me look in Shakespeare for something I might use for a title. And the find is
"pale fire." But in which of the Bard's works did our poet
cull it? My readers must make their own research. All I
have with me is a tiny vest pocket edition of *Timon of
Athens*—in Zemblan! It certainly contains nothing that
could be regarded as an equivalent of "pale fire" (if it had,
my luck would have been a statistical monster).

English was not taught in Zembla before Mr. Campbell's
time. Conmal mastered it all by himself (mainly by learning a lexicon by heart) as a young man, around 1880, when
not the verbal inferno but a quiet military career seemed
to open before him, and his first work (the translation of
Shakespeare's *Sonnets*) was the outcome of a bet with a
fellow officer. He exchanged his frogged uniform for a
scholar's dressing gown and tackled *The Tempest.* A slow
worker, he needed half a century to translate the works of
him whom he called "dze Bart," in their entirety. After
this, in 1930, he went on to Milton and other poets, steadily drilling through the ages, and had just completed Kipling's "The Rhyme of the Three Sealers" ("Now this is the
Law of the Muscovite that he proves with shot and steel")
when he fell ill and soon expired under his splendid painted
bed ceil with its reproductions of Altamira animals, his last
words in his last delirium being *"Comment dit-on 'mourir'
en anglais?"*—a beautiful and touching end.

It is easy to sneer at Conmal's faults. They are the naïve
failings of a great pioneer. He lived too much in his library,
too little among boys and youths. Writers should see the
world, pluck its figs and peaches, and not keep constantly

meditating in a tower of yellow ivory—which was also John Shade's mistake, in a way.

We should not forget that when Conmal began his stupendous task no English author was available in Zemblan except Jane de Faun, a lady novelist in ten volumes whose works, strangely enough, are unknown in England, and some fragments of Byron translated from French versions.

A large, sluggish man with no passions save poetry, he seldom moved from his warm castle and its fifty thousand crested books, and had been known to spend two years in bed reading and writing after which, much refreshed, he went for the first and only time to London, but the weather was foggy, and he could not understand the language, and so went back to bed for another year.

English being Conmal's prerogative, his *Shakspere* remained invulnerable throughout the greater part of his long life. The venerable Duke was famed for the nobility of his work; few dared question its fidelity. Personally, I had never the heart to check it. One callous Academician who did, lost his seat in result and was severely reprimanded by Conmal in an extraordinary sonnet composed directly in colorful, if not quite correct, English, beginning:

> I am not slave! Let be my critic slave.
> I cannot be. And Shakespeare would not want thus.
> Let drawing students copy the acanthus,
> I work with Master on the architrave!

Line 991: horseshoes

Neither Shade nor I had ever been able to ascertain whence precisely those ringing sounds came—which of the five families dwelling across the road on the lower slopes of our woody hill played horseshoe quoits every other evening; but the tantalizing tingles and jingles contributed a pleasant melancholy note to the rest of Dulwich Hill's evening sonorities—children calling to each other, children being called home, and the ecstatic barking of the boxer dog whom most of the neighbors disliked (he overturned garbage cans) greeting his master home.

It was this medley of metallic melodies which surrounded me on that fateful, much too luminous evening of July 21 when upon roaring home from the library in my powerful car I at once went to see what my dear neighbor was doing. I had just met Sybil speeding townward and therefore nursed some hopes for the evening. I grant you I very much resembled a lean wary lover taking advantage of a young husband's being alone in the house!

Through the trees I distinguished John's white shirt and gray hair: he sat in his Nest (as he called it), the arborlike porch or veranda I have mentioned in my note to lines 47-48. I could not keep from advancing a little nearer—oh, discreetly, almost on tiptoe; but then I noticed he was resting rather than writing, and I openly walked up to his porch or perch. His elbow was on the table, his fist supported his temple, his wrinkles were all awry, his eyes moist and misty; he looked like an old tipsy witch. He lifted his free hand in greeting without changing his attitude, which although not unfamiliar to me struck me this time as more forlorn than pensive.

"Well," I said, "has the muse been kind to you?"

"Very kind," he replied, slightly bowing his hand-propped head: "Exceptionally kind and gentle. In fact, I have here [indicating a huge pregnant envelope near him on the oilcloth] practically the entire product. A few trifles to settle and [suddenly striking the table with his fist] I've swung it, by God."

The envelope, unfastened at one end, bulged with stacked cards.

"Where is the missus?" I asked (mouth dry).

"Help me, Charlie, to get out of here," he pleaded. "Foot gone to sleep. Sybil is at a dinner meeting of her club."

"A suggestion," I said, quivering. "I have at my place half a gallon of Tokay. I'm ready to share my favorite wine with my favorite poet. We shall have for dinner a knackle of walnuts, a couple of large tomatoes, and a bunch of bananas. And if you agree to show me your 'finished product,' there will be another treat: I promise to divulge to you *why* I gave you, or rather *who* gave you, your theme."

"What theme?" said Shade absently, as he leaned on my arm and gradually recovered the use of his numb limb.

"Our blue inenubilable Zembla, and the red-capped Steinmann, and the motorboat in the sea cave, and—"

"Ah," said Shade, "I think I guessed your secret quite some time ago. But all the same I shall sample your wine with pleasure. Okay, I can manage by myself now."

Well did I know he could never resist a golden drop of this or that, especially since he was severely rationed at home. With an inward leap of exultation I relieved him of the large envelope that hampered his movements as he descended the steps of the porch, sideways, like a hesitating infant. We crossed the lawn, we crossed the road. Clink-clank, came the horseshoe music from Mystery Lodge. In the large envelope I carried I could feel the hard-cornered, rubberbanded batches of index cards. We are absurdly accustomed to the miracle of a few written signs being able to contain immortal imagery, involutions of thought, new worlds with live people, speaking, weeping, laughing. We take it for granted so simply that in a sense, by the very act of brutish routine acceptance, we undo the work of the ages, the history of the gradual elaboration of poetical description and construction, from the treeman to Browning, from the caveman to Keats. What if we awake one day, all of us, and find ourselves utterly unable to read? I wish you to gasp not only at what you read but at the miracle of its being readable (so I used to tell my students). Although I am capable, through long dabbling in blue magic, of imitating any prose in the world (but singularly enough not verse—I am a miserable rhymester), I do not consider myself a true artist, save in one matter: I can do what only a true artist can do—pounce upon the forgotten butterfly of revelation, wean myself abruptly from the habit of things, see the web of the world, and the warp and the weft of that web. Solemnly I weighed in my hand what I was carrying under my left armpit, and for a moment I found myself enriched with an indescribable amazement as if informed that fire-flies were making decodable signals on behalf of stranded spirits, or that a bat was writing a legible tale of torture in the bruised and branded sky.

I was holding all Zembla pressed to my heart.

Lines 993-995:   A dark Vanessa, etc.

One minute before his death, as we were crossing from his demesne to mine and had begun working up between the junipers and ornamental shrubs, a Red Admirable (see note to line 270) came dizzily whirling around us like a colored flame. Once or twice before we had already noticed the same individual, at that same time, on that same spot, where the low sun finding an aperture in the foliage splashed the brown sand with a last radiance while the evening's shade covered the rest of the path. One's eyes could not follow the rapid butterfly in the sunbeams as it flashed and vanished, and flashed again, with an almost frightening imitation of conscious play which now culminated in its settling upon my delighted friend's sleeve. It took off, and we saw it next moment sporting in an ecstasy of frivolous haste around a laurel shrub, every now and then perching on a lacquered leaf and sliding down its grooved middle like a boy down the banisters on his birthday. Then the tide of the shade reached the laurels, and the magnificent, velvet-and-flame creature dissolved in it.

Line 998:   Some neighbor's gardener

Some neighbor's! The poet had seen my gardener many times, and this vagueness I can only assign to his desire (noticeable elsewhere in his handling of names, etc.) to give a certain poetical patina, the bloom of remoteness, to familiar figures and things—although it is just possible he

might have mistaken him in the broken light for a stranger
working for a stranger. This gifted gardener I discovered by
chance one idle spring day when I was slowly wending my
way home after a maddening and embarrassing experience
at the college indoor swimming pool. He stood at the top of
a green ladder attending to the sick branch of a grateful
tree in one of the most famous avenues in Appalachia. His
red flannel shirt lay on the grass. We conversed, a little
shyly, he above, I below. I was pleasantly surprised at his
being able to refer all his patients to their proper habitats.
It was spring, and we were alone in that admirable col-
onnade of trees which visitors from England have photographed from end to end. I can enumerate here only a few
kinds of those trees: Jove's stout oak and two others: the
thunder-cloven from Britain, the knotty-entrailed from a
Mediterranean island; a weather-fending line (now lime), a
phoenix (now date palm), a pine and a cedar (*Cedrus*), all
insular; a Venetian sycamore tree (*Acer*); two willows, the
green, likewise from Venice, the hoar-leaved from Denmark;
a midsummer elm, its barky fingers enringed with ivy; a
midsummer mulberry, its shade inviting to tarry; and a
clown's sad cypress from Illyria.

He had worked for two years as a male nurse in a hospital
for Negroes in Maryland. He was hard up. He wanted to
study landscaping, botany and French ("to read in the
original Baudelaire and Dumas"). I promised him some
financial assistance. He started to work at my place the
very next day. He was awfully nice and pathetic, and all
that, but a little too talkative and completely impotent
which I found discouraging. Otherwise he was a strong
strapping fellow, and I hugely enjoyed the aesthetic pleasure
of watching him buoyantly struggle with earth and turf or

delicately manipulate bulbs, or lay out the flagged path which may or may not be a nice surprise for my landlord, when he safely returns from England (where I hope no bloodthirsty maniacs are stalking him!). How I longed to have him (my gardener, not my landlord) wear a great big turban, and shalwars, and an ankle bracelet. I would certainly have him attired according to the old romanticist notion of a Moorish prince, had I been a northern king—or rather had I still been a king (exile becomes a bad habit). You will chide me, my modest man, for writing so much about you in this note, but I feel I must pay you this tribute. After all, you saved my life. You and I were the last people who saw John Shade alive, and you admitted afterwards to a strange premonition which made you interrupt your work as you noticed us from the shrubbery walking toward the porch where stood—(Superstitiously I cannot write out the odd dark word you employed.)

Line 1000: [= *Line 1:* I was the shadow of the waxwing slain]

Through the back of John's thin cotton shirt one could distinguish patches of pink where it stuck to the skin above and around the outline of the funny little garment he wore under the shirt as all good Americans do. I see with such awful clarity one fat shoulder rolling, the other rising; his gray mop of hair, his creased nape; the red bandanna handkerchief limply hanging out of one hip pocket, the wallet bulge of the other; the broad deformed pelvis; the grass stains on the seat of his old khaki pants, the scuffed

back seams of his loafers; and I hear his delightful growl as
he looks back at me, without stopping, to say something like:
"Be sure not to spill anything—this is not a paper chase," or
[wincing] "I'll have to write again to Bob Wells [the town
mayor] about those damned Tuesday night trucks."

We had reached the Goldsworth side of the lane, and the
flagged walk that scrambled along a side lawn to connect
with the gravel path leading up from Dulwich road to the
Goldsworth front door, when Shade remarked: "You have
a caller."

In profile to us on the porch a short thickset, dark-haired
man in a brown suit stood holding by its ridiculous strap a
shabby and shapeless briefcase, his curved forefinger still
directed toward the bell button he had just pressed.

"I will kill him," I muttered. Recently a bonneted girl
had made me accept a bunch of religious tracts and had
told me that her brother, whom for some reason I had pictured to myself as a fragile neurotic youth, would drop in to
discuss with me God's Purpose, and explain anything I had
not understood in the tracts. Youth, indeed!

"Oh, I will kill him," I repeated under my breath—so
intolerable was it to think that the rapture of the poem
might be delayed. In my fury and hurry to dismiss the in-
truder, I outstripped John who until then had been in
front of me, heading at a good shamble for the double treat
of revel and revelation.

Had I ever seen Gradus before? Let me think. Had I?
Memory shakes her head. Nevertheless the killer affirmed to
me later that once from my tower, overlooking the Palace
orchard, I had waved to him as he and one of my former
pages, a boy with hair like excelsior, were carrying cradled
glass from the hothouse to a horse-drawn van; but, as the

caller now veered toward us and transfixed us with his
snake-sad, close-set eyes, I felt such a tremor of recognition
that had I been in bed dreaming I would have awoken with
a groan.

His first bullet ripped a sleeve button off my black
blazer, another sang past my ear. It is evil piffle to assert that
he aimed not at me (whom he had just seen in the library—
let us be consistent, gentlemen, ours is a rational world
after all), but at the gray-locked gentleman behind me. Oh,
he was aiming at me all right but missing me every time, the
incorrigible bungler, as I instinctively backed, bellowing
and spreading my great strong arms (with my left hand
still holding the poem, "still clutching the inviolable shade,"
to quote Matthew Arnold, 1822-1888), in an effort to halt
the advancing madman and shield John, whom I feared he
might, quite accidentally, hit, while he, my sweet awkward
old John, kept clawing at me and pulling me after him, back
to the protection of his laurels, with the solemn fussiness of
a poor lame boy trying to get his spastic brother out of the
range of the stones hurled at them by schoolchildren, once
a familiar sight in all countries. I felt—I still feel—John's
hand fumbling at mine, seeking my fingertips, finding them,
only to abandon them at once as if passing to me, in a sublime relay race, the baton of life.

One of the bullets that spared me struck him in the
side and went through his heart. His presence behind me
abruptly failing me caused me to lose my balance, and,
simultaneously, to complete the farce of fate, my gardener's
spade dealt gunman Jack from behind the hedge a tremendous blow on the pate, felling him and sending his weapon
flying from his grasp. Our savior retrieved it and helped
me to my feet. My coccyx and right wrist hurt badly but

the poem was safe. John, though, lay prone on the ground, with a red spot on his white shirt. I still hoped he had not been killed. The madman sat on the porch step, dazedly nursing with bloody hands a bleeding head. Leaving the gardener to watch over him I hurried into the house and concealed the invaluable envelope under a heap of girls' galoshes, furred snowboots and white wellingtons heaped at the bottom of a closet, from which I exited as if it had been the end of the secret passage that had taken me all the way out of my enchanted castle and right from Zembla to *this* Arcady. I then dialed 11111 and returned with a glass of water to the scene of the carnage. The poor poet had now been turned over and lay with open dead eyes directed up at the sunny evening azure. The armed gardener and the battered killer were smoking side by side on the steps. The latter, either because he was in pain, or because he had decided to play a new role, ignored me as completely as if I were a stone king on a stone charger in the Tessera Square of Onhava; but the poem was safe.

The gardener took the glass of water I had placed near a flowerpot beside the porch steps and shared it with the killer, and then accompanied him to the basement toilet, and presently the police and the ambulance arrived, and the gunman gave his name as Jack Grey, no fixed abode, except the Institute for the Criminal Insane, *ici,* good dog, which of course should have been his permanent address all along, and which the police thought he had just escaped from.

"Come along, Jack, we'll put something on that head of yours," said a calm but purposeful cop stepping over the body, and then there was the awful moment when Dr. Sutton's daughter drove up with Sybil Shade.

In the course of that chaotic night I found a moment to

transfer the poem from under the booties of Goldsworth's four nymphets to the austere security of my black valise, but only at daybreak did I find it safe enough to examine my treasure.

We know how firmly, how stupidly I believed that Shade was composing a poem, a kind of *romaunt*, about the King of Zembla. We have been prepared for the horrible disappointment in store for me. Oh, I did not expect him to devote himself *completely* to that theme! It might have been blended of course with some of his own life stuff and sundry Americana—but I was sure his poem would contain the wonderful incidents I had described to him, the characters I had made alive for him and all the unique *atmosphere* of my kingdom. I even suggested to him a good title—the title of the book in me whose pages he was to cut: *Solus Rex;* instead of which I saw *Pale Fire,* which meant to me nothing. I started to read the poem. I read faster and faster. I sped through it, snarling, as a furious young heir through an old deceiver's testament. Where were the battlements of my sunset castle? Where was Zembla the Fair? Where her spine of mountains? Where her long thrill through the mist? And my lovely flower boys, and the spectrum of the stained windows, and the Black Rose Paladins, and the whole marvelous tale? Nothing of it was there! The complex contribution I had been pressing upon him with a hypnotist's patience and a lover's urge was simply not there. Oh, but I cannot express the agony! Instead of the wild glorious romance—what did I have? An autobiographical, eminently Appalachian, rather old-fashioned narrative in a neo-Popian prosodic style—beautifully written of course— Shade could not write otherwise than beautifully—but void of my magic, of that special rich streak of magical madness which I was sure would run through it and make it transcend its time.

Gradually I regained my usual composure. I reread *Pale Fire* more carefully. I liked it better when expecting less. And what was that? What was that dim distant music, those vestiges of color in the air? Here and there I discovered in it and especially, especially in the invaluable variants, echoes and spangles of my mind, a long ripplewake of my glory. I now felt a new, pitiful tenderness toward the poem as one has for a fickle young creature who has been stolen and brutally enjoyed by a black giant but now again is safe in our hall and park, whistling with the stableboys, swimming with the tame seal. The spot still hurts, it must hurt, but with strange gratitude we kiss those heavy wet eyelids and caress that polluted flesh.

My commentary to this poem, now in the hands of my readers, represents an attempt to sort out those echoes and wavelets of fire, and pale phosphorescent hints, and all the many subliminal debts to me. Some of my notes may sound bitter—but I have done my best not to air any grievances. And in this final scholium my intention is not to complain of the vulgar and cruel nonsense that professional reporters and Shade's "friends" in the obituaries they concocted allowed themselves to spout when misdescribing the circumstances of Shade's death. I regard their references to me as a mixture of journalistic callousness and the venom of vipers. I do not doubt that many of the statements made in this work will be brushed aside by the guilty parties when it is out. Mrs. Shade will not remember having been shown by her husband who "showed her everything" one or two of the precious variants. The three students lying on the grass will turn out to be totally amnesic. The desk girl at the

Library will not recall (will have been told not to recall) anybody asking for Dr. Kinbote on the day of the murder. And I am sure that Mr. Emerald will interrupt briefly his investigation of some mammate student's resilient charms to deny with the vigor of roused virility that he ever gave anybody a lift to my house that evening. In other words, everything will be done to cut off my person completely from my dear friend's fate.

Nevertheless, I have had my little revenge: public misapprehension indirectly helped me to obtain the right of publishing *Pale Fire*. My good gardener, when enthusiastically relating to everybody what he had seen, certainly erred in several respects—not so much perhaps in his exaggerated account of my "heroism" as in the assumption that Shade had been deliberately aimed at by the so-called Jack Grey; but Shade's widow found herself so deeply affected by the idea of my having "thrown myself" between the gunman and his target that during a scene I shall never forget, she cried out, stroking my hands: "There are things for which no recompense in this world or another is great enough." That "other world" comes in handy when misfortune befalls the infidel but I let it pass of course, and, indeed, resolved not to refute anything, saying instead: "Oh, but there *is* a recompense, my dear Sybil. It may seem to you a very modest request but—give me the permission, Sybil, to edit and publish John's last poem." The permission was given at once, with new cries and new hugs, and already next day her signature was under the agreement I had a quick little lawyer draw up. That moment of grateful grief you soon forgot, dear girl. But I assure you that I do not mean any harm, and that John Shade, perhaps, will not be too much annoyed by my notes, despite the intrigues and the dirt.

Because of these machinations I was confronted with nightmare problems in my endeavors to make people calmly see—without having them immediately scream and hustle me—the truth of the tragedy—a tragedy in which I had been not a "chance witness" but the protagonist, and the main, if only potential, victim. The hullabaloo ended by affecting the course of my new life, and necessitated my removal to this modest mountain cabin; but I did manage to obtain, soon after his detention, an interview, perhaps even two interviews, with the prisoner. He was now much more lucid than when he cowered bleeding on my porch step, and he told me all I wanted to know. By making him believe I could help him at his trial I forced him to confess his heinous crime—his deceiving the police and the nation by posing as Jack Grey, escapee from an asylum, who mistook Shade for the man who sent him there. A few days later, alas, he thwarted justice by slitting his throat with a safety razor blade salvaged from an unwatched garbage container. He died, not so much because having played his part in the story he saw no point in existing any longer, but because he could not live down this last crowning botch—killing the wrong person when the right one stood before him. In other words, his life ended not in a feeble splutter of the clockwork but in a gesture of humanoid despair. Enough of this. Exit Jack Grey.

I cannot recall without a shudder the lugubrious week that I spent in New Wye before leaving it, I hope, forever. I lived in constant fear that robbers would deprive me of my tender treasure. Some of my readers may laugh when they learn that I fussily removed it from my black valise to an empty steel box in my landlord's study, and a few hours later took the manuscript out again, and for several days *wore* it, as it were, having distributed the ninety-two index cards about my person, twenty in the right-hand pocket of my coat, as many in the left-hand one, a batch of forty against my right nipple and the twelve precious ones with variants in my innermost left-breast pocket. I blessed my royal stars for having taught myself wife work, for I now sewed up all four pockets. Thus with cautious steps, among deceived enemies, I circulated, plated with poetry, armored with rhymes, stout with another man's song, stiff with cardboard, bullet-proof at long last.

Many years ago—how many I would not care to say—I remember my Zemblan nurse telling me, a little man of six in the throes of adult insomnia: *"Minnamin, Gut mag alkan, Pern dirstan"* (my darling, God makes hungry, the Devil thirsty). Well, folks, I guess many in this fine hall are as hungry and thirsty as me, and I'd better stop, folks, right here.

Yes, better stop. My notes and self are petering out. Gentlemen, I have suffered very much, and more than any of you can imagine. I pray for the Lord's benediction to rest on my wretched countrymen. My work is finished. My poet is dead.

"And you, what will *you* be doing with yourself, poor King, poor Kinbote?" a gentle young voice may inquire.

God will help me, I trust, to rid myself of any desire to follow the example of two other characters in this work. I shall continue to exist. I may assume other disguises, other forms, but I shall try to exist. I may turn up yet, on another campus, as an old, happy, healthy, heterosexual

Russian, a writer in exile, sans fame, sans future, sans audience, sans anything but his art. I may join forces with Odon in a new motion picture: *Escape from Zembla* (ball in the palace, bomb in the palace square). I may pander to the simple tastes of theatrical critics and cook up a stage play, an old-fashioned melodrama with three principles: a lunatic who intends to kill an imaginary king, another lunatic who imagines himself to be that king, and a distinguished old poet who stumbles by chance into the line of fire, and perishes in the clash between the two figments. Oh, I may do many things! History permitting, I may sail back to my recovered kingdom, and with a great sob greet the gray coastline and the gleam of a roof in the rain. I may huddle and groan in a madhouse. But whatever happens, wherever the scene is laid, somebody, somewhere, will quietly set out —somebody has already set out, somebody still rather far away is buying a ticket, is boarding a bus, a ship, a plane, has landed, is walking toward a million photographers, and presently he will ring at my door—a bigger, more respectable, more competent Gradus.

Index

The italicized numerals refer to the lines in the poem and the comments thereon. The capital letters G, K, S (which see) stand for the three main characters in this work.

A., Baron, Oswin Affenpin, last Baron of Aff, a puny traitor, *286.*

Acht, Iris, celebrated actress, d. 1888, a passionate and powerful woman, favorite of Thurgus the Third (*q.v.*), *130.* She died officially by her own hand; unofficially, strangled in her dressing room by a fellow actor, a jealous young Gothlander, now, at ninety, the oldest, and least important, member of the Shadows (*q.v.*) group.

Alfin, King, surnamed The Vague, 1873–1918, reigned from 1900; K.'s father; a kind, gentle, absent-minded monarch, mainly interested in automobiles, flying machines, motorboats and, at one time, sea shells; killed in an airplane accident, *71.*

Andronnikov and Niagarin, two Soviet experts in quest of a buried treasure, *130, 681, 741;* see Crown Jewels.

Arnor, Romulus, poet about town and Zemblan patriot, 1914–1958, his poem quoted, *80;* executed by the Extremists.

Aros, a fine town in E. Zembla, capital of Conmal's dukedom; once the mayorship of the worthy Ferz ("chessqueen") Bretwit, a cousin of the granduncle of Oswin Bretwit (*q.v.*), *149, 286.*

B., Baron, involuntary father-in-law of Baron A. and imaginary old friend of the Bretwit (*q.v.*) family, *286.*

Bera, a mountain range dividing the peninsula lengthwise; described with some of its glittering peaks, mysterious passes and picturesque slopes, *149.*

Blawick, Blue Cove, a pleasant seaside resort on the Western Coast of Zembla, casino, golf course, sea food, boats for hire, *149.*

Blenda, Queen, the King's mother, 1878–1936, reigned from 1918, *71.*

Boscobel, site of the Royal Summerhouse, a beautiful, piny and duny spot in W. Zembla, soft hollows imbued with the writer's most amorous recollections; now (1959) a "nudist colony"—whatever that is, *149, 596.*

Botkin, V., American scholar of Russian descent, *894;* king-bot, maggot of extinct fly that once bred in mammoths and is thought to have hastened their phylogenetic end, *247;* bottekin-maker, *71; bot,* plop, and *botelïy,* big-bellied (Russ.); botkin or bodkin, a Danish stiletto.

Bregberg. See Bera.

Bretwit, Oswin, 1914–1959, diplomat and Zemblan patriot, *286.* See also under Odevalla and Aros.

Campbell, Walter, b. 1890, in Glasgow; K.'s tutor, 1922–1931, an amiable gentleman with a mellow and rich mind; dead shot and champion skater; now in Iran; *130*

Charles II, Charles Xavier Vseslav, last King of Zembla, surnamed The Beloved, b. 1915, reigned 1936–1958; his crest, *1;* his studies and his reign, *12;* fearful fate of predecessors, *62;* his supporters, *70;* parents, *71;* bedroom, *80;* escape from palace, *130;* and across the mountains, *149;* engagement to Disa recalled, *275;* parenthetical passage through Paris, *286;* and through Switzerland, *408;* visit to Villa Disa, *433;* night in mountains recalled, *597, 662;* his Russian blood, and Crown Jewels (*q.v.* by all means), *681;* his arrival in the U.S.A., *691;* letter to Disa stolen, *741;* and quoted, *768;* his portrait discussed, *894;* his presence in library, *949;* identity almost revealed, *991;* Solus Rex, 1000. See also Kinbote.

Conmal, Duke of Aros, 1855–1955, K.'s uncle, the eldest half-brother of Queen Blenda (*q.v.*); noble paraphrast, *12;* his version of *Timon of Athens, 39, 130;* his life and work, *962.*

Crown Jewels, 130, 681; see Hiding Place.

Disa, Duchess of Payn, of Great Payn and Mone; my lovely, pale, melancholy Queen, haunting my dreams, and haunted by dreams of me, b. 1928; her album and favorite trees, *49;* married 1949, *80;* her letters on ethereal paper with a watermark I cannot make out, her image torturing me in my sleep, *433.*

Embla, a small old town with a wooden church surrounded by sphagnum bogs at the saddest, loneliest, northmost point of the misty peninsula, *149, 433.*

Emblem, meaning "blooming" in Zemblan; a beautiful bay with bluish and black, curiously striped rocks and a luxurious growth of heather on its gentle slopes, in the southmost part of W. Zembla, *433.*

Falkberg, a pink cone, *71;* snowhooded, *149.*

Flatman, Thomas, 1637–88, English poet, scholar and miniaturist, not known to old fraud, *894.*

Fleur, Countess de Fyler, an elegant lady-in-waiting, *71, 80, 433.*

G, see Gradus.

Garh, a farmer's daughter, *149, 433.* Also a rosy-cheeked gooseboy found in a country lane, north of Troth, in 1936, only now distinctly recalled by the writer.

Glitterntin, Mt., a splendid mountain in the Bera Range (*q.v.*); pity I may never climb it again, *149.*

Gordon, see Krummholz.

Gradus, Jakob, 1915-1959; alias Jack Degree, de Grey, d'Argus, Vinogradus, Leningradus, etc.; a Jack of small trades and a killer, *12, 17;* lynching the wrong people, *80;* his approach synchronized with *S*'s work on the poem, *120, 131;* his election and past tribulations, *171;* the first lap of his journey, Onhava to Copenhagen, *181, 209;* to Paris, and meeting with Oswin Bretwit, *286;* to Geneva, and talk with little Gordon at Joe Lavender's place near Lex, *408;* calling headquarters from Geneva, *469;* his name in a variant, and his wait in Geneva, *596;* to Nice, and his wait there, *697;* his meeting with Izumrudov in Nice and discovery of the King's address, *741;* from Paris to New York, *873;* in New York, *949¹;* his morning in New York, his journey to New Wye, to the campus, to Dulwich Rd., *949²;* the crowning blunder, *1000.*

Griff, old mountain farmer and Zemblan patriot, *149.*

Grindelwod, a fine town in E. Zembla, *71, 149.*

Hiding place, *potaynik* (q.v.)

Hodinski, Russian adventurer, d. 1800, also known as Hodyna, *681;* resided in Zembla 1778-1800; author of a celebrated pastiche and lover of Princess (later Queen) Yaruga (*q.v.*), mother of Igor II, grandmother of Thurgus (*q.v.*).

Igor II, reigned 1800-1845, a wise and benevolent king, son of

Queen Yaruga (*q.v.*) and father of Thurgus III (*q.v.*); a very private section of the picture gallery in the Palace, accessible only to the reigning monarch, but easily broken into through Bower P by an inquisitive pubescent, contained the statues of Igor's four hundred favorite catamites, in pink marble, with inset glass eyes and various touched up details, an outstanding exhibition of verisimilitude and bad art, later presented by K. to an Asiatic potentate.

K, see Charles II and Kinbote.

Kalixhaven, a colorful seaport on the western coast, a few miles north of Blawick (*q.v.*), *171;* many pleasant memories.

Kinbote, Charles, Dr., an intimate friend of *S,* his literary adviser, editor and commentator; first meeting and friendship with S, *Foreword;* his interest in Appalachian birds, *1;* his good-natured request to have S use his stories, *12;* his modesty, *34;* his having no library in his Timonian cave, *39;* his belief in his having inspired S, *42;* his house in Dulwich Road, and the windows of S's house, *47;* Prof. H. contradicted and corrected, *61, 71;* his anxieties and insomnias, *62;* the map he made for S, *71;* his sense of humor, *79, 91;* his belief that the term "iridule" is S's invention, *109;* his weariness, *120;* his sports activities, *130;* his visit to S's basement, *143;* his trusting the reader enjoyed the note *149;* boyhood and the Orient Express recalled, *162;* his request that the reader consult a later note, *169;* his quiet warning to *G, 171;* his remarks on critics and other sallies endorsed by S, *172;* his participation in certain festivities elsewhere, his being debarred from S's birthday party upon coming home, and his sly trick next morning, *181;* his hearing about Hazel's "poltergeist" phase, *230;* poor who? *231;* his futile attempts to have S get off the subject of natural history and report on the work in progress, *238;* his recollection of the quays in Nice and Mentone, *240;* his utmost courtesy towards his friend's wife, *247;* his limited knowledge of lepidoptera and the sable gloom of his nature marked like a dark Vanessa with gay flashes, *270;* his discovery of Mrs. S's plan to whisk S to Cedarn and his decision to go there too, *288;* his attitude towards swans, *319;* his affinity with Hazel, *334, 348;* his walk with S to the weedy spot where the haunted barn once stood, *347;* his objection to S's flippant attitude towards celebrated contemporaries, *376;* his contempt for Prof. H. (not in Index), *377;* his overworked memory, *384;* his meeting with Jane Provost and examination of lovely lakeside snapshots, *385;* his criticism of the 403-474 lines section, *403;* his secret guessed, or not guessed, by S, his telling S about Disa, and S's reaction, *417;* his debate on Prejudice with S, *470;* his discussion of Suicide with himself, *493;* his surprise at realizing that the French name of one melancholy tree is the same as the Zemblan one of another, *501;* his disapproval of certain flippant passages in Canto Three, *502²;* his views on sin and faith, *549;* his editorial integrity and spiritual misery, *550;* his remarks on a certain female student and on the number and nature of meals shared with the Shades, *579;* his delight and amazement at a portentous meeting of syllables in two adjacent words, *596;* his aphorism on the slayer and the slain, *597;* his logcabin in Cedarn and the little angler, a honey-skinned lad, naked except for a pair of torn dungarees, one trouser leg rolled up, frequently fed with nougat and nuts, but then school started or the weather changed, *609;* his appearance at the H——s, *629;* his severe criticism of quotational titles, from *The Tempest* etc., such as "pale fire," etc., *671;* his sense of humor, *680;* his arrival at Mrs. O'Donnell's country house recalled, *691;* his appreciation of a quodlibet and his doubts anent its purported authorship, *727;* his loathing for a person who makes advances, and then betrays a noble and naïve heart, telling foul stories about his victim and pursuing him with brutal practical jokes, *741;* his not being able, owing to some psychological block or the fear of a second G, of traveling to a city only sixty or seventy miles distant, where he would certainly have found a good library, *747;* his letter of April 2, 1959, to a lady who left it locked up among her treasures in her villa near Nice when she went that summer to Rome, *768;* divine service in the morning and ramble in the evening with the poet finally speaking of his work, *802;* his remarks on a lexical and linguistic miracle, *803;* his borrowing a collection of F. K. Lane's letters

from the motor court owner, *810;* his penetrating into the
bathroom where his friend sat and shaved in the tub, *887;* his
participation in a Common Room discussion of his resemblance
to the King, and his final rupture with E. (not in the Index),
894; he and S shaking with mirth over tidbits in a college
textbook by Prof. C. (not in the Index), *929;* his sad gesture of
weariness and gentle reproach, *937;* a young lecturer in Onhava
University vividly recollected, *957;* his last meeting with S in
the poet's arbor, etc., *991;* his discovery of the scholarly gardener recalled, *998;* his unsuccessful attempt to save S's life,
and his success in salvaging the MS, *1000;* his arranging to have
it published without the help of two "experts," *Foreword.*

Kobaltana, a once fashionable mountain resort near the ruins of
some old barracks now a cold and desolate spot of difficult
access and no importance but still remembered in military
families and forest castles, not in the text.

Kronberg, a snow-capped rocky mountain with a comfortable
hotel, in the Bera Range, *70, 130, 149.*

Krummholz, Gordon, b.1944, a musical prodigy and an amusing
pet; son of Joseph Lavender's famous sister, Elvina Krummholz, *408.*

Lane, Franklin Knight, American lawyer and statesman, 1864-
1921, author of a remarkable fragment, 810.

Lass, see Mass.

Lavender, Joseph S., see O'Donnell, Sylvia.

Male, see Word Golf.

Mandevil, Baron Mirador, cousin of Radomir Mandevil (*q.v.*),
experimentalist, madman and traitor, *171.*

Mandevil, Baron Radomir, b.1925, man of fashion and Zemblan
patriot; in 1936, K's throne page, *130;* in 1958, disguised, *149.*

Marcel, the fussy, unpleasant, and not always plausible central
character, pampered by everybody in Proust's *A la Recherche
du Temps Perdu, 181, 691.*

Marrowsky, a, a rudimentary spoonerism, from the name of a
Russian diplomat of the early 19th century, Count Komarovski,
famous at foreign courts for mispronouncing his own name—
Makarovski, Macaronski, Skomorovski, etc.

Mass, Mars, Mare, see Male.

Multraberg, see Bera.

Niagarin and Andronnikov, two Soviet "experts" still in quest of a buried treasure, *130, 681, 741;* see Crown Jewels.

Nitra and Indra, twin islands off Blawick, *149.*

Nodo, Odon's half-brother, b. 1916, son of Leopold O'Donnell and of a Zemblan boy impersonator; a cardsharp and despicable traitor, *171.*

Odevalla, a fine town north of Onhava in E. Zembla, once the mayorship of the worthy Zule ("chessrook") Bretwit, granduncle of Oswin Bretwit (*q.v., q.v.,* as the crows say), *149, 286.*

Odon, pseudonym of Donald O'Donnell, b. 1915, world-famous actor and Zemblan patriot; learns from K. about secret passage but has to leave for theater, *130;* drives K. from theater to foot of Mt. Mandevil, *149;* meets K. near sea cave and escapes with him in motorboat, *ibid.;* directs cinema picture in Paris, *171;* stays with Lavender in Lex, *408;* ought not to marry that blubber-lipped cinemactress, with úntidy hair, *691;* see also O'Donnell, Sylvia.

O'Donnell, Sylvia, nee O'Connell, born 1895? 1890?, the much-traveled, much-married mother of Odon (*q.v.*), *149, 691;* after marrying and divorcing college president Leopold O'Donnell in 1915, father of Odon, she married Peter Gusev, first Duke of Rahl, and graced Zembla till about 1925 when she married an Oriental prince met in Chamonix; after a number of other more or less glamorous marriages, she was in the act of divorcing Lionel Lavender, cousin of Joseph, when last seen in this Index.

Oleg, Duke of Rahl, 1916-1931, son of Colonel Gusev, Duke of Rahl (b. 1885, still spry); K.'s beloved playmate, killed in a toboggan accident, *130.*

Onhava, the beautiful capital of Zembla, *12, 71, 130, 149, 171, 181, 275, 579, 894, 1000.*

Otar, Count, heterosexual man of fashion and Zemblan patriot, b. 1915, his bald spot, his two teenage mistresses, Fleur and Fifalda (later Countess Otar), blue-veined daughters of Countess de Fyler, interesting light effects, *71.*

Paberg, see Bera Range.

Payn, Dukes of, escutcheon of, *270;* see Disa, my Queen.

Poems, Shade's short: The Sacred Tree, 49; The Swing, 61; Mountain View, 92; The Nature of Electricity, 347; one line from *April Rain, 470;* one line from *Mont Blanc, 782;* opening quatrain of *Art, 957.*

Potaynik, taynik (q.v.).

Religion: contact with God, *47;* the Pope, *85;* freedom of mind, *101;* problem of sin and faith, *549;* see Suicide.

Rippleson Caves, sea caves in Blawick, named after a famous glass maker who embodied the dapple-and-ringle play and other circular reflections on blue-green sea water in his extraordinary stained glass windows for the Palace, *130, 149.*

Shade, Hazel, S's daughter, 1934-1957; deserves great respect, having preferred the beauty of death to the ugliness of life; the domestic ghost, *230;* the Haunted Barn, *347.*

Shade, John Francis, poet and scholar, 1898-1959; his work on *Pale Fire* and friendship with *K, Foreword;* his physical appearance, mannerisms, habits, etc., *ibid.;* his first brush with death as visualized by *K,* and his beginning the poem while *K* plays chess at the Students' Club, *1;* his sunset rambles with *K, 12;* his dim precognition of *G, 17;* his house seen by *K* in terms of lighted windows, *47;* his starting on the poem, his completing Canto Two, and about half of Three, and *K's* three visits at those points of time, *ibid.;* his parents, Samuel Shade and Caroline Lukin, *71; K's* influence seen in a variant, *79;* Maud Shade, S's father's sister, *86; K* shown S's clockwork *memento mori, 143; K* on S's fainting fits, *162; S* beginning Canto Two, *167; S* on critics, Shakespeare, education, etc., *172; K's* watching S's guests arriving on his and S's birthday, and S writing Canto Two, *181;* his worries over his daughter recalled, *230;* his delicacy, or prudence, *231;* his exaggerated interest in the local fauna and flora, *238, 270;* the complications of *K's* marriage compared to the plainness of S's, *275; K's* drawing S's attention to a pastel smear crossing the sunset sky, *286;* his fear that S might leave before finishing their joint composition, *288;* his waiting vainly for S on July 15th, *338;* his walk with S through old Hentzner's fields and his reconstitution of S's daughter's expeditions to the Haunted Barn, *347;* S's pronunciation, *367;* S's book on Pope, *384;* his grudge against Peter Provost, *385;* his work on lines 406-416 synchronized with G's activities in Switzerland, *408;* again his prudence, or considerateness, *417;* his having possibly glimpsed twenty-six years ago Villa Disa and the little Duchess of Payn with her English governess, *433;* his apparent assimilation of the Disa material and K's promise to divulge an ultimate truth, *ibid.;* S's views on Prejudice, *470;* K's views on Suicide, *493;* S's and K's views on sin and faith, *549;* S's crabbed hospitality and delight in meatless cuisine at my house, *579;* rumors about his interest in a female student, *ibid.;* his denial of a stationmaster's insanity, *629;* his heart attack synchronized with K's spectacular arrival in the USA, *691;* K's allusion to S in a letter to Disa, *768;* his last ramble with S and his joy at learning S is working hard on the "mountain" theme—a tragic misunderstanding, *802;* his games of golf with S, *819;* his readiness to look up references for S, *887;* S's defense of the King of Zembla, *894;* his and K's hilarity over the rot in a textbook compiled by Prof. C., psychiatrist and literary expert (!), *929;* his beginning his last batch of cards, *949;* his revealing to K the completion of his task, *991;* his death from a bullet meant for another, *1000.*

Shade, Sybil, S's wife, *passim.*

Shadows, the, a regicidal organization which commissioned Gradus (*q.v.*) to assassinate the self-banished king; its leader's terrible name cannot be mentioned, even in the Index to the obscure work of a scholar; his maternal grandfather, a well-known and very courageous master builder, was hired by Thurgus the Turgid, around 1885, to make certain repairs in his quarters, and soon after that perished, poisoned in the royal kitchens, under mysterious circumstances, together with his three young apprentices whose pretty first names Yan, Yonny, and Angeling, are preserved in a ballad still to be heard in some of our wilder valleys.

Shalksbore, Baron Harfar, known as Curdy Buff, b. 1921, man of fashion and Zemblan patriot, *433.*

Steinmann, Julius, b. 1928, tennis champion and Zemblan patriot, *171*.

Sudarg of Bokay, a mirror maker of genius, the patron saint of Bokay in the mountains of Zembla, *80;* life span not known.

Suicide, K's views on, *493*.

Taynik, Russ., secret place; see Crown Jewels.

Thurgus the Third, surnamed The Turgid, *K's* grandfather, d. 1900 at seventy-five, after a long dull reign; sponge-bag-capped, and with only one medal on his Jaeger jacket, he liked to bicycle in the park; stout and bald, his nose like a congested plum, his martial mustache bristling with obsolete passion, garbed in a dressing gown of green silk, and carrying a flambeau in his raised hand, he used to meet, every night, during a short period in the middle-Eighties, his hooded mistress, Iris Acht (*q.v.*) midway between palace and theater in the secret passage later to be rediscovered by his grandson, *130*.

Tintarron, a precious glass stained a deep blue, made in Bokay, a medieval place in the mountains of Zembla, *149;* see also Sudarg.

Translations, poetical; English into Zemblan, Conmal's versions of Shakespeare, Milton, Kipling, etc., noticed, *962;* English into French, from Donne and Marvell, *678;* German into English and Zemblan, *Der Erlkönig, 662;* Zemblan into English, *Timon Afinsken,* of Athens, *39;* Elder Edda, *79;* Arnor's *Miragarl, 80*.

Uran the Last, Emperor of Zembla, reigned 1798-1799; an incredibly brilliant, luxurious, and cruel monarch whose whistling whip made Zembla spin like a rainbow top; dispatched one night by a group of his sister's united favorites, 681.

Vanessa, the Red Admirable (*sumpsimus*), evoked, *270;* flying over a parapet on a Swiss hillside, *408;* figured, *470;* caricatured, *949;* accompanying *S's* last steps in the evening sunshine, *993*.

Variants: the thieving sun and moon, *39-40;* planning the Primal Scene, *57;* the Zemblan King's escape (*K's* contribution, 8 lines), *70;* the Edda (*K's* contribution, 1 line), *79;* Luna's dead cocoon, *90-93;* children finding a secret passage (*K's* contribution, 4 lines), *130;* poor old man Swift, poor—(possible allusion to *K*), *231;* Shade, *Ombre, 275;* Virginia Whites, *316;* The

Head of Our Department, *377;* a nymphet, *413;* additional line from Pope (possible allusion to *K*), *417;* Tanagra dust (a remarkable case of foreknowledge), *596;* of this America, *609-614;* first two feet changed, *629;* parody of Pope, *895-899;* a sorry age, and Social Novels, *922.*

Waxwings, birds of the genus *Bombycilla, 1-4, 131, 1000; Bombycilla shadei, 71;* interesting association belatedly realized.

Windows, Foreword; 47, 62, 181.

Word golf, S's predilection for it, *819;* see Lass.

Yaruga, Queen, reigned 1799-1800, sister of Uran *(q.v.);* drowned in an ice-hole with her Russian lover during traditional New Year's festivities, *681.*

Yeslove, a fine town, district and bishopric, north of Onhava, *149, 275.*

Zembla, a distant northern land.

ABOUT THE AUTHOR

Vladimir Nabokov was born in St. Petersburg on April 23, 1899. His family fled to the Crimea in 1917, during the Bolshevik Revolution, then went into exile in Europe. Nabokov studied at Trinity College, Cambridge, earning a degree in French and Russian literature in 1922, and lived in Berlin and Paris for the next two decades, writing prolifically, mainly in Russian, under the pseudonym Sirin. In 1940 he moved to the United States, where he pursued a brilliant literary career (as a poet, novelist, memoirist, critic, and translator) while teaching Russian, creative writing, and literature at Stanford, Wellesley, Cornell, and Harvard. The monumental success of his novel *Lolita* (1955) enabled him to give up teaching and devote himself fully to his writing. In 1961 he moved to Montreux, Switzerland, where he died in 1977. Recognized as one of the master prose stylists of the century in both Russian and English, he translated a number of his original English works—including *Lolita*—into Russian, and collaborated on English translations of his original Russian works.